COUNTY LINES

CJ WOOD

Chapter One

Jason Hamilton had spent the night at his luxury apartment on floor twenty, in one of Manchester's new luxury apartment tower blocks. The exclusive apartment didn't come cheap but cost wasn't a problem for Jason these days. Criminality had made him a rich man. He was driven by achieving such decadence and the need to be top of the pile. It was a perfect place from which to run his criminal enterprise, importing and supplying drugs, whilst eluding the police and any other unwanted attention. Even so, he didn't spend as much time there as he would like. Jason's days were split between the apartment and a house in the Manchester suburbs which he shared with his partner, Kirsty. The house was part of his new legitimate business enterprise, Hamilton Properties. Although he had developed a successful portfolio of properties, it didn't hit the spot quite like his original business empire.

Jason walked from the shower room across the smooth wooden flooring, a white towel wrapped around his waist. He stood at the plate glass window looking out over the city. The heat of the morning sun felt comforting on his skin. Catching a glimpse of his reflection in the window, Jason thought, *not looking bad for a 40 year old.* He stood at six feet tall and had maintained his broad shoulders and muscular physique. His jet black hair and tanned skin gave him an almost Mediterranean appearance. He walked through the vast open-plan lounge, passing the two black leather sofas that dominated the room, to the kitchen area.

The kitchen was minimalist. Stainless steel cupboards and accessories were in chic contrast to the black marble worktops. As with everything else in the apartment, each item in this room came from top of the range brands. It was an exclusive development after all, marketed towards the higher end of city professionals. He switched the kettle on. Jason was in a good place. He was reaping the rewards of his ruthlessness. He had served his time running pub doors and small time drug dealing. But he hadn't stopped there. Jason always wanted bigger and better things, and it didn't matter who he had to tread on to get them. Having created a fearsome reputation on the drugs scene, he built a successful criminal business and was now enjoying the financial rewards. It seemed a long time since he was 'hands on' managing door security at the pubs in Warrington.

"I'd love a coffee." Jason looked around towards the bedroom door, he'd almost forgotten she was still here. It was the one night stand from last night. Jason couldn't remember her name. She looked ready for the walk of shame, wearing her black dress and high heels. "You need to go, I've got a busy schedule today." Jason said. He didn't even look towards her, whilst he made coffee. The clicking of her heels on the floor was irritating him.

"Charming, I guess we won't be swapping numbers then." An uncomfortable silence followed. She picked up her bag and walked towards the door. "Bye then, I'll see myself out." The door closed shut behind her.

It was the morning after the night before. Jason had been out on the town with his lieutenants, Wayne, Ryan and Carl, watching the football match at the pub. The beers flowed following the City win. Things were on the up at City and the fellas were making the most of it, City had been in the football wilderness and beyond for far too long. Jason hadn't had too much to drink though. He preferred to be in full control. The effects of alcohol weakened his judgement, which was not a good option for a man in his position. Unlike Ryan, who was wasted by the end of the night and had to be carried to a taxi by Jason and Wayne. Carl had scored with a woman earlier and left them to it. Jason had known Ryan since their school days and he thrived on being the alpha male, Ryan always came off second best.

Jason got dressed into his training sweats ready for a good workout at the gym. Fitness was a priority for him. Healthy body, healthy mind, survival of the fittest, being one of his core mantras. He walked back to the kitchen and grabbed a protein shake from the fridge. Whilst he was drinking, his mind drifted back to Ryan, *I need to keep an eye on Ryan, looks like he's going off the rails again.*

After leaving the apartment Jason took the lift to the main exit. The brightness of the sun made him squint, but the warmth was spot on. Jason walked for a short distance to warm up before breaking into a jog. He was looking forward to lifting some weights with Wayne.

Jason was hardly out of breath when he arrived at the gym, which looked like a rundown industrial building from the outside, its Victorian crumbling red brick interspersed with weeds growing from the cracks. The two buildings on either side of it were boarded up and derelict. He pushed open the industrial metal door. It felt cool as he walked inside. Wayne was already there, setting up the plates on the bench press, where the session always began.

"Going to start heavy, big man, can you hack it today?"

"You put more beer away than I did last night, do you think you'll be able to keep your breakfast down?" Jason replied.

"Don't worry about my breakfast. You need to focus on the weights. I'm guessing you didn't get much sleep last night. How was blondie? Jason gave Wayne a look of derision and didn't answer. "I'm going to kick your ass, like last time." Wayne laughed.

It was no laughing matter for Jason. *Come on, focus, I can do this. Wipe that smile off his face.* Leaving the banter for later, Jason lay down on the bench. He took the bar and did his best to make the reps look easy. They had been on the weights together since they were kids, at a back street gym in an old Victorian factory in Warrington. They both took the sessions seriously, no pain, no gain.

Jason loved it here. This was a proper back street gym, loose weights and racks, no cross trainers, seated cycles or running machines. Just rough and ready, in contrast to the leisure club, where he and Kirsty were members. Two hours later they were done. Jason relished the feeling of being pumped up at the end of a workout, it made him feel alive and ready to take on the challenges before him. His build would let him pass for an athletic rugby league player. It gave him an intimidating edge.

"Are you using the booze as an excuse, pal? Thought you were going to kick my ass? Welcome to man town," Jason goaded.

"Enjoy the moment,'' Wayne replied. "You don't experience it that often. Normal service will resume next time."

"You running back home or are you tired?" Jason asked, ignoring his last remark.

"Yeah, sounds good, I'll show you how it's done, fat boy."

Wayne took the bragging rights when it came to running, he was muscular but sleek, more like a footballer than a rugby player. At sixteen he had joined the army but had been discharged after three years, a sliding doors moment in his life. He had been convicted of assault following a fight with some local lads outside a pub in Salisbury. He still had a short military hairstyle and the demeanour of a soldier. In fact, he often used it as a cover story, hinting at a Special Forces background when chatting up women. It was a rumour that he didn't actively dismiss, and rather enjoyed.

They left the gym and started to jog down the dog-shit alley that led to the canal tow path. This part of the canal was still derelict and neglected, not like central Manchester's trendy canal network.

The pace was getting quicker, helped by the flat tow path and a bit of healthy competitive spirit which they both had in buckets.

"There's been a few robberies along here, some woman had her bike taken last week. She tried to fight them off and took a good kicking," Wayne said.

"What's it coming to, beating women up and nicking their bikes? Low life scum is all they are, mate. Anyway, how's business?" Jason replied.

"We're doing well in Glasgow. The boys up there want us to double the shipment. We could sort that from some of the gear we brought back from Bristol."

"Yes, that was a bit of a mess," Jason agreed. "I think we underestimated the locals in Saint Paul's. We did right to get out, last thing we need right now is a turf war. We've got better markets elsewhere. Where did you get the kids from, that you sent down to Bristol?

"Usual kids home in Salford. High maintenance, they created more aggravation rather than getting on with selling the gear. Apparently, Ryan had to intervene to save them from getting tortured."

"You need to instil more fear, give them a kicking, it's all they understand."

"There's plenty more, the kids from Rochdale, we sent to Macclesfield did a good job for us. I'll use them again."

"We're due a visit to Amsterdam, I think they respect us more now with the amount of gear we're shifting. Might have to haggle that price down a bit."

A guy in a black hoodie and grey camouflage combat trousers caught Jason's attention. He was walking along the tow path towards them in the distance. He had his hoodie up, covering his head, and was walking with a confident swagger about him which oozed bad attitude. *What's he up to? This doesn't feel right, if he thinks he's robbing us he's in for a shock, bring it on, boy.* Jason recognised trouble when he saw it. He looked around to see if there were any others with him. *That's all we need, a gang of kids wanting to turn us over.*

"You see what I've seen?" Jason asked.

"Yeah, what's his game? He looks like trouble," Wayne replied.

"Barge him into the canal mate, that'll knock some attitude out of him." Wayne laughed.

"Probably the scum that robbed the woman's bike," he said.

Jason's focus was on the hooded figure, weighing up the threat. He saw him pull out an automatic pistol from his hoodie pocket and was first to react, shouting, "He's got a gun."

The guy in the black hoodie faced them square on, his legs shoulder width apart in a firing stance. He was holding the pistol with his right hand, sideways on like a gangster in a rap video, rather than closing one eye and looking at his target through the sights. It was pointing roughly towards Jason and Wayne. *At least he doesn't know how to use it,* thought Jason.

There was a noise. Jason knew it was a pistol shot with a silencer, since there was no loud bang. Instinctively, Jason crouched and darted to the side. *Nowhere to run, make yourself small, he looks like he's never fired that before, got to drop him.* Jason accidentally ran into Wayne at speed. Caught off balance, Wayne fought to stay on the tow path. Gravity won and he landed in the water feet first. The splash sounded louder than it should have to Jason's heightened senses.

Shit, where did that bullet go? Has Wayne been hit? Out of the corner of Jason's eye he saw Wayne had disappeared from the tow path. *He's no hit man; he doesn't know how to use it.*

The attacker had fired the pistol using only one hand. He had snatched at the trigger causing the pistol to recoil back, moving all over the place, pointing well above his targets.

All of Jason's survival senses and attention became focused on the pistol in the hand of the hoodie. His adrenalin kicked in. It was flight or fight time. His brain went into self-preservation mode, processing the circumstances rapidly. *Fight time.* He was now only five metres from the hoodie and gaining ground rapidly, his whole focus was on survival.

Jason continued to run at full pelt. Experiencing an energy surge like never before, he heard another bullet pass by too close for comfort. His eyes closed as he flinched in reaction to the noise and he waited for the pain of being hit to register, which never came. Moments later he reached the attacker.

Jason launched himself off the ground towards the hoodie, with the momentum of his charge and one hundred kilograms of muscle behind him. He had a fleeting glance at his face, which now looked panic-stricken and showed real fear. Jason rugby tackled the attacker and bear hugged his arms around his waist. *Got the bastard, get the pistol off him. Where is it? Can't see it. Shit.* The force took them both to the ground with a heavy thud. Jason saw the pistol was on the floor, *he's dropped the pistol, get the pistol.* The hoodie looked winded, shocked and disorientated.

The odds were suddenly getting better for Jason. He was instinctively punching the hoodie's head. The hoodie stretched out his arm, struggling to reach the pistol. But Jason's hand was closer. Jason grabbed the pistol and tried to roll away to safety. The hoodie grappled him back in to the scrum. He had a thin wiry build but this guy could fight. His hoodie had fallen, uncovering his head. He looked in his twenties with jet black unruly hair. He punched Jason hard, his fist connecting with Jason's nose. The pain made Jason feel physically sick. He looked up and saw Wayne standing above them both, water dripping off him. *Thank god for that, I could do with some help here.*

Jason had a ringside view and saw Wayne's right foot connect with the attacker's face. There was a sickening crunch noise and his head whipped backwards. His body went limp for a stunned moment before he lunged back towards Jason. But Jason was pointing the pistol at him now, the muzzle only a foot away from the attacker's body. He fired three shots, creating three distinct sounds as the bullets hit the attacker's chest. His body went limp again, this time for good.

Jason could taste iron in his mouth but couldn't tell if it was blood from his nose or some chemical reaction to stress and fear. He felt exhausted.

"Check his pockets, Wayne. Do you know him, who the hell is he?" Jason shouted, catching his breath.

"Never seen him before, strong bastard, and he didn't like you, pal." Wayne said this as he rummaged through the assailant's pockets. "Just a phone, I'll have that. I don't recognise him. Surely, he's not one of our dealers, looks in his twenties. You been hit?"

They both scanned Jason's body but couldn't see any wounds or blood. Jason felt euphoric, pumped up with adrenalin. His exhaustion left him so quickly that it was almost like an out of body experience. He started to laugh now the danger had dissipated.

"You been for a nice swim in the canal whilst I gave him some?" he asked.

Wayne was soaking wet.

"Come on, let's move," he said. "You look okay, don't think he hit you."

Jason watched as Wayne did a visual and touch check of his own body. He didn't find any wounds.

"Get him into the water, we need him out of the way," Jason said. He started rolling him over, pushing with his feet. Wayne did likewise. The body was hard to move. Together, they managed to edge it over the side of the tow path and into the canal. There was a quiet splash as the surface of the water was broken. With nothing to weigh it down, the current pulled the body to the side, where it became partly hidden amongst the weeds, grasses and other debris at the water's edge. Seeing this, Jason had a worrying thought and asked, "Any cameras about?"

Both of them scanned the area. There was a thick border of bushes, small trees and brambles with polythene bags and other litter strewn around. It separated the canal from the industrial units on the other side.

"The only camera is on the building over there, we'll need to get rid of it," Jason said, answering his own question. The building he was referring to was the closest industrial unit to the canal and had a camera pointing along its length, possibly covering the tow path. Jason looked at the body in the canal. It was floating, lifeless, face down. The back of the black hooded jacket was bulging with air like a bin bag in the water, covered in part by the grass. Jason looked around on the ground. "Make sure we haven't dropped anything."

"Shit. There's a jogger coming," Wayne said, looking to Jason.

Jason looked along the tow path and saw the jogger in the distance. He could just make out that the guy was wearing a Manchester United shirt.

"He's too far away, he can't have seen anything. The body is covered by the grass. He'll probably not see it."

The jogger was a few hundred metres away on the tow path, having appeared from around a bend. Luckily, he didn't appear that fit, his jogging was more of a labour, his pace slowing even as they watched.

"Let's do one, back to the alley, as long as he doesn't see our faces we're okay," Wayne said. He picked up a plastic bag from the shrubbery and handed it to Jason, who put the pistol inside. As they began to jog back Jason's legs would hardly move. They felt like lead weights, it was like he had lost some control over them after the adrenaline rush.

"What was that all about? He chose a good quiet stretch to take us out, but struggled to use the pistol properly," Jason said.

"But that's now worked to our advantage," Wayne pointed out. "The closest flats were far enough away and the windows didn't cover us. I think we should be okay with this one. No witnesses. We just need that cctv."

"I was lucky he didn't know his arse from his elbow with a pistol. I don't think he expected me to run at him, it spooked him good style. Did you see his face? He shit himself."

"Amateur, I need to find out who he is, and what it was all about. There's no way someone's hired him, he couldn't hit a barn door. I should have taken a photo of him," Wayne said. They reached the alley and left the canal tow path by the edge of the industrial estate, where they concealed themselves alongside a fence at the back of a works unit. Wayne put a call in to Ryan's burner phone.

"I'm with Jason. We've just had some wanker try to shoot us on the canal. Pick us up in the van soonest, mate, we're next to the carpet warehouse further down from the Spinners Arms. Bring some towels and spare sweats for us, Ryan. I'm pissed wet through. Jason threw me in the canal."

Jason looked at Wayne and started laughing, "You're lucky it's hot, mate, you're drying out already. Still can't believe you went for a swim whilst some lunatic is taking pot shots at me."

"And there's me thinking you pushed me to safety out of harm's way, you psycho," Wayne replied.

Ryan ended the call with Wayne. He knew the score, he had been working for Jason for a long time. They worked well together, like a well-oiled machine. He threw some sweats and hoodies into a holdall bag and walked to the builders yard, which was Wayne's legitimate cover business. He opened the roller-shutter door of the unit and went inside. After climbing into the driver seat of the van, Ryan grabbed the keys from behind the sun visor.

It looked like any other builder's van, off white, filthy and battered around the edges, having been a workhorse for many years. On the back someone had written in the grime, 'I wish my wife was this dirty.' It did have one significant difference though, false registration plates. Ryan knew this came at a risk but there were far fewer cops on the streets these days, so the chances of being pulled over were low. Besides, if he did get pulled, he could easily outrun the plod on foot. The protection the plates gave was well worth the risk. He set off to pick the fellas up.

Jason saw Ryan pull the van over alongside the kerb.

"He's here, let's go."

Jason scanned the area from the alley. It looked all clear. They got into the back of van, *no one about, looking good, keep focused,* Jason reminded himself.

"Where to, fellas?" shouted Ryan, above the noise of the diesel engine.

"Back to the yard, pal," replied Jason, adding, "We've just been shot at by some lunatic. I took the pistol off him and slotted him. He's now floating in the canal."

"Any idea who it was?" Ryan asked.

"Not a clue," Jason answered honestly. "Lad in his twenties, black hair, wiry and strong, looked like he may have done some boxing. He knew where to find us though. He'd been waiting for us. It looks like he'd done some homework. We need to find out who he is, pronto, and find out if anyone else was involved or if someone put him up to it. It needs to be stamped on."

There was no time to lose. The plans to cover their tracks were discussed in the back of the van. This was nothing new. They knew the threats that needed to be addressed. Jason took charge as usual, he shouted to Ryan to make himself heard over the engine noise.

"The cctv camera at the electrical supplies industrial unit needs grabbing straight away. When you've got it, destroy it. I couldn't see any more but a sweep will need doing from the gym to the bridge near the flats along the canal. There are no cameras at the gym, we're okay there. Did you notice any strangers in the gym Wayne?"

"No, Dean and his mate were training, and the lads from the Racecourse estate, that was it," Wayne said. "And they know better than to talk to the cops if they come sniffing around. We need to get rid of these clothes and have a shower. We've probably got traces from the pistol shots."

Ryan drove the van into the yard. It was the perfect business cover for their drug dealing activities. Wayne once ran it as a legitimate building company, but he didn't need to anymore. The money from his new venture was much better. The exterior red brick walls, finished with razor wire provided them with the anonymity they sought. The yard was cluttered with timber, bricks and builder's machinery which made it unspectacular to the passer by. At the far end of the yard was a steel fabricated unit with a roller shutter door. "Ryan you get straight back to the canal and sort out the cctv, we haven't got much time." Jason said.

"Leave it with me, I'll check for any other cameras whilst I'm there." Ryan replied. Jason and Wayne got out of the van, the side door slid shut and Ryan set off.

Ryan parked the van a few streets away from the gym. He walked towards it, over the rough ground and to the tow path. He was left in no doubt where they had been attacked. He saw an area of the tow path sealed off with police cordon tape and a uniform cop stood guarding the scene. It looked like they had just arrived. He needed to move fast to beat them to any incriminating cctv footage.

It wasn't difficult to work out which building had the cctv. Ryan made sure his baseball cap and hoodie concealed his identity and made his way onto the industrial estate. He wasn't too concerned about the cop on the canal, he was too focused on protecting the crime scene before the detectives and forensic people arrived. Even if the cops rumbled him, he would just assume the role of an unlucky burglar with no involvement in the death.

The industrial unit was one of three adjacent to the tow path, separated by a wire fence and shrubbery that gave Ryan cover from the cop at the scene. He walked along the side of the building and saw the camera that Jason had mentioned. It didn't look like a dummy. From this position he could see there were no cameras on the other two units. He couldn't see any on the other side of the canal either. The would-be assassin had chosen his location well.

As Ryan walked around to the side of the building, the adrenaline started to kick in. He was in the zone. The door was protected by the usual bog-standard roller-shutter with a cheap padlock securing it. He took out his jemmy bar from under his hoodie and forced the padlock. The roller-shutter retreated easily with one firm push and he quickly lay on the floor, using his legs to boot the bottom panel of the door through. He sprang up and was inside the building in seconds.

Easy, these places need some proper security. Even better, there's no alarm. Ryan couldn't believe his luck. He ran down a corridor and opened the first door he came to. It was the kitchen.

The alarm activated with a loud piercing screeching noise and made him jump. *Shit, the pressure's on, the cop will be able to hear it.* He ran further down the corridor, opened the next door along and ran into a large workshop area. There was a lean-to office in the corner. Ryan was now feeling the pressure. He knew that if the cops were switched on they'd be on their way, which meant he had only minutes to get this sorted.

He headed straight for the office. The door was unlocked, and there on a desk was the cctv hard drive next to a monitor. He ripped it from its wires, dropped it into his carrier bag and sprinted across the workshop passed the parked vans to a fire door in the corner. Opening the door so that it was ajar, Ryan took a peep. He couldn't see anyone about so he slipped out of the building and made his way up the entry back towards the road.

Not bad at all, in and out in minutes, he thought. These skills had been refined over many years of misspent youth, during which time he was in the care of the local authority. Ryan made his way back to the van, sticking to the shadows. *Job done.*

Wayne and Jason entered the unit, it was a large open area with two floors of porter cabin offices at the far end. They made their way to the shower room and stripped off their clothing. They washed themselves down in detergent, hoping to rid themselves of any traces of gunshot residue. They didn't know for sure if it worked, but they'd always done it as routine. Jason was first into the shower. He threw his clothing onto the shower tray. The hot water felt good, and the fading smell of the detergent felt even better.

"I enjoyed that. Makes you feel alive," Jason shouted from the shower.

"He didn't stand a chance," Wayne replied. "Good effort, pal, you've still got what it takes. Took some balls to run at him, it's the last thing he expected to happen."

"Well I had to. I didn't see the man from Atlantis getting stuck in," Jason laughed.

Wayne got into the shower as Jason left. He threw Jason's sodden clothing on the floor and replaced them with his own. Jason started to dry himself off. He still felt on a high with the rush of endorphins and adrenaline. He felt great and his reputation, as a psycho who shouldn't be messed with, had been reinforced. One question still burned away at him though. Who was it and what was his game? He needed to know.

They got dressed into the spare gym sweats that Ryan had brought. Jason put a pair of surgical gloves on and removed a panel from the kitchen wall. He wiped the pistol down and placed it with the wet clothing into the wall recess and returned the panel. The gloves went into his pockets to be ditched safely later on, away from the unit.

"I think we're sorted here, let's go." Jason said.

They left the unit by the rear door and began to jog towards the edge of the housing estate, known locally as 'The Concrete' in recognition of the soulless architecture. They continued through the rabbit-warren back alleys. They looked like two regular Joes, out for some exercise. The conversation was anything but that of two regular Joes, but this gave them the advantage of not being overheard by anyone.

"It doesn't make sense. He's definitely not a pro. But he targeted me and was happy to take me on. He must have known my reputation," said Jason.

"He must have thought he was Billy big bollocks with the pistol, he didn't bank on you taking it off him?" Wayne replied, almost to himself.

"We've no issues at the Amsterdam end, and everything is tidy in Manchester and Liverpool. We could have trodden on someone's toes whilst dealing in Cheshire? I can't see anyone from Bristol coming up, but it's a possibility. We pissed a lot of people off dealing down there. I'm not too worried. It might just have been some buck wanting to make a name for himself."

"That's the likeliest explanation. We'll have to wait until the cops find him to find out who he is. I thought your time was up, mucker. First thing I knew I was in the canal."

"We'll keep it tight between the three of us for now, ears to the ground but we won't task any of the lads to go digging. We need to distance ourselves from it for the time being. If there's been a conflict with our lads we will soon find out."

"The cops will have him identified by tonight I guess. He looked like they would have known him," Wayne said.

"We'll need to keep our heads down. It's no manslaughter, that's a murder charge all day long."

"It sends the right message back to the fuckers though."

"Yeah, they can bring it on. I do enjoy a bit of sport, it makes you feel alive."

"It stops us getting complacent too," Wayne said.

"Time for a pint, whilst we wait for Ryan." Jason said as they approached The Wagon & Horses.

It was a typical backstreet Manchester boozer, off the beaten track. A brick building painted white with a black door and rotting window frames in need of more than a lick of paint. It was a well-known haunt for local shoplifters selling their joints of meat and shaving razors in the snug. It was a bit moody, not very welcoming to outsiders and most importantly it was a well-known fact that the punters minded their own business. The landlord was an older fella who looked like he had aged prematurely because of smoking and boozing. He looked like he hated his job, or maybe he just hated the punters. Either way, he'd struggle to look more disinterested if he tried. A local sat at the end of the bar looking at a racing paper, keeping himself to himself. The only other customers were two lads in council work gear sat at a table.

Wayne and Jason were on their second pint when Ryan entered the pub. They were sitting in the corner, well away from the other punters. The inside of the pub was dark and dingy, the tables and chairs were well past their sell by dates and the carpet should have been condemned years ago. The pattern on this last item had disappeared under the grime. Ryan ordered three pints and joined them in the corner. "Bet you needed that, fellas," Ryan laughed.

"How've you got on Ryan," Jason replied.

"The camera on the industrial unit is sorted, just a simple system, so I got in and took the hard drive. The alarm didn't go off until I was well inside, Jesus it was loud, my ears are still ringing. I nearly jumped out of my skin when it went off."

"Any other cctv around?" Jason asked.

"No, it's a good location, I can't see you having any comebacks."

"Good man," Jason acknowledged, and then gave his instructions. "I want you to destroy the hard drive, pistol and clothes. Thinking on, let's get rid of the van to be on the safe side. It's time we changed it, we've had it for far too long anyway. Get it scrapped. Let's not make it easy for the cops. I need you to hold the fort and keep your ears to the ground. We need to know who we're up against. The cops will do the monkey work for us. Me, Carl and Wayne will head out to the Dam tonight, it gets us out of the way in case the cops get a lucky break. I've got a meeting with the Dutch boys and the Columbian wants to meet up too. Probably wants to put the prices up."

“Shall I get some of the lads to do some digging?” Ryan asked.

“No, keep it low key pal. I suspect it’s a maverick trying to make a name for himself, so let the info come to us. We don’t want to show too much interest and alert the cops to us.” They finished their drinks and got into Ryan’s car.

Ryan dropped Jason off outside his flat.

“Thanks, Ryan,” he said. “You can use my car whilst I’m away, don’t prang it though. I’ll give you a bell when I know the flight times.”

Wayne got out from the back of the car and jumped in the front passenger seat.

“Looking forward to Amsterdam, I might enjoy a bit of indulgence once the meetings are done,” he said, as Ryan drove the car away.

“It’s okay for some. I’ll take on the role of taxi driver and odd job man, being careful not to prang his car of course,” Ryan replied.

“Ouch, do I sense some bitterness in the air?”

“I just get a bit sick of it. He’s always been the same with me. It’s like I need to know my place, I’m sure he gets a kick out of it.”

Wayne stayed silent. If there was a rift growing between Jason and Ryan, he was staying well clear of it. Jason made sure Ryan never went short, but it still rankled with Ryan that he was at the bottom of the food chain. After he had dropped Wayne off he headed into town to pick up some charlie. He was more than ready for a few lines, a perk of the job. Perhaps one he could do without. He didn’t know when he’d had enough, as with the booze.

Jason walked into his flat and placed his keys down on the kitchen worktop. The smell of industrial detergent had followed him home. He decided to have another shower to get rid of the stench and any remaining gunshot residue. It was this kind of attention to detail that had kept him below the radar of the police for all these years.

Now on his own, he had time to reflect. His mind was racing with questions. *Who put the hit on me? That was no chance robbery. I've pissed nobody off in Amsterdam, Carl has had no issues in Manchester, same with Wayne in Liverpool, the supply has been smooth, and the merchandise is good quality. Is there a new supplier on the scene?*

Away from the lads and without the need for public bravado, Jason admitted to himself that he had been up against it today. It could easily have ended far worse for him.

His attention was brought back to the moment by his mobile phone ringing. He left the shower, wrapped a towel around his waist and walked over to the kitchen. The phone displayed 'Kirsty'.

"Hi babe, what are you up to?" Jason said.

"Just back from the gym, that personal trainer is a right evil bastard," she laughed. "Lee and his girlfriend Samantha were there again. I had a coffee with them, they're a nice couple, we should take them out for a curry one night."

"No pain, no gain, you know the routine. Yes, they seem okay, he said he was in the military, served in Iraq and Afghanistan. He works down in London guarding VIP's but gets back to Manchester to see Sam. What does she do for a living?"

"I think she works at a solicitors firm, or something like that. What time are you back tonight? I was thinking we could go for a curry, at the new place on the in Rusholme," Kirsty suggested.

"Sounds great, but I was just going to phone you. The Algarve apartment complex I invested in has hit a problem, probably some bent official who wants to get his grubby hands on more money. The solicitor out there wants a meeting. I'm going to fly out with Wayne and Carl tonight and get it sorted."

"I might go and visit my mum and dad for a few days then, not seen them for ages."

"Good idea, I'll phone you when I know what's happening out there. I might extend it a few days and have a bit of a jolly, which reminds me, we are due some chill time. Give some thought to where you fancy. Ryan is staying in town, looking after things, so if you need anything, give him a bell."

Jason still experienced a gut feeling of anxiety when he mentioned Ryan's name to Kirsty. He had first met Kirsty years ago when she was going out with Ryan. Jason was 23 years of age and they were 18, the 5 year age difference was significant at that age. They had got together whilst she was out on the town in Warrington with her pals and Ryan was working the doors for Jason. It didn't take long for Jason to charm her away. Of the two of them, Jason was the better looking guy and the better catch. What Ryan had, Jason wanted, especially an athletic, attractive, blonde girlfriend. In those days Kirsty was a hairdresser hiring a chair in a salon. Soon after she hooked up with Jason, he set her up with her own business and premises which she developed into a successful chain under her own steam independently from Jason. They had been together now for over ten years. These days the relationship came second to their respective businesses, especially in Jason's case. They didn't have much in common anymore, and spent a lot of time apart.

Once he was settled on the sofa with a coffee, Jason booted up his laptop and booked the tickets for the flight from Manchester airport. Dirk would sort out their accommodation at the other end. His mind was taken back to the shooting on the canal. In the past there had always been rising tensions prior to any conflict or trouble. But there had been no indication that this was going to happen today. He had been caught totally unaware. Although he was still in the dark, Jason took solace in the fact that the hoodie gunman was incompetent and now dead in the canal. *Could it be one of the care home kids we've been using to deal? They're mad reckless little bastards.*

Jason was mainly hands-off now, apart from the importation meetings in Amsterdam to sign off the shipments. The day to day management of the charlie, heroin and weed supply was overseen by Wayne and Carl. Today's incident had rocked Jason's boat and made him question their ability to keep a lid on things. It made him question whether he had gone hands off too soon. He knew he had to be patient, the identity of the shooter and his motivation would be revealed soon enough.

Chapter Two

Whilst Ryan was doing a runner from the industrial estate, Detective Inspector Andrea Statham was at the Force Training School. She was delivering a case study of one of her murder investigations to the latest trainee detective course. It was a regular date in her diary. She was probably the most experienced and respected Detective Inspector in the Force.

Andrea had learned her trade with the Metropolitan Police in London. Being an ambitious young female detective in those days wasn't easy. But she now reaped the rewards of learning in the school of hard knocks. It helped her to develop her persistence, guile and tenacity. Andrea had transferred up north following her acrimonious divorce. Her ex worked for the Met too, and she had needed to put some miles between them. Andrea's phone display lit up on the desk in front of her, but she was too far away to see the caller ID. She needed a coffee anyway, and directed the class to break off into their groups, to discuss interview plans for the suspect in her case study.

The corridor was decorated with group photographs of previous course attendees. Some would argue it was more of a rogues-gallery. The crime training staffroom was empty. Andrea put the kettle on. She also fancied a cigarette, but she was three weeks into quitting. *Better make the coffee a bit stronger*, she thought, putting an extra spoonful in her cup. The room was a basic kitchenette with cheap wall cabinets. An A4 piece of paper was taped onto the cupboard door, 'Please clean up after using the kitchen facilities.' Another notice was stuck to the fridge, 'Do not take food from this fridge that does not belong to you.' *Jeez, Detective Training school. What has it come to? Must be part of the theft syllabus.* She took her coffee and sat at the plain white dining table.

The missed call was from DS Pete Higgs. Andrea pressed return call. He answered almost immediately.

"Hi, Ma'am, are you free to speak?" Pete asked.

"Yes, I'm just having a coffee, everything okay?" Andrea asked the perfunctory question but she already knew the answer. Pete was an experienced Detective with 28 years in the job, one year more than herself. He didn't phone her unless it was something serious.

"I've just turned out to a job, a body in the canal. A local dog walker discovered it about half an hour ago. It's a male, mid-twenties, several wounds which look like gunshots. The police surgeon is on route to certify death. Incident log number 1028, if you want to get a heads up."

"I'm virtually done here. I'll wrap it up and meet you at the crime scene. Can you get the fast track actions allocated?" Andrea was quietly relieved to be leaving the desk top exercise world of the training school for a real case to get stuck into.

"I'm on with it, the scene is secured, the police surgeon is sorted, and the crime scene manager is on her way. I'll not bother calling the pathologist to the scene. The body has been moved anyway. The team are making their way over to get on with a witness trawl and cctv enquiries. The press office has been onto me already so I've put out an initial holding statement, usual routine."

"Sounds good," Andrea sighed. "I'll contact the Coroner and set up a Home Office post mortem for later on. It's going to be a long day, see you in a bit."

Andrea finished her coffee. She enjoyed working with Pete. They had worked together on and off over the years in various crime squads. Their current posting on the Major Incident Team would probably see both of their careers to a conclusion.

Back in the classroom, Andrea made her apologies to the Training staff and students. On her way to the car she rang the Coroner and requested permission for a Home Office Pathologist to undertake a post mortem. Permission was granted as expected.

About half an hour later she parked up in the cul-de-sac near to the canal and walked over the black metal foot bridge to the scene. She could see a white forensic tent covering the body. Pete was talking to the crime scene manager, Aisha, who was wearing her protective forensic suit, ready to get started.

"The doctor's been," Pete said, in lieu of greeting. "Life has been pronounced extinct."

"Let's have a look then. Have you got a suit for me, Aisha?" Andrea asked.

Aisha handed her the protective suit, mask, gloves and boots. Andrea hated wearing the protective equipment on hot days like this. It was like a boil in a bag experience. Once suited up, Andrea and Aisha signed the crime scene log proffered by the bored uniform PC and approached the tent.

"I escorted the doctor in," Aisha said. "From an initial examination there are three gunshot wounds to the chest. All three have exit wounds so we'll need a search for the bullets."

"So, it's looking like he's been shot from close range with a grouping like that, unless it was a military sniper," Andrea observed. "I think we can rule the Manchester canal pusher out of this one, unless he's upped the ante. The water has no doubt weakened our chances of forensics, what do you think? Photos, swabs for what it's worth and tape lifts, then body recovery?''

"Yes, we can do the rest at the mortuary, it's worth a try," Aisha said.

"Can we take fingerprints too, in case the identification isn't straight forward?" Andrea asked.

"Yes, I'll write up a forensic strategy for you to sign off. If you look at his face, near his nose and lips, there is a little grazing. It could be consistent with a fight, it looks recent."

"Interesting, he doesn't look familiar. I'm guessing he's known to us. My hunch is a gang dispute, quiet location, no witnesses, pre-meditated."

Andrea left the tent and walked the short distance up the tow path to Pete at the cordon.

"I need to get this suit off, it's too hot," she said. "Let's head back to the nick and take stock of where we're at. And where's that bloody annoying alarm coming from? I need a cigarette right now."

"It was going off when I arrived. It's over there somewhere on the industrial estate. I've radioed it in to get a patrol to check it out. I think you need some more nicotine patches on. Let me get you a coffee, that'll chill you out."

Andrea removed the forensic protective suit and felt instant relief. She could feel sweat under her blouse, she hoped it couldn't be seen through her blouse. They both walked back to their cars and headed back to the police station.

Pete walked into the DI's office with two black coffees. It was a modern office, glass partition walls with horizontal blinds separating it from the main detective office. Andrea was sitting behind her desk, reading through the incident log on her computer. Pete took one of the four chairs at the meeting table.

"Cheers, Pete, just what I need. How are we doing?"

"There are no house to house enquiries as such, but as a cautionary measure we will do the block of flats further up the canal, you never know. I've extended the cctv capture parameters wider as there's nothing much near the scene. We might get the offenders on their way to or from the scene. I've requested fingerprints to be taken from the deceased for identification then we can get on with the victim lines of enquiry. I've tasked the Informant Handling Unit for any intelligence. The teams are all busy on outside enquiries. Coffee time?"

"Looking good," Andrea said. "The post mortem is all set. I'll have to head over there shortly. Hopefully we'll find out who he is soon from the fingerprints. Oh, and by the way, it's called the Covert Human Intelligence Source Unit these days, you dinosaur."

"Sounds like some sci-fi movie. What's wrong with old fashioned Informants Unit?" Pete laughed.

"Don't knock it. People get promoted on the back of re-inventing the wheel. We'll be working late tonight; did you have any plans?" Andrea asked.

"No, me and the Mrs had a few drinks and a curry in Rusholme last night with some mates. I was looking forward to some telly and an early night tonight. I'm betting you had plans?"

"Picking this job up may be for the best, I was meeting a new internet date in town. I'm not doing so well with the internet dating, so these long hours save me the disappointment, and keep me out of the pub. Have you got any nice single mates, Pete?"

"None who are brave enough to take you on," Pete laughed, knowing she was joking. Andrea was an attractive woman who had many admirers around the force, and she knew it. She was a good catch for the right guy.

"Right, thanks for that vote of confidence. I'll get off to the mortuary for the post mortem. Keep me up to speed with any updates."

Andrea put her jacket on and grabbed her handbag. She enjoyed the banter with Pete. Their relationship did not go beyond work but their mutual trust and respect for each other was solid.

Andrea pressed the intercom button at the mortuary entrance. The metal gates slowly opened and she drove into the small enclosed back yard. The mortuary staff had recognised her car on the monitor screen. She had become a regular visitor over the years. The CSI van was already parked up alongside the black Range Rover which she knew belonged to the Home Office Pathologist Sarah Lovick. Andrea walked in through the back doors which led directly to the refrigerated units where the bodies were stored.

The bright lights and pungent smell hit Andrea's senses straight away. She signed in and walked along the corridor to the viewing room, where she was the last to arrive, as usual. Aisha, Sarah, Graham the mortuary technician, and DC Morris the exhibits officer were drinking coffee and eating biscuits. Andrea declined Graham's offer of a brew and got on with the briefing. She sensed they were all eager to get going and could see through the viewing window that the deceased was laid out on the examination table.

At the end of her briefing, Andrea nipped into the kitchen and made a coffee whilst the other three put on their protective clothing and entered the mortuary post mortem examination area. It wasn't long ago that she would have been in there with them, but new health and safety guidelines restricted her to the viewing area. As Andrea returned to the viewing room, she took out her phone and sent a message to her date, Martin, the car sales executive from Bury. *Really sorry I've had to work late, love to meet another time ... genuine x.* She took out her case book and caught up writing her notes, whilst awaiting the start of proceedings.

The intercom speaker broke her line of thought.

"Andrea, I'm going to start. Aisha has completed your forensic requests. My first impression is that the body was not in the water for long, between one and two hours at the most."

Andrea continued to update her notes and policy decisions from earlier. She had worked alongside Sarah many times, and awaited the next observation. Sarah had been a pathologist for years and was good at her job. They had worked together often, investigating unexplained and suspicious deaths. Andrea didn't expect Sarah to discover any surprises at this post mortem. Andrea's mobile started to ring.

"Hi, Pete, you solved it yet?"

"Nearly, you'll love this one. The alarm that was pissing you off at the scene was the industrial workshop unit with the only cctv camera we could find covering the scene. The cheeky bastards have broken in and removed the cctv hard drive. It's the best chance we had of catching the offenders on video footage. I've got forensics at the Unit now, we may get some fingerprints. The gunman chose a good location here, it's isolated, a good bit of planning has gone on I think. Not many people about on a Sunday and half of the units are empty anyway. Have the fingerprint bureau got back to you yet?"

"Not yet, Sarah's just started the post mortem. She reckons he hadn't been in the water for long, so that narrows down our timeline. If we can blast through the fast track enquiries today we will be good to go when he is identified and the intelligence starts coming in tomorrow."

"We need to trace a potential witness. The dog walker who discovered the body saw a jogger wearing a Man United shirt, she reckons the jogger was fifteen minutes ahead of her and could have seen something."

Sarah interrupted on the intercom, "Andrea, I've got the trajectory of the bullets for you, no surprises."

"I've got to go, Pete. I'll phone you later."

Andrea stood up and approached the viewing window and microphone intercom. She glanced at her phone. There was no reply from Martin… *No surprises there then, what a shame, he seemed a decent lad, he wasn't just interested in sexting.*

Sarah continued, "Three wounds in a very close grouping of eight centimetres around the sternum. Looks like they are from very close range. Exit wounds in the back so I'm not expecting to recover any bullets." Andrea could see the metal rods placed into the wounds to illustrate trajectory on the photographs. Aisha was busy taking photographs of the wounds. "Right, I've done with the external examination, I'll crack on with the internal examination."

Andrea wasn't expecting any breaking news from this but a thorough examination was still required of all the vital organs. She stayed at the window writing her notes and watched.

Two hours later Sarah was finished. She left the room to get changed, leaving Graham to repatriate the organs to the body.

Andrea put the kettle on and made coffee for everyone in preparation for the debriefing. DC Morris was first to return.

"All sorted, Ma'am, I'll get the Forensic examination requests done first thing in the morning if that's okay?"

"That's fine," Andrea replied. "I don't expect any surprises on this one. You get going if you like. It's been a long day."

"That's great, thanks. I'll get back to the nick and book this into the fridge, see you in the morning," DC Morris said.

Sarah was next to enter, she had changed out of her blue scrubs and was now wearing her usual attire, fleece top and walking trousers. Andrea got on well with Sarah. She was down to earth and pragmatic, an outdoors woman who was into climbing, mountain biking and walking.

"How's the barn conversion going, Sarah?"

"Really well thanks, I'm enjoying it. I'm tempted to move into it and rent the cottage out instead of the barn, I'm not sure whether the other half will want the upheaval though. You still doing the internet dating?"

"Unfortunately, I'm not doing too well. I had a date for tonight and had to cancel on him."

"Hey, we need to meet up. We're overdue a drink and you can tell me all about your conquests," Sarah laughed.

"Moving on," Andrea said, as they were joined by Aisha.

"The cause of death was gunshots to the chest, inflicting fatal injury to the heart and subsequent blood loss," Sarah said, taking the hint. "He was dead before he entered the water."

"No bullets recovered from the body?" Andrea asked.

"No."

"Any signs of drug abuse?"

"No marks or signs on the body. We will have to wait for the toxicology reports. He did have injuries to his face, consistent with punches or other blunt force trauma."

"There was grazing to his knuckles as well. It's looking like there was a fight prior to him being shot," Aisha added.

"So, it's either a chance meeting, which I doubt because of the isolated area, or it's been set up which is more likely. Can I just double check there are no signs of him being tied up?" Andrea said.

"No, no markings, which I would expect to see if he had been tied up," Sarah confirmed.

"Right, thank you everyone, it's been a long day. Time for something to eat."

"I'll get the report emailed to you when I get the toxicology back."

Andrea updated Pete on her mobile from her car and set off for home. She was quite hungry now and decided to pick up a takeaway pizza on her way back. Her usual meal for one washed down with a glass of wine. *Still no reply from Martin, another one bites the dust.*

Chapter Three

Elsewhere in the City, Ryan was on taxi duty, picking the fellas up to take them to the airport. He had already collected Wayne and Carl. They were in the back of his SUV. Wayne had recounted the events on the canal to Carl.

"That must have taken some balls to run straight at the shooter," he said.

"He went into his psycho mode, pushed me into the canal to make sure I didn't spoil his fun. He looked like he enjoyed it, ran straight at him and rugby tackled him to the floor whilst being shot at. It could have easily ended badly for him. I don't know why the shooter got so close to us, he must have planned where he was going to shoot from. Jason made him have it. He was like an animal going in for the kill."

"It's probably as simple as that. The shooter never expected Jason to run at him. Then he panicked, happens to the best of us. It's like we've gone back in time running the clubs in Warrington, would-be gangsters taking a pop at us," Wayne said.

"Happy days, Jason loves it. He was on a massive high afterwards. I'm not sure if he realised how close he came to the end, or maybe that's what he gets off on. It's a reminder of how mad he is. Do you remember the guy who tried to chat Kirsty up in Benidorm?"

"I must have missed that one, what happened?" Carl asked.

"After the initial bust up, Jason shook his hand and invited him for more drinks. After that they ended up walking to a hotel to score some charlie. The fella was absolutely wasted. Jason went into psycho mode and threw him over the balcony. Local police weren't interested, just another pissed up tourist dead."

"My gut feeling is that it's some wannabe young buck trying to make a name for himself. He could be one of the Liverpool lads. They always have that edge of intimidation about them."

"Have any of your lads had any aggravation recently, Carl? The local lads know better and wouldn't dream of taking Jason on."

"No, nothing that would escalate to that, whoever it was did their homework on him. They knew where to find him."

"And they chose their location well. It was deserted around there. We took the only cctv, so hopefully we've covered our tracks. There must have been others involved," Ryan said, as he parked the car near to Jason's place. His mind was elsewhere, on the night in Benidorm, he had asked Kirsty to return to the last bar they visited, on the pretext that he had lost his wallet. He wanted to protect her from seeing Jason go psycho on her hopeful suitor. It wasn't the first time he had protected her from the dark side of Jason. It was a pure act of love for her, not seeking any reward or favour.

The front passenger door opened and Jason slid into the car.

"Cheers Ryan, I appreciate you holding the fort. Keep us up to date with developments. I've got us some new burner phones. Give Ryan your old ones fellas and use these."

He handed them out and put Ryan's in the cup holder.

"Make sure these old phones are destroyed, Ryan," he said. "No slip ups."

Ryan was pissed off. Once again, he was being condescended to, as the runt of the litter, whilst they did the serious stuff and got to enjoy a trip to Amsterdam. He felt like Jason's errand boy.

The drive only took twenty minutes to terminal two at Manchester airport. The M60 was quiet at this time of night. The fellas got out of the car and headed for departures. Ryan headed back to town with his pocket full of charlie. He knew he was hitting it hard these days, but so what? Work hard, play hard. *I can handle it, and I know when to stop.* He was going to meet some of the firm's lads for a drink at the arches near Deansgate. Nothing needed doing tonight so it was party time, and he would be top dog for a change. The courier lads assumed Ryan was ensconced in Jason's inner sanctum.

He parked the car and walked over towards Deansgate. He wished he'd not been reminded about the night in Benidorm. He knew of many instances like it and had witnessed quite a few. There was no doubt Jason was a dangerous psycho, but killing a guy for chatting Kirsty up. That was just so wrong, even for him. Jason never mentioned Kirsty to Ryan, the mere fact he stole her from him said it all. Ryan had never forgiven Jason for that, especially because of the way he treated her and cheated on her. He still held a grudge after all these years.

Jason, Wayne and Carl checked in for the flight and went through security. They all started laughing when the security officer took Wayne aside for a pat-down search. It wasn't too busy so security didn't take long. They grabbed their hand luggage from the grey plastic trays and walked through the array of duty-free shops selling booze and perfumes. When they reached the boarding concourse, Wayne checked the departures monitor.

"The flight's on time, fellas. Not boarding yet. Beers?"

Nobody needed to answer. They gravitated towards one of the smaller bars. Jason went to the bar and returned to their table with three pints.

"It will be interesting to find out who our would-be assassin is when the dust settles in the next few days," he said. Jason loved the feel-good factor from the fear he generated, not just on his enemies. If any of his own lads were getting ideas of grandeur or ideas above their station, incidents like this were a sobering reminder of the pecking order.

"I think Ryan was sulking because he wasn't joining us," Carl said.

"He doesn't seem interested anymore," Wayne added. "He needs to ease off the charlie and the booze. It's like he's got a self-destruct button. He's still in small time mode. Cracking thief though."

Jason's ears pricked up. It was the first time any of his boys had badmouthed Ryan in his presence. He knew they wouldn't do that lightly either, but now he knew that his concerns were mirrored.

Even though it was useful to have a second opinion, this was not the time to run the rule over Ryan. Jason wouldn't deny that he had always kept Ryan at his heel. It hadn't started out as a conscious behaviour, but it just developed naturally over time. Having a whipping boy made Jason look good, and more importantly it made him feel good. Taking Kirsty from him was the ultimate buzz, but as is often the case,

Jason found the chase to be better than the catch. The current state of their relationship reflected that.

"Dirk will be meeting us at the train station," he said, changing the subject. "He'll drive us to the hotel. I'm taking it easy tonight. A few beers in the hotel will do me then hit the town tomorrow after business."

"Are we arranging the shipment with Dirk whilst we're here?" Wayne asked.

"Yes, we've one from Turkey to sort out. It's coming through Liverpool. Hope our dead boy isn't one of their lads, that could complicate matters."

"I don't think it was, they would have done it properly. I reckon it's a lone wolf."

"A misguided wolf," Carl corrected, laughing.

Jason was deep in thought. *If someone put the hoodie up to shooting me, I'll torture them to the slowest possible death.*

After a few beers they boarded their flight to Schiphol and took the opportunity to get their heads down. It had been an eventful day. They were only in the air for an hour and a quarter before touching down in Holland. Again, they cleared security quickly and picked up the train into the city.

"These trains are the business, modern, clean and fast," Carl said. "Christ, we still have pacer trains in Manchester which sound like they're going to break down any minute."

"Never had you down as a train spotter, you weirdo," Jason joked.

As they left the train station, Jason spotted Dirk standing beside his 4x4, parked in the taxi rank. He was a big fella with long straight hair tied into a pony tail and a goatee beard. He was wearing a long black leather coat. Jason started laughing.

"You can't miss Dirk, can you? He must be 6'2" and built like the proverbial, we could have done with him in the old days."

"He looks like an aging rock star from the seventies more than an enforcer," Wayne mocked.

"Welcome, gentlemen, good flight I trust? I will drive you to the hotel. Throw your bags in the trunk." The four of them got into the car and Dirk set off. "I will not talk business tonight. We can save that until tomorrow. That being said, all is going to plan."

After a short drive they arrived outside their hotel near Dam Square. Dirk stayed at the wheel.

"See you tomorrow, guys, don't enjoy yourselves too much."

Jason, Wayne and Carl got out of the truck and walked up the grand stone steps to the hotel lobby. The building had a stone exterior, probably about a hundred years old. They checked in and sat at the hotel bar.

"I'm not going out, lads. I want to run through my numbers and stuff then I'm ready for tomorrow. I've got a hunch they want to change something."

"Why don't we have a quick beer in the bar? Then me and Wayne can go for a leg stretch along the canal and see what's on offer," suggested Carl.

"No, I'll use room service. You boys have a good time. Don't bring any attention to yourselves."

As Wayne and Carl headed for the exit, Jason took the lift to the third floor. He walked along the wide, purple-carpeted corridor, it felt calm and quiet. He opened the room door with his card. The room lights came on when he slipped the card into the receiver. It was a spacious junior suite with a super king size bed.

Hope that's a newish mattress. Bet this room's seen some action. It was decorated in beiges and browns and had brass light fittings. The pictures on the wall were still-life sketches of naked women.

Jason retrieved a bottle of beer from the fridge, took a swig then sat at the dressing table with a pad and pen. He started scribbling numbers and weights, just to refresh his memory. *All looks good, got to be right, a lot more coke than usual and a decent amount of heroin. I must remember to get them to run over the routes again.* Satisfied his numbers were right, Jason ripped the paper into tiny pieces and dropped them out of the window.

Wayne and Carl hadn't made it far along the canal before they found a lively bar. They walked inside. The rock music was loud and the lighting was low accentuating the Seventies style disco lights. It was very small and the few tables were taken already.

"I think we're standing at the bar, pal," Wayne said.

He caught the attention of the woman behind the bar and ordered two beers.

"We're in interesting times, Wayne. That may have been the first of more challenges to come on Jason."

"I think it rattled him more than he's letting on, but he'll never admit it. You've got to respect him though, he's never taken shit from anyone."

"It'll be interesting to see what deal he strikes tomorrow. The shipments have doubled in size and he wants more. I think the Dutch boys are taking him more seriously now. Ryan is causing me concern, something isn't right with him, we need to watch him," Carl said.

“Have you got a downer on Ryan, what’s he done to upset you?” Wayne asked.

“No not at all, I actually like the guy, but he obviously isn’t happy and could potentially cause us some issues.”

“I just noticed you mentioned it a few times to Jason today, you need to be careful. Jason might see a problem when there isn’t one, we don’t need any more dramas. You and I can handle Ryan without bothering Jason.”

They carried on chatting over the current situation over a few beers. Women seemed to have slipped off the agenda.

Back in Manchester, Ryan was being helped into a taxi by two of his lads. He could just about walk but was slurring his words and talking bollocks.

“Cheers, lads. Here, take this with you, we need to keep an eye on them kids we’ve got dealing for us. They’re too young to be in this game. A liability too we need to keep things tighter.”

He held out one of his packets of charlie, which was received gratefully by his boys. The door was closed and the taxi set off. Within moments, Ryan was asleep.

Chapter Four

Andrea Statham was back in the office early the following morning. She started the day by reading through reports of enquires completed by her detectives. It wasn't long before the main office started to get busy with members of the team arriving. She could hear the banter and discussions about the case and orders going in for coffee. There was a tap on her door.

"Morning, Ma'am, I feel like I've not been away," Pete said. "I finished about one o'clock this morning. You ready for a catch up?"

"Morning, Pete. Yes, grab a drink and we'll make a start. Can you ask the team to carry on with their enquiries? We'll have a team briefing later on this afternoon."

Pete left and returned a short time later. He sat down and opened his case book, ready to run through the events of yesterday. Andrea left her desk and joined him at the meeting table, opening her book with pen poised.

"No surprises at the post mortem. Pretty much as we suspected, it looks like he was shot from close range, possibly during a fight or struggle," Andrea began.

"We have an identification on our victim, Paul Smethurst, aged twenty-seven, from Macclesfield. He has previous convictions for assaults and drugs possession. Current intelligence suggests he was involved in running heroin and coke street dealers around Chester and Wrexham. He had no obvious links to Manchester. His next of kin is his elderly mother. A family liaison officer has made contact and is arranging formal identification of the deceased to be carried out today."

Pete paused whilst Andrea was writing in her policy book and slid a bundle of previous conviction computer printouts across the table to her. He then continued, "Not much intelligence is forthcoming but this one is interesting, it appears to be from a reliable source. Our victim has had a dispute with Manchester lads moving in and dealing on his patch. He faced them up and put one of them in hospital. The intelligence suggests the Manchester lads were county lines drug dealing for an Organised Crime Group, headed by a guy called Jason Hamilton. He has previous from a while ago for assault whilst running the pub doors in Warrington. He lives on us now but we've nothing recent about him."

"Interesting line of enquiry, it fits the circumstances too. Who's researching Hamilton?" Andrea asked.

"I've not allocated it yet, but he needs a good looking at. I'll ask the intelligence cell to do some digging."

"He's the best option we've got to look at right now," Andrea agreed. "Can you get back onto the Force Intelligence Unit with a request for further tasking? Right, I'd better get going, I'm going to be late again. I've got some media interviews at Force Headquarters."

"I'm meeting the Tactical Aid Unit at the crime scene to brief them. They will do a final search for the missing rounds of ammunition and anything else we haven't found yet. If we can recover a bullet it will give us a chance of identifying the weapon. Once the search is complete I'll release the scene. I've had the uniform Inspector on my back wanting his officers released. They're thin on the ground for patrols. Catch up with you later," Pete said.

Ryan climbed out of bed. He was starting to get flashbacks from his night out, and for a moment he couldn't remember how he got home. Then he recalled being shaken awake by an irate taxi driver demanding his fare. He switched on the television ready for the local news and went for a shower.

An hour later, whilst making a coffee, he heard the presenter announce the discovery of a body by a dog walker in a Manchester canal. As she handed over to the reporter at the scene, Ryan walked back into the lounge and took a seat.

"At around 4.30pm yesterday, the police were contacted by a man who had discovered a body in the canal." The reporter was on the tow path, with an area cordoned by police tape visible in the background. Ryan could also see a white forensic tent and police officers walking in a line searching the tow path. "At this time a police spokeswoman has confirmed that the body is that of a male, possibly in his twenties, who had been shot. The death is being treated as suspicious."

The reporter continued with a request from the police for anyone who saw anything suspicious in the area, or had any information surrounding the death, to come forward. Ryan switched off the television. He had work to do.

Ryan decided to put some distance between himself and Manchester before disposing of the incriminating evidence. Bristol would be a good location. He could spend a few days with Lisa, a woman he was seeing down there. He had met her, back when he was overseeing the drug dealing in the clubs. The burner phones and SIM cards were already sorted, he had thrown them into the waterway at Castlefields the previous night.

With a quick call, he tasked one of his courier lads to keep his ear to the ground about the guy shot on the canal, in case there were any repercussions that might affect the firm. Ryan made it clear that he wanted it low key, no digging for info, just listening. They needed to keep their distance and not create any links between their lads and the death. Local villains would soon pick up on such interest.

He packed some clothes in a rucksack and set off jogging to the lock-up, his baseball cap and hoodie providing him with cover from any cameras. On arrival he gave the shower unit a dowsing in bleach and double-checked that nothing had been overlooked. Next, he retrieved the bagged clothing and pistol, concealing them with the hard drive in the hidden storage space in the van's bulkhead. Once in Bristol he planned to take the van to a breakers yard and have it converted into a jagged metal cube.

For now, he fixed the original registration plates onto the van just in case he was picked up by ANPR cameras or the motorway cops. He set off, looking forward to seeing Lisa but not looking forward to spending hours on the M6. Jason had pulled them out of dealing in Bristol a while ago, after the local gang had taxed their dealers and a bit of a battle broke out.

That was the official version of events given to Jason. In reality the dealers who got taxed were only teenagers, vulnerable kids in local authority care from

Manchester. Two of them had been kidnapped by the Bristol gang, and tortured with a steam iron. Ryan had handed over a substantial amount of cash and cocaine in return for their safety. Having been in care himself, Ryan despised Jason for exploiting such vulnerable kids and tried to look out for them. He had taken a big risk, Jason couldn't have given a toss about the kids, they were expendable. If Jason ever found out he had handed over drugs and money, he'd be in deep shit.

Ryan was gutted to leave. He enjoyed it down there, especially once he met Lisa, but Jason didn't need the aggravation they were getting.

Five hours later Ryan pulled the van up, halfway onto the pavement, on a quiet road near to a housing estate. It was dark now, with a yellow glow from the street lamps. The dark gave him more cover. Not that anything looked amiss.

He recovered the pistol from the bulkhead, stripped it down into the component parts, washed them over in de-greaser spray and spread them about his pockets. He placed the bags of clothing and hard drive in his rucksack and locked the van. It didn't look out of place here on the edge of the industrial estate. He would get it scrapped later in the week.

Ryan set off jogging towards the docklands area. He looked like any other runner and blended right in. Once he reached the docks he was in familiar territory. He knew which route to take, and one by one the parts of the pistol were launched into the water, not to be seen again. If he was honest with himself, Ryan was relieved the pistol was gone. It was the only item he would have struggled to explain away to the cops. The clothes and hard drive could be sorted later. Now it was time to hook up with Lisa.

Lisa's flat was a short distance away in one of the new build waterfront developments, he ran the long way around to arrive from the opposite direction of the docks. This was purely a precaution. Lisa answered the door, she was a petite, good looking woman with brown hair tied back. Ryan thought she looked happy to see him.

"Didn't think you'd be here 'til later Ryan, I've missed you," she said.

They hugged. Ryan was chuffed to be back. This was the world he most enjoyed at the moment. The relationship had started off as being just drunken sex after they met in a club, but Lisa was growing on him.

"Missed you too, babe, I need to move down here and get a proper job. I've brought us some charlie to be getting on with."

As they were walking up the stairs to the flat, Lisa said, "I'm off for three days, then I'm working for four. How long are you down for?"

"Probably a week, I'll ditch my gear," Ryan said.

He walked into the bedroom. It smelt of Lisa's perfume. The walls were pink designer wallpaper, decorated with stylish pictures of exotic destinations. They contrasted against the white furniture. The room was immaculately tidy, everything in its place. He took the rucksack off his back, grabbed his packet of cocaine, and placed the rucksack in the bottom of the wardrobe. It was pretty safe here. He was off-grid from the cops.

He returned to the lounge and walked through to the kitchen, where Lisa passed him a glass of beer and picked up her G and T. It was like a show house or boutique hotel. The kitchen was pristine white, with metal accessories. The worktops were gloss black with silver glitter. Ryan placed his pack of powder onto one of them and prepared some lines.

"Ladies first," he said and beckoned to her. Lisa took two lines and left three for Ryan. She began to kiss and started to undo the buttons on his shirt. Ryan responded kissing her neck, whilst slowly moving, embraced together, towards the bedroom where they made up for lost time.

It was late afternoon when Andrea Statham and Pete Higgs met back at her office. The main office was virtually empty, but for the exhibits officer and intelligence officer. Andrea had been busy. Straight after filming the media witness appeals she had attended organisational management meetings at headquarters. She was a dyed in the wool detective with twenty seven years' experience and preferred to be doing the job. This meant she didn't care much for such meetings, especially as most were talking shops for those pitching their promotion ambitions.

"It's good to be back," she said. "What a day. The media releases should be aired on the local news tonight. Hopefully we might get some response from them."

"We could do with it. The searches of the scene have been completed, no luck finding the ammunition. It probably ended up in the water. It would have been good to link it to the weapon and open a few more lines of enquiry. Anyway, I've released the scene now. How did your meetings at headquarters go?" Pete asked.

"Nothing significant really. The usual management bullshit bingo, along with the promotion of hot-desking."

“You’re getting more cynical by the day, Andrea. Either that or you need to start smoking again. Are they still pressing ahead with rotating detectives back to uniform every few years?”

“It’ll never happen, just a fad idea. I had an interesting call from Dave Ferguson at the Drugs Unit. Our PNC checks on Jason Hamilton were flagged up to them. They are looking at him on a joint operation with the regional crime squad. Apparently, he’s top dog in an organised crime group, importing drugs and money laundering. Their problem is, he’s hands-off now, and they’re struggling to get evidence directly on him.”

“He’s been well under our radar,” Pete said. “I’ve never heard of him, I must be losing my touch. If the dispute with the deceased is right, it looks like we’re getting somewhere.”

“Apparently he’s in Amsterdam at the moment. He flew out there about six hours after the murder. I wonder why? We’ve not got a lot of evidence on him, just circumstantial and intelligence. So, I think we’ll speak to him from the angle of him being targeted by Paul Smethurst, on the pretext that there may still be a threat to his life, if others are involved. He’d only go ‘no comment’ if we arrested him.”

“It makes sense. If he does talk we may get something useful out of him to work on. We’ve drawn a blank up to now trying to trace the Manchester drug dealer who was assaulted by Paul Smethurst in Chester. The hospital has a record of a teenager attending A & E at about the right time. But he refused to give his details, so they stitched up some cuts and he was on his way before the police or social services had a chance to get involved.”

“At least we’re getting somewhere,” Andrea mused. “It looks like we’re on the right track. Hamilton’s boys go dealing heroin on Smethurst’s turf in Chester. Smethurst isn’t happy, gives them a beating and probably interrogates them to find out who they are dealing for. He then goes after their boss to send a strong message. What isn’t clear yet is how Smethurst ends up dead in the canal. Could it have been an arranged meet with Hamilton’s boys?”

“If we go with that hypothesis, it would make sense that Smethurst had the pistol. Maybe he went to shoot Hamilton and had the pistol taken from him. He did have injuries consistent with a fight.”

“They must have taken his mobile phone, I wish we had that.”

“We might get his number from intelligence. Shame we haven’t recovered any bullets to link to the pistol. There’s still a chance we might recover the pistol I suppose,” Andrea said, more in hope than expectation.

“We’ve made a good contact with Cheshire Police in their Force Intelligence Unit. Paul Hampton, he’s a switched on cookie and is working hard to help from his end.”

“I bet he is. It’s a bit more exciting for him than investigating sheep worrying in the sticks,” Andrea laughed.

Chapter Five

It was the second day in Amsterdam. The fellas had another free night since Dirk had cancelled the meeting to deal with an urgent problem. They had returned to one of their favourite bars to drink and watch some football. It was spacious, with plenty of hidden alcoves offering some privacy. The lights were low. They blended in well with the other groups, which were mostly stag and hen parties making a lot more noise.

Jason was at the table on his own, nursing a beer. Wayne and Carl returned from the basement, an even darker and dingier area where pot was sold and smoked.

"You should have come with us, Jason. They've got some good stuff down there. It's a cool place," Carl said.

"Next time, mate," Jason replied, with some regret. "I'm just running through some details for the meeting. Business first, you know me."

"Is the meeting on for tonight?" Wayne asked.

"Not had a call yet," Jason replied. "I bet he's knocking it on to tomorrow. I'm guessing he's waiting on the Columbian. I hope the problem doesn't involve our shipment."

Wayne stood up and walked over to the bar. He returned with three large beers and placed them on the table.

"Any word from Ryan yet?" asked Carl. Wayne gave him a quizzical look.

"No, but then I'm not expecting to hear from him. I told him not to call unless it was significant. No news is good news, eh?"

"Right then, shall we go and check some entertainment out?" Wayne asked.

The three of them finished their beers and left the bar. They walked alongside the windows looking at the prostitutes behind them, wearing lingerie and beckoning them inside on the promise of a good time.

"Spoiled for choice, fellas," Jason said.

"There's a place down here," Wayne said, "more civilised. It's like a lap dancing bar and the different girls come over to you. Leave this lot for the gawping tourists."

They continued on, brushing aside the pimps doing their best to entice them into their establishments, until they reached the bar that Wayne had mentioned. The low lighting in ambient colours made it feel later than it was. An attractive blonde woman in her twenties, wearing black leather pants and bra top, escorted them to a booth and took the orders for three beers. The music was loud from a quality sound system. The bass vibration travelled through the floor and furniture. They could hardly hear themselves speak.

"Cool music, it's like the Ibiza scene," Wayne said.

Jason nodded, taking in the surroundings. Three scantily-clad women approached their table, dancing to the music. Jason was looking passed them to a stunning looking woman at the bar who was talking to a disinterested punter. When he saw that the woman had given up on the guy at the bar, Jason said, "I know where I'm going. See you back at the hotel later."

He approached the woman and started to talk, then followed her towards the rooms beyond the dance floor. They had made it halfway when Jason felt an aggressive push in his back. He stumbled forward, almost falling over to the floor. The woman made a run for it and disappeared into the darkness.

"She's with me, dickhead."

It was the punter from the bar, a bald guy with face piercings in a black t shirt, his arms covered in tattoos. He was of smaller build than Jason and unsteady on his feet, he was well pissed.

"Don't think so," Jason growled. "She's with me now. Why don't you fuck off back to the bar before I slice you up, boy?"

Jason was right up in the punter's face, glaring with his psycho eyes. His threat had the desired effect. The older guy wasn't up for it and walked back to the bar holding on to chairs for support as he went. The woman reappeared from the shadows.

"Well done, he's a slimy creep," she said.

You're obviously not too bothered. You were rubbing his leg five minutes ago, Jason thought, as they walked through a door that led into a dingy corridor. The woman took him into a tiny room with the dimmest of red lights. All Jason could make out was a narrow single bed. He closed the door behind them.

When Jason returned to the bar, the pissed up bald guy with the face piercings was nowhere to be seen. He ordered a G and T and looked around. Wayne and Carl were no longer in the booth. The place was still busy but the loud music was growing on him. He liked it here. Jason finished his drink and walked to the gents.

The door swung open. As Jason entered he nearly bumped straight into the bald guy who had pushed him earlier. There was an instant look of recognition and fear in his eyes. He attempted to turn towards the sanctuary of a toilet cubicle but was too slow in his drunken state. Jason launched into him with a series of punches to his head. The guy tried to throw a punch back but failed to hit anything but air. Once he was down, Jason repeatedly kicked him, then stepped over his limp form and went to take the piss he had initially come in for.

"Say thank you, you piece of shit," Jason said over his shoulder.

"Thank you," the bald guy mumbled.

"Stay down, or you get more."

The punter lay still on the floor, groaning. Jason stepped over him again on the way out, and made his way back to the hotel. *He was off his head, doubt he'll even remember anything in the morning, apart from the pain.* Jason felt no shame or compassion for the hapless drunk he had just assaulted.

Kirsty was driving home to Manchester along the M6 having spent some time with her parents in Stockton Heath, Warrington. She always enjoyed her visits. Her mum and dad had been married for over forty years and were enjoying their retirement. Their rural cottage was idyllic and peaceful. Kirsty loved their walks along the country paths, particularly in autumn. She looked forward to the beautiful colours on display in the trees and to the log-burning fire on their return to the cottage. It always brought back nostalgic memories of her childhood, and in truth still felt like home. Driving along the tree-lined Avenue to her house, Kirsty noticed that the automated security gates were open. *That's strange, I'm sure they closed when I left*, she thought. *Jason must be home, but surely, he would have called me, or was it a surprise? No, he wouldn't have left the gates open. Maybe they have a fault. It wouldn't be the first time.* She turned the car into the drive and parked by the front door, activating the security light sensors on the porch.

The house was in darkness. Jason was not home. She pressed the button on her fob and the gates slowly closed.

Feeling uneasy, Kirsty entered the house and locked the front door behind her. She picked up the mail and headed for the kitchen. She was well overdue a caffeine hit. After she had flicked the kettle on Kirsty sat at the breakfast bar on a stool, opening the mail. Nothing new, just bills and clothing catalogues. The peace was disturbed by the sound of a dog barking. *It must be the neighbours with the kids on the right,* Kirsty thought.

The kettle began to whistle. Kirsty got up and made a cafeteria of coffee. A cool breeze made goose bumps rise up along her arms as she sat back down. Instinct told her that something wasn't right.

Kirsty walked into the orangery and was startled to find that the doors were wide open. An electric shock of fear and adrenaline descended upon her. *That's why I could hear the dog,* she thought. *Oh my god, is someone in the house? I need to get out.* Her mind started to race, trying to make sense of what was unfolding in front of her. There was no damage to the doors. She grabbed her car keys and ran out of the front door to her car, the hairs on the back of neck standing up. Consumed by fear, Kirsty wished she was back in Stockton Heath by the fire. She got into the car and couldn't lock the doors fast enough. As soon as the gates were open she drove through out of the drive and up the road, creating a safe distance.

Kirsty kept driving until she reached a supermarket car park. It seemed like a safe place to park up. Taking out her mobile phone, Kirsty wondered who to call. Jason wouldn't want her to call the police. She knew he kept them at arm's length because of his 'other business dealings'. It was an effort to focus and pull herself together. At least she felt less vulnerable in public, away from the unwanted intrusion of her home. With only a brief hesitation, she selected Ryan from her contacts. Somehow it felt right to be reaching out to Ryan when she was afraid and needed help, even though Jason said he was holding the fort. Try as she might to ignore them, she still had feelings for him.

Ryan returned from the bar with two G and Ts. They were enjoying their time together. It had been a great few days of snorting coke, drinking and intimacy.

"Thanks, babe," said Lisa. "What do you fancy eating later? Shall we go to the waterfront?"

Ryan was thinking pizza. He was about to answer with his suggestion of Italian when his phone began to ring. Looking at the phone, he was about to press the red circle when he noticed it was Kirsty calling. The sight of her name put him on edge instantly. Kirsty didn't call him much these days, so what did she want?

"Hi, Kirsty, how are you doing?"

"Not good, Ryan, something weird is happening. I'm scared. Someone's been in the house."

Ryan stood up and walked away from the table, towards the door. Outside he sat on a wooden bench.

"What, have you been burgled? What have they taken?"

"I don't think so. I got home, the gates were open. I went in and made a coffee. I saw that the patio doors were wide open, nothing else looked disturbed. I just got out quick, what should I do now?"

"Where are you?"

"I'm parked up at the retail park. I'm too scared to go back. They might have still been upstairs when I was there."

"No worries, you're safe now, don't go back to the house. Get a room for the night just to be on the safe side. I'll drive back up to Manchester and meet you. It just sounds like some kids. I'll sort things out." Ryan didn't believe his own explanation for a moment, but his main concern was to get Kirsty to calm down.

"The patio doors are still open though," Kirsty said.

"It's fine, I'll make a call and get a couple of the lads to keep an eye on things 'til I get back. I'll give you a bell when I'm coming off the motorway. Have you told Jason?"

"No, what use is he in Portugal, or wherever he really is."

Ryan felt a tinge of satisfaction at this.

"Okay, I'll be with you ASAP. Stay away from the house."

Ryan walked back into the bar, sat down and placed his phone on the table.

"Sorry, babe, I need to get back up to Manchester." Lisa clasped her hands on her lap and looked downwards. He could tell she was disappointed. "There's been an issue with one of our properties, a break in. She's one of our best clients. It won't wait and I'm the only one available to sort it out."

"I could come with you," Lisa said hopefully.

"I'd love you to come up, but I'm going to be tied up for a few days. I'll get it sorted and come back down. You're back in work the day after tomorrow anyway and we need to give our livers a rest."

In reality his reasons were more selfish than that. He wanted to keep distance between Lisa and his life in Manchester, not just because of the criminality. He didn't want her to see him as the errand boy either.

They walked back to Lisa's place and said their goodbyes. He felt a pang of guilt, knowing he was actually looking forward to the opportunity of seeing Kirsty.

Ryan's phone rang whilst he was walking back to his car. This time it was Eddie, one of the enforcers.

"Ryan, the fella who was found dead in the canal is called Paul Smethurst. He's the dealer we upset when we moved onto his patch in Chester. Do you remember, he battered two of our care home kids and taxed them?"

"Yeah, I remember that, the block of flats in Blacon. I'll speak to Carl. I think he went down to Chester and sorted it out. There's nothing for us to worry about then. It won't affect our business. Listen, Eddie, I'm back in Manchester tonight, I'm going to need you to drop some charlie off for me. I'm running low, mate."

"Jeez, Ryan, have you gone through that last bag already? If you paid me for it, you'd be my best customer."

"You cheeky little bastard, it was for some of Jason's associates, not me. Wind your neck in."

"No worries, mate, I always like to keep the addicts sweet. Catch you later," Eddie said, and hung up, not giving Ryan the chance to reply to his cheap shot.

Ryan didn't like banter like that. He knew Eddie was right. It was getting out of hand again. *I need to rein him, he's taking the piss out of me. Christ I'm sounding more like Jason now.*

Ryan filled his hire car with fuel and set off for Manchester. He thought about calling Jason, but decided against it. *Kirsty didn't sound very happy with Jason. Who could blame her?* Besides, he didn't want any unnecessary contact on the mobile, and hopefully he could sort it out.

As he drove, Ryan's mind was running through every possible explanation for the break in at Kirsty's place. Was it linked to the shooting on the canal? Was someone putting the frighteners on Jason? They must not have wanted to hurt Kirsty, because they obviously could have done that already. *Shit, just think if they had taken her hostage to get at Jason. What is she doing with him?* So, it's just intimidation or burglars disturbed. Who was behind all this? He was still drawing a blank. There were no obvious contenders other than Smethurst and his cronies who had the motive of revenge.

As Ryan drove north, Jason and Wayne were in a bar watching some Premier League football. Carl appeared from the lift and walked over across the lobby.

"Can't believe you're watching United, you must be bored," he laughed.

As Carl lowered himself into a wingback chair, the waitress approached the table and placed down their three beers. She walked back to the bar area, followed by Jason's eyes.

"Wonder what she's doing later," Jason said.

"Nothing that involves you I guess, she's young enough to be your daughter," Wayne replied, without missing a beat. They all laughed.

"Did you two see the idiot who tried it on with me when I approached the hooker in the lap dancing bar?"

"No, what happened?" asked Wayne. Feeling almost duty bound to show an interest.

"He squared up to me and said she was with him. I told him to do one before I ripped a strip off him. He scurried back under his stone at the bar. Anyway, when I was leaving, I bumped into him in the gents. His face was a picture. He looked like he'd bumped into Freddy Kruger. So, I gave him a good hiding."

"The fella who shot at you on the canal has been identified, he's called Paul Smethurst," Carl said, changing the subject. Jason was a little disgruntled that his tale of unbridled aggression and dominance hadn't been met with the usual show of admiration he had been expecting.

"Paul Smethurst, never heard of him, have you?" Jason replied, letting it slide for now.

"Ryan got a call from one of our street dealers. Apparently, there's history with him that goes back to March. We got some kids to cuckoo in an addict's flat on the estate in Blacon near Chester. Anyway, they took over the addict's flat in the tower block, seeing him right with some gear. They started dealing from there. This Smethurst, who took a pop at you, took an exception. It was his turf and we undercut his dealers, meaning he was losing a lot of money. He sees himself as a bit of a local Pablo Escobar. So, he visited the flat with a few of his thugs, gave our kids a good kicking and taxed their gear. But before he left he gave them some additional pain to find out who they were dealing for. He gave one of the kids some dental work with a pair of pliers."

Jason cringed inside at the memory, and asked, "Did the kids keep their mouths shut? We don't want the cops and social service all over us. Who was he dealing for?"

"Not sure," Carl replied. "We know he gets his gear from Liverpool, but we think that's the only connection. No gang ties. Apparently, he was feared down in Chester. He had a bit of a reputation as a local lunatic."

"More like the local idiot. So, it's a one off, nobody wants to go to war with us. That's good. I can get back to buying and selling property. I'm an upstanding citizen now you know."

Jason laughed at his own joke and took a swig of beer.

"What time is Dirk meeting us?" Wayne asked.

"Not sure, just said we'd be watching the footie here when he was ready."

"It's time for another one then." Wayne beckoned over the waitress and ordered some more beer.

A short while later Dirk entered the bar area and walked over to their table. He towered over the table, his Viking like physique almost shading the light. "Goedenavond mijne heren."

"Same to you my friend," Jason said. After a round of handshakes the four men settled around the table.

"How is the hotel, are you being looked after?" Dirk asked.

"Can't complain, good Dutch hospitality as usual, with a bit of quality sleaze thrown in," Jason answered.

"Good, after we have talked business, I will take you to an excellent bar tonight. Top quality sleaze." Dirk smiled as he said this.

"Excellent, we look forward to it." Jason looked over to Wayne and Carl. "Gentleman, I'm sure you won't mind visiting De Wallen whilst I have a chat with Dirk. There's a few quid, choose wisely and enjoy. Don't go to the same place twice. See you back here at ten."

He handed a wad of Euros to Wayne as the two of them stood up to leave.

"Let's walk, Jason. I know a good place on Zeedijk," Dirk said. They left the bar, and any prying ears or listening devices, behind.

"I'm a bit more cautious walking by canals these days," Jason said.

"You cannot swim, Jason?" Dirk answered, looking puzzled.

"I can swim, but I came across a shark on my last canal visit and nearly got eaten."

"Ha-ha, English humour, I still don't get it." Dirk looked bemused.

"Anyway, to business," Jason shrugged. "My new banker is phenomenal. Dubai based and mostly launders through France and Spain. Was my last payment okay?"

"All fine, we have one small change to make. This time your products will enter the UK through Felixstowe with different drivers. Just precautionary, we have used Liverpool for the last few runs and don't want be predictable. It's the usual Balkan route from Turkey. I will give you details of the vehicle and timings for your boys to monitor."

"I've got some talented spotters; the cops and customs surveillance teams don't stand a chance. Can you get the driver to stop at Keele services and take a rest for half an hour? Then leave the M6 at Warrington, junction 21, north, before getting back on the M6 at junction 22, south, then onto the M62, followed by the usual drop-off routine. If we identify any problems I'll call you to abort the delivery."

"No problem, I like your attention to detail. We have new drivers and some innovative storage in the chassis. The merchandise will be safe there, under the cargo of tulips and bulbs."

"Where's Ronnie, your partner in crime?" Jason asked. "He usually never leaves your side. Is he not joining us tonight?"

"No, poor Ronnie was somewhat careless, and had an accident. You won't be seeing him again."

"Creepy bastard, I never liked him anyway. Look, you need to be straight with me here. It sounds like you have some problems. Is there any risk of a compromise with the law?"

"No, everything is sweet, no problems for you to worry about. Here we are, sir, a fine establishment. We can amuse ourselves before returning to meet Wayne and Carl."

"One last bit of business first. I'm moving upstairs soon, call it a non-exec position. I would like Wayne to attend future meetings, but only with yourself. I need to know if you want to introduce someone new because I will need to be present."

"That's fine with me. We can better acquaint ourselves tonight. You deserve your retirement, Jason, you have worked hard and it's been a pleasure to do business with you."

"Yeah, because I pay your inflated prices on time," Jason said. They both laughed and entered the club. *Meeting done and dusted, he obviously doesn't want to tell me about Ronnie. Probably been grassing or on the take. Now time for some entertainment.* "Actually, there is one last thing. What about the Columbian?"

"He had to cancel, but he wants you to go and visit him. In fact, he insists, because of the quantities you are now buying. He wants to see the whites of your eyes and discuss further business opportunities. You are a VIP customer Jason. He is okay now we have vouched for you."

"You can tell him I look forward to it. I'm sorry but I'm not convinced here, first the meeting is delayed, then Ronnie has had an accident, then the Columbian cancels. What's going on, Dirk? I smell a rat, so I'll ask you again, are we in danger of a compromise? I know you guys wouldn't turn me over because of the consequences that would follow."

"All is good my friend, you have no reasons to be concerned."

"I hope so, for all of our sakes," Jason replied. He felt rattled.

After visiting the lap dancing bar, they moved on to a Chinese restaurant and got stuck into the buffet. The tension eased with the help of a few more beers.

As they were leaving, Dirk called back, "I've arranged for a guest to call on you tonight. Enjoy, Jason. I'll be in touch. All is going to plan, trust me." *Well if she's like his previous guests I'm in for a good night,* thought Jason. He texted Wayne to let him know the meeting had gone well and he was heading back to his room.

There was a knock at his door. Jason walked over and looked through the spy hole. Two gorgeous women were standing outside. He opened the door.

"Hi, Jason, we're friends of Dirk. He said you could do with unwinding after your business meetings."

Wow, two of them, and they're stunning, I'm liking this.

"Well, you'd better come in, girls. Sounds like a good idea to me."

He closed the room door after them and followed them inside. They both slipped their coats off, revealing their nakedness underneath.

"Shall we leave drinks until later?" Jason suggested.

Chapter Six

Ryan was feeling tired as he drove the car into the hotel car park. He got out and stretched his back, pushing his arms upwards and backwards into the air. His whole body was stiff from the journey. Since he hadn't received any calls from his lads, he suspected the break in was low-key intimidation or a burglary. He strolled lethargically into the hotel reception area and scanned the comfy sofas in the lobby for Kirsty, but he couldn't see her. Unconcerned, he made his way into the bar area. It looked pretty full, with people dining and business types trying to convince each other that their option was the best.

Kirsty was sitting in a chair near to the fireplace, engrossed on her tablet. She was dressed in a black top, black thigh-length skirt, and black tights. All of this black was in contrast against her long, naturally blonde hair.

As Ryan approached, Kirsty looked up and gave him a welcoming smile.

"Hi, Ryan, thanks for driving up. I've calmed down a bit now. It gave me a bit of a shock. I wish Jason would get his act together and move on, he's got the property development to keep him busy. I don't like the danger his other stuff puts me in and this has been another wake up call."

"No worries, I was going to come back to Manchester tomorrow anyway," he lied.

"What would you like to drink?"

"I'll leave it 'til later. I'll have a run over to the house first, have a quick look and get it secured. Can I have your keys?"

"I'd rather come with you. What do you think's going on, Ryan? Jason said he had to fly out to Portugal urgently, and now this. Has he pissed somebody off? I need to know if he has. Where is he and what's he up to?"

Kirsty was a bright and determined woman. Ryan knew this, so he thought better of telling her to wait at the hotel.

"I've not heard anything, Kirsty, but I suppose once you've got money, and a big house like this, you become more of a target, especially in the networks where Jason operates," he said, hoping she didn't delve any further. "I'll just pay a visit to the gents then we can get going."

Ryan walked into the toilets and relieved himself. He'd not had a break on the way up. After closing the cubicle door, he prepared a few lines of coke. He was feeling agitated and tired and he needed a hit. Even though he hated using toilets it was better than going without.

All sorted, he returned to Kirsty.

They left the hotel bar and walked into the car park.

"We'll take my car. If anyone's watching, we don't want them to think it could be Jason returning," Kirsty said.

She's switched on, thought Ryan, and he wondered exactly how much she knew about Jason's criminal enterprises. She obviously must have known about him running the doors of pubs, and controlling the dealing of heroin, speed and charlie around Warrington. But since then his legitimate property business had provided a decent cover for the present drug dealing. But did she realize how big his empire had grown?

Ryan left his thoughts and came back to the present when Kirsty deactivated the car alarm. They got into the car and set off in silence.

As Kirsty turned the car into her road, Ryan was running through possible scenarios. He felt satisfied that neither he nor Kirsty were the targets. They could be collateral, held as hostages, but had that been the case they could have taken Kirsty already. He was conscious that he was not tooled up, but content there would be knives in the kitchen if needed. Jason probably had a pistol stashed somewhere but he guessed Kirsty knew nothing about it. His gut told him that they were okay in this situation. Ryan didn't think there would be any drama. Not that it mattered, he would protect Kirsty at any cost.

Kirsty activated the gates and parked the car on the drive. Ryan noted that she closed the gates behind them.

There were no signs of life in the house as they approached the door. Kirsty got her keys out and unlocked it. If she was frightened, she was not showing it. Ryan had known her from the Warrington days, great Saturday nights out on Bridge Street, then onto the night clubs. Those had been halcyon times. He realised his mind was wandering but that's what Kirsty did to him. Her presence had made Lisa a distant memory already. This was the woman Ryan really wanted to be with. Ryan snapped himself back into focusing on the task at hand. His coke-induced confidence was overwhelming, *bring it on.*

They entered the house cautiously. Kirsty flicked the lights on as they entered. It looked pretty much as she had described it. No signs of damage or that the place had been searched. In a strange way this made it more sinister.

The ground floor was clear. Ryan started to climb the stairs, Kirsty followed him. Room by room it became evident that no one was here. The place looked undisturbed.

"Where is the cctv security unit?" Ryan asked.

"It's in Jason's office, in the loft conversion."

"Let's go and find out who our mystery guest is."

They entered the office.

"I almost feel like a visitor," Kirsty said. "I never have a reason to come in here."

They both noticed that the wires from the monitors were hanging from the LCD screen. The cctv hard drive unit was gone. An area of dust on the desk left a tell tail sign.

"Clever boys covering their tracks," Ryan said.

"So, who do you suspect, Ryan? I'm not having it that you know nothing."

"I honestly don't know. But we both know Jason has made a few enemies over the years. Your guess is as good as mine."

"Is he really in Portugal sorting out new apartments?" Ryan was silent. "No, I thought not."

"Look, Kirsty, you can't put me on the spot like this. Stuff like that is between you and Jason. I'm keeping out of it."

They went back down to the kitchen. Kirsty locked the patio doors and fixed them both a G and T. She took a long drink, like she needed it.

"Now look, Ryan, you're talking to me now. What's said in the room stays in the room. I'm not stupid. I know there is still some 'need to know' stuff going on. Who are we messing with?"

"If I knew I would tell you, Kirsty, you know that. I trust you one hundred per cent. I've not got a clue, and it's not for the lack of trying to find out. Go and have a look around to see if anything's missing."

Kirsty maintained eye contact with an intense stare. Ryan could sense the old chemistry between them, which hadn't gone away since he took her virginity years ago. Ryan laughed nervously. Every bone in his body just wanted to embrace her, and take care of her.

"I don't know," he said again. "If I did, I would tell you so that you could protect yourself, honest."

He would still do anything for her even though she chose Jason ahead of him. Which he hadn't seen coming. At the time he thought Jason was flexing his muscles, and that the relationship wouldn't last. But here they were, years down the line. *She's really got a downer on Jason,* Ryan couldn't help feeling a sense of smug satisfaction.

The gin and tonic, and the ones that followed, took the edge off the tension caused by the break in. They chatted about the old days. Conversation flowed easily, Ryan believed that the mutual attraction was still there. They always picked up where they left off, even after months of not seeing each other. Ryan was reliving feelings of old, he realised. He could so easily make a move on Kirsty right now. *I'm definitely feeling something here, but is she feeling the same? But it's too risky*. Then his line of thought changed, *get a grip of yourself, it's a no go*, he thought reluctantly.

"I'll call us a taxi and drop you off at the hotel," Ryan said. "It's not worth risking the cops pulling us over at this time of night. We're well over the limit."

Kirsty replied, "I'm staying here, I'd feel safer if you slept on the sofa though."

She said this with a mischievous smile.

Ryan knew his will power was non-existent. He lived for the moment. He was also aware of his self-destructive tendency to act on hedonistic impulses. He knew he should leave. He knew he was on dangerous ground. *Time to get out of here,* he thought.

Instead, he said, “Okay, pour the drinks.” It was as if the words came out before he had even thought about it. Ryan was reckless and he knew it, it had always been his weakness.

Kirsty returned to the breakfast bar. She spun Ryan’s stool around so she was facing him and sat astride his legs. Slowly, she moved closer to him, taking his head in her hands. They started to kiss slowly. Ryan knew he should push her away and leave. Yet he continued the kiss and wrapped his arms around her. Kirsty’s hand slowly moved down between his legs. There was no turning back, this Ryan knew for sure. They started to undress each other and stumbled towards the sofa.

“Are you sure Kirsty,” Ryan whispered.

“Shut up Ryan,” Kirsty replied.

Earlier that evening, whilst Ryan was heading north on the motorway, a debriefing was taking place in Manchester. Detective Inspector Dave Ferguson was ruing the shambles that had just taken place. He was the head of the force’s drug unit, leading the fight against Organised Crime Groups networking controlled drugs across Greater Manchester and beyond. This was the latest of many setbacks. His task wasn’t easy.

Detective Constables; Walsh and Nolan were seated on the opposite side of the table. They were in a sparse, tired, magnolia-coloured windowless office, which apart from the desk contained nothing more than an antique-looking green metal filing cabinet.

Walsh broke the silence.

"We just had to get out and we were lucky to manage it. It was shit or bust."

"There was no time for discussions," interrupted Nolan. "I heard the car on the drive. It was time to go, or we would have blown the whole operation. At least we live to fight another day."

Walsh continued, "We left nothing there to say it was us."

"No, you didn't," Ferguson said. "Still, they might suspect us. They don't know it was us for sure. It could have been a disturbed burglary, but there was no damage or ransacking. It could be worse I suppose."

"It is what it is, we can't change it now," Nolan said.

"The RIPA authority was for fitting a listening device, not removing the cctv system from the house. We will have to be transparent with our explanation on the authority document. In the circumstances it was the right decision," Ferguson said, almost to himself, pre-empting the questions from the Surveillance Commissioners on their next review.

"We couldn't have left it. It was in bits with the job half done. We might as well have left a police calling-card," said Nolan. He sounded defensive, despite that fact that Ferguson had just agreed with their actions.

"Cheers fellas, not your fault. And you got out in time without compromising the operation. If the Regional Crime Squad surveillance team had alerted us to her leaving her mum and dad's house, none of this would have happened. Happy days," Ferguson mused.

Walsh and Nolan left the office to go and get something to eat.

DI Dave Ferguson got on the phone to DI Andrea Statham. He was glad it was her leading the murder investigation. They had worked together as Detective Sergeants in the CID at Longsight years ago. There was a mutual respect and trust between them.

"Evening, Dave. Don't tell me, you've charged Hamilton and he's admitted to the murder as well."

"I wish. This is proving difficult and just to make matters worse our lads were in the middle of fitting a listening device in the house when his partner arrived home. They had to leg it over the gardens with his cctv hard drive. The crime squad had her under surveillance but lost her. We needed that like a hole in the head."

"It's not much better for us, so don't be feeling sorry for yourself. Our time will come. It always does in the end. We're going to speak to him when he gets back. He'll know we haven't much on him, so you never know, he might get cocky and complacent."

Andrea proceeded to update Dave on the progress of the murder investigation.

"So, we have a good idea of what has happened, but no evidence, yet," she concluded.

Chapter Seven

Ryan was awoken by drawers opening and closing and other noises from the kitchen. For a split second he struggled to establish where he was. The events of the previous night resurfaced in his mind. *Shit, what have I done? what was I thinking? Why me, again*, he thought. He rolled off the sofa onto all fours and stood up, a bit too fast for his gin headache. It wasn't a dream, their clothing was still strewn across the floor from the breakfast bar to the sofa, and the empty bottles and glasses were still on the table. He grabbed his trousers and put them on.

Kirsty was in the kitchen, putting the kettle on.

"Coffee?" she asked as he walked in.

"Nice one. Black. No sugar please."

"How are you this morning?" asked Kirsty.

"I feel okay. That sofa is spot on, the best sleep I've had in ages."

"You went out like a light, snoring your head off, so I thought I'd leave you to it and went to bed."

Ryan felt like they were both dancing around the elephant in the room. He had to say something, but what?

"Kirsty, last night was fantastic, but we shouldn't have gone there."

"It's done now, Ryan. We both know how we feel about each other. It was bound to happen sooner or later. It's our secret."

She handed him a coffee and sat at the kitchen table. Ryan followed and sat across from her.

"I know you're right," he said, "but if Jason found out he'd go ballistic." *Wonder if she found out about the bloke he threw from the balcony for chatting her up?*

"He isn't going to find out though, is he? What's good for the goose is good for the gander, Ryan. I know more than you think. He's probably with some slag right now."

That's a path I don't want to go down. Thought Ryan.

"Nice coffee," he said, before a silence developed that made him feel uncomfortable. "Well, the visitors didn't return in the night, that's a plus."

"And we still don't know who they are, or what they wanted," replied Kirsty. "Or do you, Ryan?"

Ryan assumed it was a tease rather than a question. He guessed she believed him.

"I'm going for a shower. Help yourself to something to eat if you like."

Kirsty pushed her chair back and headed upstairs. Ryan put some bread in the toaster and sipped at his coffee. He had to fight his instinct, which was to follow her upstairs. He could easily take on from where they left off last might. He had crossed the line already. *Does she want me to follow her? Or was it a one off?* The toast popped up, bringing his attention back to the mundane. He buttered the toast instead.

Kirsty walked back into the kitchen wearing her gym gear. The sight of her made Ryan wonder if Jason appreciated what he had. "What are you up to today, Ryan?"

She sounded very matter of fact, like she had moved on from last night already and it was now history.

"I've got stuff to sort up here, so I'll be around 'til Jason gets back on Saturday, just in case there are any more dramas. I'll do a bit of digging and see if I can shed any light on this."

"Cheers, I appreciate that. I'm calling Jason later so I'll tell him what happened." She paused and started to laugh. "Don't worry, I won't tell him everything that happened."

Ryan suddenly felt vulnerable and paranoid. Could he trust her? Of course, he could. He just needed to chill out.

"Can you give me a lift to my car?" he asked.

"Yes of course, I'll drop you off on the way to the gym."

On the way to his car Kirsty broke the silence.

"You must have guessed all isn't well with me and Jason?"

"I hadn't to be honest, he never mentions you to me and I don't see you that often."

"Between you and me, I've come close to leaving him a few times. I'm just a trophy wife for him, another one of his chattels. He's a bastard with me most of the time. He won't give up the crime and he won't have kids. I'm not getting any younger and I definitely want kids. I need to move on really. Most of the time I just keep busy with my salons. I enjoyed last night Ryan. We should do it again."

Kirsty had taken Ryan by surprise. He didn't have an inkling she felt like that.

"I look forward to it," he said. "I'll be in touch." Ryan felt guilty that he knew he would drop Lisa like a stone for Kirsty.

Ryan got out of the car and walked over to his hire car. *Christ, as if my life isn't complicated enough already.* He set off to meet the lads from the care home, it had become a habit now, even a vocation. He did his best to steer them away from the dealing and put them back on track. Even though he felt like he was fighting a losing battle most of the time. They would more than likely make the same mistakes he did. It was an unforgiving world to live in, succumbing to peer pressure and petty crime made life easier.

Two days later the flight from Schiphol touched down at Manchester International Airport. Jason, Carl, and Wayne were glad to be back. They had enjoyed it in the Dam, it was their favourite playground, but Manchester was always home.

Jason would never admit it to the others but he was experiencing some pangs of anxiety as they approached customs control. An element of irrational fear created an expectation of a hand being placed on his shoulder, with a request of, '*would you follow me, sir. My name is Detective Constable…*' He snapped back into the present. Ryan's update about Smethurst had given them the nod that there would be no drama. It was just a phobia at airports exacerbated by the amount of 'in your face' authority and intrusion.

The three of them exited the airport without incident. Jason couldn't get hold of Ryan on his mobile.

"What is it with Ryan? He's trying my patience, and it's working," Jason said as he flagged down a taxi.

The three of them got in, eager to get the last part of the journey over with. The tiredness generated by the trip was now kicking in. Each of them retired to their thoughts and the conversation dried up. It was almost like a transition period from Amsterdam mode to Manchester mode.

Jason was first to be dropped off. He handed Carl £60 for the fare and looked over his shoulder into the back of the taxi.

"Cheers fellas, lets meet up tomorrow night with Ryan. We need to make sure we're on the ball with everything."

He walked up the driveway, the crunching noise of the stones under foot making him feel at home, back on familiar territory. The lights were on inside. Jason was looking forward to seeing Kirsty. He knew that he neglected her and took her for granted but they were both busy with their own businesses. He didn't know how long he could string her along in the hope of him leaving his life of crime. He had the finances to make it a reality, but doubted whether he could live without the edge that his criminality provided?

He unlocked the front door and walked into the kitchen. Kirsty looked up from reading her magazine at the breakfast bar.

"How was your journey?" Kirsty asked.

"It's good to be back."

"How was Spain, did you get the problem sorted?" Kirsty tested.

"Portugal, Kirsty. Yes, all done, it's a cracking project. We should clean up on this one." It was as if they were both going through the motions of passing pleasantries.

Kirsty made coffee and went on to tell Jason about the break-in at the house whilst he was away. Jason felt a shiver down his neck, but he also felt a rising swell of anger. He was seething. *They've crossed the line, breaking into my house, they'll fucking pay for this.*

Jason got up to examine the patio doors and concluded that there was no damage. After establishing this, he made his way to his office and studied the area where the cctv hard drive had once been. *Why the cctv?*

Kirsty followed on behind, recounting the events as they walked.

"Are you sure nothing else was taken?" Jason asked her.

"I don't think so, but you have to check too. Do you think I disturbed them?"

"Probably," Jason replied. "Are you sure the patio doors were locked?"

"Definitely, I double-checked everything before I went to Warrington."

As Kirsty spoke, Jason removed the books from the middle bookshelf. He removed the rear of the casing, blocking Kirsty's view with his body. He saw that his semi-automatic pistol and a stash of cash was still there.

"The money is still there," Jason said. *This is the work of a professional, which the canal shooting wasn't. Or more likely it could have been the police.*

Jason came back downstairs behind Kirsty.

"Don't forget your coffee," she said.

"I'll be back in a minute. I just need to take a look around the garden."

Out on the patio, Jason scanned the garden. There were no obvious signs of intruders. He walked across the lawn towards the summer house. The footprints in the flowerbed caught his attention. *Two sets of prints I reckon, and scuffing on the fence. They left in a hurry, she must have disturbed them. My money is on the cops planting a listening device. But why take the hard drive without a warrant?*

Jason took out his phone and selected Wayne from the contacts.

"Hey, how you doing, Jason? Thought you'd be busy," Wayne said.

"Bit of an issue, mucker, whilst we were away someone broke into the house through the patio doors. No damage, nothing ransacked, nothing stolen except the cctv hard drive. It doesn't add up. It's got to be the cops."

"Shit, that's all we need."

"I've found two sets of footprints, as if they've fled over the fence. I reckon Kirsty disturbed them when she came home. I'm going to have a look around outside for any camera devices."

"It's feasible I suppose. We need to pull up the drawbridge. I wonder if they've got a lead on Smethurst."

"We can't take any chances here," Jason said. "We need to be on our game. I'm going to take Kirsty out for something to eat. I'll leave you a key in the usual place. Will you come over and do a full electronic sweep for any surveillance devices?"

"Yes, no worries, luckily it's not that long ago since I did one. It sounds like it's worth doing another though. If I find anything it confirms our suspicions, leave it with me."

Jason returned to the house and took a long drink of his lukewarm coffee. It hit the spot.

"I've just booked us a table in China Town," he told Kirsty. "Are you hungry?"

"Good idea, I've not had a Chinese in ages. Buffet for two looking good."

They locked up the house and drove to China Town in Kirsty's Coupe.

"Kirsty, I reckon it's the police who broke into the house. It all adds up to them wanting to plant a surveillance camera. I need you to think hard. Whilst I was away did you have any conversations that they'd be interested in?"

Jason watched Kirsty's face, which was still and thoughtful before she spoke.

"No, I've hardly been there. Ryan came up obviously to sort things out. But he didn't stay long. I doubt we said anything they'd be interested in." It wasn't a convincing answer, and Jason sensed that she was eager to change the subject. "That couple we've been seeing in the gym, Lee and Samantha, were in there again today. I had a coffee with them in the café. I really get on with them. They're on our wavelength. I suggested we should go out for a meal sometime. It's a new friend who could be part of our new life, away from your other stuff."

"I've only met the bloke a couple of times. He seems like a top fella, you can tell he's ex forces. I'll have to give him a run for his money on the weights in a proper gym," Jason said.

"I'll diary something in for us then."

"What does he do now?"

"Samantha said he was a bodyguard or something like that, he's away in London a lot. He gets a lot of attention from the women in the gym. I'm having a coffee with Samantha next week whilst he's away."

There's something moody about Lee, wonder what his new line of business is? Thought Jason.

Wayne turned up at Jason's house. He had driven around the long way checking for any police surveillance teams lurking around. This latest request was routine for him, if there were any listening devices in the house he would find them. However, Wayne did feel uncomfortable with the possibility of heightened police attention. Were they watching him right now as he arrived? Were they making progress on the canal shooting? *This isn't good,* he thought. He seriously could do without the cops on his case. Wayne's life had never been better and he wanted it to stay that way. Prison at this stage of his life was not appealing. He had been there, done that, got the t-shirt.

He purposely parked on the roadside rather than enter the driveway. Once he was out of the car, Wayne lit a cigarette, using the time to take a good look at the surrounding houses, trees and anything else for tell-tale signs of surveillance cameras. A guy walking a dog was approaching him. Wayne stepped towards him.

"Nice dog, mate. I love border collies, how old is he?" Wayne asked, bending down to make a fuss of the dog.

"He's almost two now. I got him from a farm. He needs a couple of big walks every day," the fella replied.

"He'll keep you fit then."

The fella walked on, oblivious to the fact Wayne had just made an assessment that he was not part of a police surveillance team. In fact, he hadn't noticed anything of concern. Wayne threw his cigarette into the road, got his bag of tricks out of the car boot and walked up the driveway.

Kirsty parked the car. They walked along Faulkner Street, under the Chinese Archway, and entered their favourite restaurant.

"I'm ready for this," said Jason. "Shall we do the Emperor Banquet?"

"Sounds good to me. As long as it includes crispy aromatic duck, I'm happy."

They were seated at a table and ordered drinks. Menus weren't needed.

"Do I need to know anything about what's going on?" Kirsty asked.

Jason hated talking business with Kirsty, she was part of his other life and he wanted to protect her, and subsequently himself, from his 'other' activities.

"A few problems have arisen, but we're on it. Nothing we can't handle." *Now shut the fuck up interfering and stuff your face with aromatic crispy duck.*

The dim sum arrived at the table. Jason enjoyed the short respite from the irritating questions whilst they both tucked in.

"Is that what the trip was really about?" asked Kirsty.

His respite was over.

"I didn't want you to be concerned. There's no need to be, it's stuff you don't need to know. It's to protect you and me. If things came on top with the cops, you can't let anything slip out if you don't know anything in the first place." *Now shut the fuck up and eat your food.*

"I do need to know about it when the police start breaking into our house. I thought you were moving on from all that now. You're making enough from the property rentals, quit while you're ahead. Let's move on, no more looking over your shoulder. I'm getting really pissed off with all this. I've had enough of it."

There was a pause whilst they finished off the dim sum. *It's not that easy*, thought Jason.

"Christ, we are under police surveillance, it's definitely time for you to move on then, surely. Are you really going to risk going down?" Kirsty was like a dog with a bone. "I don't like this, Jason. I don't need it, and you don't need it, let's move away from Manchester."

Jason could see the anguish and fear in her face.

"I know, I'm on with it, whilst we were away I set Wayne up with some contacts to take my place on the front line. I'll need to sort things out then we'll go for it, away from Manchester, out in the sticks somewhere."

It was the best he could do, although he knew that Kirsty had heard it all before.

After their meal they visited a few bars. Jason's mobile rang.

"Wayne, how you doing?"

"It's all clear, pal, looks like Kirsty must have disturbed them and they left sharpish. I saw the two sets of footprints in the soil. Looks like it was the cops all right, we could do without this attention though."

"Tell me about it. Cheers, Wayne, thanks for sorting it. Catch up soon."

Chapter Eight

Jason, Wayne and Carl were having a beer at the City match.

"I'm thinking it's time for me to step back more, fellas. The legitimate stuff is taking more of my time and Kirsty's getting pissed off, which doesn't help." *I didn't even convince myself there.*

"Is this because of the cops snooping?" asked Carl.

"No, we can handle the cops, we always have. And it's not the shooting on the canal either. I'll miss all that stuff, seriously. I've earned enough from the grafting. The income from the property business is legit. I'm in a good place to step back, virtually hands-off the day to day stuff. You two can earn me a nice pension and take control. I told Dirk that Wayne would be taking the lead on meetings in the future."

Wayne was quiet. Jason wondered whether he was thinking along similar lines.

"Can't argue with that, mate," Carl said.

"I think it's time for you and Wayne to step up to the plate. You're in the perfect position. You manage operations on the ground already and you know the Amsterdam boys, they trust you both."

"I think it's Wayne's gig, I'm okay with things as they are," Carl said.

Wayne nodded in agreement, but Jason could see he didn't look too enthusiastic.

"You can use the same banker through Dubai, nothing needs to change, not even the account numbers." *Am I trying to convince myself here*? Jason wondered.

Wayne spoke up.

"I've been thinking about the cops entering your place. I'd just like us to make sure we haven't got a grass. The timing is weird. Nothing has happened within the firm to put us on the cops' radar, so it must be the shooting on the canal."

"Good thinking," Jason said. "It can't do any harm."

"Anybody in the frame, or just precautionary?" asked Carl. Jason thought Carl was a bit eager with the question. *Wayne would have said if he knew who the rat was, and action would have been taken.*

"Precautionary," Wayne answered. "I think we need to check the money laundering side as well as the lads dealing the product on ground. It's time to ensure we are watertight. Anyway, I'm on with it, if there's a snitch I will find them. I've spoken to our lads in Liverpool, they know of Smethurst. He buys from another firm in Liverpool but they have no loyalty to him. They described him as a buck with a bad attitude and ideas above his station."

They necked the last of their beer and made their way to their seats, ready for kick-off.

As they entered the seating area, Jason was still thinking through his decision. He knew the timing was right. He'd had a good run recently. The cops had fallen behind due to all the cuts in their budget. They couldn't keep up with the Organised Crime Groups. Jason had read somewhere that there were a similar number of OCG members as per the population of Ipswich. He'd never visited Ipswich, but it sounded like a lot of people. Drug dealing was now back in the media and political agendas, rebranded as county lines. Tackling the drugs trade was a vote-winner for the politicians.

After the match Jason drove into the city centre to his apartment. He'd booked his usual escort. He parked the car and walked towards the entrance. She was standing by the doors waiting as planned. She was tall and slim, wearing a light grey rain coat, her long jet black hair tied into a pony tail. "I've not got long, we need to be quick," Jason instructed.

"It's great to see you again too," She laughed and followed him through the entrance to the lift, struggling to keep up with him in her stilettos. They took the lift to Jason's apartment and walked straight to the bedroom, it was a familiar routine to both of them, Jason didn't see the need for small talk. The bedroom door was shut behind them.

Jason was secretly wishing he was back at the apartment as he drove into the driveway of his home. He felt Kirsty was on his back too much lately, he didn't need the grief. "I'm back, the bringer of good news," he shouted.

"I'm up here, I'll be down in a minute," Kirsty shouted back.

Jason grabbed himself a beer from the fridge, walked through to the lounge and fell back onto the sofa. Kirsty walked in and sat on the chair opposite.

"Go on then, what's the good news?"

"I've told Wayne I'm out and it's down to him. I've finally got out, babes, we can move on."

"Good, but I hope you're not too late. We had a visitor this afternoon."

Kirsty passed Jason a business card, almost with glee, as if her argument had been officially accepted. He spotted the police badge straight away.

"DS Peter Higgs, Serious Crime Division. What did he want?" Jason asked, suddenly feeling anxious.

"He said he was investigating a murder. A fella was shot on the canal a couple of weeks ago. He said it was nothing to worry about but needed to speak to you."

The news took Jason by surprise. His mind flashed back to Wayne's suggestion about hunting for a grass.

"Not got a clue why he needs to speak to me. I'll give him a call." With the look of disdain on Kirsty's face, he now questioned his decision to return from his apartment.

Jason left the house. He stood on the driveway and found himself scanning around for any signs of the cops keeping an eye on him. He selected Wayne from his contacts.

"Wayne, have you had any contact from the cops today?"

"No, mate. Why, should I be expecting a call?"

"Whilst we were at the football the CID called at our place. They told Kirsty they needed to speak to me about the shooting on the canal. Is there anything else concerning you about grasses that you didn't mention before?"

"No, nothing specific, just with the extra attention we're getting from the cops, it's put me on my guard. They can't have anything on you. They would have locked you up otherwise. A bit concerning though, we need this attention like a hole in the head."

"I'll arrange to see them and find out what they've got to say. I'm not going to involve my solicitor at this stage. It might look like I've got something to hide. They can show me their cards first. I'll give you a bell when I know more, catch you later."

Jason took the business card from his pocket and dialled the mobile number.

"DS Higgs," came the reply.

"It's Jason Hamilton. You called at my house today. I believe you need to speak to me."

"Hi, Jason thanks for getting back to me. Is it okay for me to call in and see you? I know it's getting late, but we can sort things out quicker that way."

"Why do you need to speak to me?" Jason asked.

"It's just that your name has been linked to a person of interest in our investigation, that's all. You may have some information that could be useful for us."

"Sorry, I'm not available tonight. I've got some business meetings in Manchester tomorrow morning, I could see you then?"

Jason didn't want to give the impression that he was eager to meet. He also wanted to control the time and place, around his legitimate business meetings.

"Okay, where and when are you free?" DS Higgs asked, sounding unconcerned.

"Saint Anne's Square, on the benches near the church, one o'clock?"

"That's great, see you then, Jason."

Kirsty was still in the kitchen when Jason returned to the house. He picked up his coffee and took a drink.

"I've arranged to see DS Higgs tomorrow, whilst I'm in town," he said.

Looking at Kirsty, he could tell she was trying to be nonchalant. It was evident to him that she was pretty worried and pissed off.

"These are all warning signs, Jason. You really need to leave all that shit behind you before it's too late. I'm tired of it. Leave it behind. You've got enough on your plate with the property developments. I'm not prepared to sit back and watch our lives go down the sink hole. If you want to that's fine, but not me. And let's hope it's not too late for you."

"I know, I know, babe. You're right. It's happening but it can't be done overnight. I'll sort it."

They walked into the lounge and Jason crashed out on the sofa. His mind was preoccupied with the attention he was getting from the police. *What do they know?*

Jason was up early the following morning. He took his car down to the gym so that he could drive straight on to his meeting afterwards. Wayne wasn't there yet, so Jason started putting the weight plates on the bench press. He knew a good workout was what he needed mentally before meeting the plod. He lay down on the bench and started pushing out some reps.

"Mister Keen, at it all ready, how long you been here?" Wayne said as he approached the bench.

"Just got here, mate. Your turn," Jason said, as he got up off the bench and stood waiting to spot for Wayne.

"Anything further from last night?" Wayne asked.

"No, I'm going to meet him at one o'clock today after I've been to the solicitors."

Wayne began pushing out his reps. He released his grip on the bar, onto the stand, with a clunk.

"Give me a bell afterwards, unless you're remanded to Risley," Wayne laughed. "Although I think you may be allowed one call."

"Who needs enemies with friends like you?"

The banter hid the tension they were both experiencing. They were more than curious to discover what the cops had to say, but neither would have admitted to the other. The workout allowed them to forget the about the cops for an hour or so.

After showering, Jason got dressed into his business attire and left the gym. He drove into the city, parked up, and walked to his conveyancing solicitor's office. He needed to discuss some concerns before signing on the dotted line for a new riverside development opportunity in Lancaster.

The office was modern in design, with white walls and glass partitions. Men and women in suits were going about their business and off to meetings. There was a clean, efficient and friendly feel about the place.

The meeting went as planned. Jason was soon to be the owner of four more luxury apartments by the River Lune. When he walked out again he felt relaxed in his legitimate-businessman skin. The feeling was fleeting though, as his mind switched to the next meeting.

He walked to Saint Anne's Square along Deansgate. It was a nice warm sunny day. The pavement was bustling with people. Saint Anne's Square was full of shoppers and workers enjoying their lunch-break under the sun. This also meant that most of the benches were taken, including the ones by the church. It wasn't a problem because he'd developed a habit of spotting the cops from a mile away, as if it was second nature to him. Surely enough, as he approached the church he saw a middle-aged guy, grey short hair, with a beer belly putting a strain on the buttons of his shirt. He was wearing a grey suit that had seen better days. The fella was chatting on his mobile phone. Jason approached him and purposely stepped right into his personal space. The fella instinctively stepped back and said, "I've got to go, catch you later." He placed his mobile in the inside pocket of his jacket.

"Peter Higgs?" Jason asked.

"Yes, you must be Jason?"

Jason nodded his head and said, "How can I help you?"

"I'm investigating the death of a man called Paul Smethurst. He was shot on the canal about two weeks ago."

"I remember reading about that on the internet, poor bastard."

"Did you know Smethurst?"

"No. Should I have?"

"The reason I ask brings me onto why I wanted to meet up. We've received some intelligence from a reliable source that he was intending to shoot you. Have you any idea why he would want to do that?" DS Higgs asked, not leaving any time for this news to sink in.

"Absolutely no idea. Jesus, that's a bit of a shocker. Are you sure it was me? It's no secret that I was a bad lad back in the day and got up to things I now regret, but I can't see it being a grudge from that long ago. You've obviously done your checks on me. I've left all that behind me. I'm now a property developer helping to build the tax man's bank balance. This Smethurst guy wasn't involved in property ventures, was he?"

"No, we've not come across anything to suggest that. Give it some thought. Something may come back to you. He may have had connections with people you've crossed. Because we are aware of the alleged threat we have a duty of care to make you aware of the threat. Even though he is deceased, he may have other associates involved, who may still pose a risk to you.

Would you sign these papers to confirm we have made you aware?"

DS Higgs passed the papers and a pen to Jason. He scribbled a signature on each and handed one back.

"You've got my mobile, if you remember anything or need assistance regards the threat, give me a call, and I'll let you know if anything further comes to our attention. Thanks for meeting up."

"No worries," Jason said, as he walked away. He sensed that Higgs knew more than he was letting on. He came over as an experienced detective. Jason had an unnerving feeling that they would meet again in the future. And a battle would commence.

DS Higgs walked away in the opposite direction. The meeting went pretty much as he had anticipated, neither of them giving much away. He was hungry and knew he should get something healthy. His middle age spread had appeared from nowhere and showed no signs of abating. His kids had even started teasing him, having grown up with a dad who was well into his sports and fitness. However, Pete believed he deserved a treat in view of the long hours he had been working. He made his way to his favourite all day breakfast café. Before entering he put a call in to Andrea Statham.

"Hi, Pete, how you getting on?" Andrea said.

"I've just left Jason Hamilton. I kept it very brief and left him wanting more. He looks like a switched-on fella, confident and intelligent. He was courteous and polite, the stereotypical clean-cut businessman. My gut-feeling is that we are on the right track. If he didn't shoot Smethurst, he knows who did."

"Did you serve the Threat to Life Notice?" Andrea asked.

"Yes, the Chief Constable's back is covered, he can sleep easy tonight."

"You're very cynical, Pete. I was just concerned for Hamilton's safety."

They both started laughing.

"Of course, Ma'am, I wouldn't expect anything less."

Pete enjoyed their banter, particularly the gallows cop humour. It helped him deal with the horrendous situations that the job had placed him in over the years. He had to be careful though these days. The political correctness regime took no prisoners.

"So, you think we're on the right lines?" Andrea asked.

"Definitely, it's a classic drugs dispute. It may work to our advantage having the Drugs squad chasing him too, it might put some pressure on associates to start talking."

"Okay, nice work, Pete, catch you when you get back."

Pete's mind was elsewhere already. He was looking at the menu through the café window.

Jason made his way to one of the pubs at the opposite end of the square. It was busy and noisy with laughter and chatter. There was a great choice of beers. He opted for an IPA. There were no available seats so he stood at the bar. An incoming text vibrated his mobile. It was Ryan again. 'Any chance of an advance mate, I'm on my arse down here at the minute.'

Part of Jason had some sympathy with him. He knew he had treated him like a sidekick over the years. But Ryan brought it on himself. He was becoming reckless and unreliable. Since he'd been going down to Bristol with his new woman he was back on the charlie and booze. No doubt waking up with the blackouts again, not remembering the shit-storm he had created the night before.

Jason knew he was being too soft but decided to transfer him a few hundred. In a weird way it made Jason feel good that Ryan was so dependent on him. It would keep him out of trouble too, if he went off the rails anything could happen. They'd caused enough havoc already and stepped on some toes with their dealing in Bristol. Ryan had been a bit distant since the trip to Amsterdam. This was probably down to the new love interest. He'd no doubt be back up North when it all ended.

'I'll transfer you an advance, how you doing?' Jason texted.

'All good, I've got my ear to the ground, there's some opportunities for us to do business down here again. I've met some interested parties,' Ryan texted back.

Sounds like bull to me, justifying the advance. 'When are you back up in town Ryan?'

He didn't receive a reply to this last one. Nothing new there, Ryan now had what he wanted.

After his second pint, Jason left the boozer and headed for the car park. He blended in well in his businessman attire, cutting a fine figure in his pinstripe suit. *Is it time to leave the past in the past? Or will I miss it too much?* His criminal enterprises were almost hands-off now anyway. He was passing the baton to his trusted lieutenant, returning the loyalty

Wayne had given him over the years. He felt he owed Wayne his opportunity, and more importantly they would continue to deliver his cut of the profits.

He had been enjoying the transition until DS Higgs came on the scene. His assessment was that this cop was no mug. He looked capable, an old-fashioned Jack who would stalk his prey with patience and guile. Jason knew he had to be on guard and take the threat seriously, more seriously than the threat of some 'wannabe' who tried to shoot him. He took out his mobile and called Wayne.

"So, you've not been locked up. I was about to arrange a visiting order to fetch you a food parcel," Wayne laughed.

"I don't think he showed his hand. He looks capable, and he looks focused on getting his man. He was just having a poke about, watching my reaction. Not good, we could do without this."

"Is it worth getting Frank Burton to do a bit of homework on him, you never know what he might find… a bit of intimidation or threats can go a long way?"

"Can't do any harm. On the face of it, he wanted to serve a threat to life notice. They've had intelligence that this Smethurst wanted to take me out. I hope that's come from one of Smethurst's boys rather than one of ours." Frank Burton, Jason's solicitor was a good option, he had crossed the line into criminality and was now a trusted associate of Jason's. An invaluable member of their firm.

"We've been here before, we just need to go into lockdown. I wonder where the information came from. I think we need to disclose some misinformation to see if we've got a rat grassing amongst us," Wayne said.

"Mate, I don't like saying this but the canal incident was kept tight. Ryan's in self-destruct mode again, we can't rule him out. You and Carl need to keep an eye on him."

"I can see where you're coming from, Jason, but we can't jump to conclusions. Carl's obviously got a downer on him, I can't see Ryan being the grass. But I'm keeping an open mind. Whoever it is, we can flush them out. Leave it to me. You take a backseat, especially as the cops are looking at you. Give them the run around to nowhere whilst I crack on with business."

"Makes sense, mate. Good timing for us too. Catch up later."

Jason put his mobile away and walked to his car. *Good man Wayne, the voice of reason, top fella and the right man to steady the ship.*

Chapter Nine

Lee McCann felt as if his heart was going to burst out of his chest and slapped the red stop button on the running machine. He didn't mess about in the gym, a proper session on every visit. Old habits die hard. He was still super fit from his time in the Paras.

The fitness regime helped his mental health, too. Tours in the Middle East had taken their toll. Some would say Lee suffered from PTSD. Not Lee though, he felt he had reached the point of burnout but was coping well. Since leaving the forces he had never felt better.

Lee saw Kirsty. She was getting some close attention from one of the personal trainers. *Who could blame him*, he thought. Lee waved to her as he passed by, walking to the cross trainer. He stopped next to the multi-gym where his partner Samantha was working out on the lateral pull down.

"Have you seen Kirsty's in? She's over by the running machine getting chatted up by the personal trainer," Lee said.

"Any sign of Jason?" Samantha asked.

"No, she says he's been busy with work and hasn't had the time to get down to the gym."

"I don't think he comes here as often as we thought," Samantha said.

"I think you're right, I might have to visit the other gym and pin him down there."

"Hey you two, how you doing?" Kirsty asked. She was standing in their blind-spot next to the dip bars.

"Kirsty, good to see you. I think you've got a new admirer over there. Talking of admirers, I've not seen Jason in for a bit, how is he?" Lee replied.

"He's good. He's been working away on some new property development."

"I could do with a good excuse like that, I'm knackered," Samantha said.

"He's been back a few days, so we're having some pals around tonight for drinks. You're more than welcome to join us if you're free."

"Thank you, we'd love to," Samantha said.

They swapped mobile numbers and carried on chatting, whilst Lee resumed his workout.

"I think Lee will get on well with Jason," Kirsty said.

"Yes, they're very similar and Lee's hoping to spend more time back in Manchester. He's pushing for the company to open an office up here," Samantha said.

After showering, Samantha and Lee met in the cafe. It was a relaxing open-plan area, overlooking the outside pool on one side and badminton courts on the other. They took their coffees and sat on one of the sofas.

"This is my favourite bit, chilling with a cappuccino," Samantha said.

"Light weight," laughed Lee.

"How long had Kirsty been stood behind us?"

"I'm not sure but it can't have been long. I don't think she heard much, we were only saying that we'd not seen Jason anyway."

"I hope not. We need to be more careful. Anyway, the invite's a bonus, it's your chance to make a good impression on Jason. No pressure!"

"What were you two gabbing about?"

"Well, she's taken a shine to you, definitely got the hots for you," Samantha laughed. "She was saying you and Jason would get along great, she's match making you a bestie!"

"Anything about work?" Lee side stepped the bestie comment.

"Yes, she was saying that he made his money in pubs and clubs. He now has a decent property portfolio, she mentioned Lancaster and Portugal."

"Well this meal should be an interesting night then, they seem keen to get to know us."

It was about eight o'clock when Lee and Samantha approached Jason and Kirsty's house, along the tree-lined avenue.

"I'll park outside on the pavement. I Don't want to get blocked in on the drive," Lee said.

Samantha had been the first to meet Jason at the gym. He chatted her up under the guise of some weight-lifting coaching. It was a great opportunity for her to introduce him to Lee. The four of them got on well and always had a good chat if they bumped into each other.

"Nice pile, what do you reckon, £700.000?" Samantha asked.

"And the rest, how the other half live eh?"

"I'm thinking it's going to be modern and bling inside. I wonder who else is coming tonight."

"I'm not sure. I hope there are others are coming, from what you were saying earlier, and Jason chatting you up they might have other ideas!" They both burst into laughter, "It would be good to meet some of Jason's mates too. Should be a good night, hopefully."

They got out of the car and walked through the small gate up to the porch. Kirsty answered the door. Lee was always saying he thought she was a stunner, and she certainly appeared so tonight. The black dress was complimented by her athletic physique and long blonde hair. Lee gave her a bottle of Chateau Neuf De Pap, his 'go to' bottle for party hosts.

"Glad you could make it. Go straight through, Jason's in the kitchen with the others."

The expansive hallway opened into a massive open-planned kitchen and dining area with an orangery beyond it. The décor was minimalist. Jason saw them straight away and made his way over from the fellas he was talking to.

"Good to see you both. I was ready for a quiet night but Kirsty had other plans."

"You're looking good, Jason. Not seen you at the gym, so you've obviously been going to your back street boxing gym," Lee said.

"I've managed a few workouts between meetings. Business is booming so I've been run off my feet. You two aren't looking bad yourselves. Kirsty mentioned she had seen you at the health club."

Jason fixed them both a drink. Samantha couldn't argue with Lee, Jason was good looking. Short dark hair, six foot plus, strong shoulders, charismatic, and oozing confidence. He blended in well with the lavish surroundings.

Kirsty joined the three of them next to the array of drinks and poured herself a prosecco.

"Your house is beautiful, it's like a show home," said Samantha.

"It's not a house, it's a lifestyle," laughed Lee.

"Jason's never here and we've no kids so it's easy to keep tidy. Come on, Samantha, I'll give you the tour. We love it here. We've had it for about a year now."

The two women made their way to the hallway. Jason led Lee to the three fellas he was talking to when they arrived.

"Fellas this is Lee, Lee this is Wayne and Carl. Lee's an ex Para, so don't piss him off," Jason laughed.

"Hi, Lee, we met at the Arches on Deansgate," Carl said.

"I remember, it was a good night, you guys were celebrating City's win. We were on a leaving do for one of our guys. He missed the regiment too much and has re-enlisted. Pleased to meet you, Wayne."

Lee was enjoying the company. The chatter was going well and the beer was flowing. They seemed to enjoy his stories from Iraq and Afghanistan, especially Jason. There wasn't much information coming from the other direction.

When Lee went to the kitchen for another drink, Kirsty joined him for a refill.

"You were like a machine in the gym, Lee, once a soldier always a soldier?"

"It's the endorphins rush, I love it. It keeps me sane too. You know the score, you're no slouch yourself."

"Flattery will get you everywhere."

Kirsty winked at him with a flirty smile and returned to the group of women. *Jeez, perhaps Samantha was serious,* thought Lee, but he knew it was a road he couldn't go down, no matter how tempted he was.

It was about 1.00am when Lee and Samantha left the party. Samantha had got the short straw and was driving them back to the flat. Both of them had enjoyed the night out and felt chilled.

"I see what you mean, quite a likeable guy on the face of it," said Samantha.

"He deals mainly in property now. It sounds like he has an impressive portfolio. His other activities are well hidden. Not one of them let anything slip. He comes across as the typical successful business man."

"He must have millions," replied Samantha. "Kirsty gave me the full tour. They have a fully kitted-out gym and exercise studio in the basement."

"It was a good night. I didn't get a chance to work the room. I was chatting with Jason and got an introduction to Carl and Wayne. They were quite cagey and didn't divulge much. They work with Jason and run a small building firm."

Samantha laughed. "They didn't look like successful business men. More like a couple of gangsters, you wouldn't want to meet them in a dark alley."

"Did you get to meet anyone of interest?" asked Lee.

"Not really, just Kirsty and a bit of small talk with some of her friends. They were mostly the women who worked in her hairdressing salons. She has three shops. It sounds like she works hard."

After showing Lee and Samantha to the door, Jason sat down for cigars and whiskey with Wayne and Carl. Kirsty was sitting near them, listening but not appearing to be listening, whilst flicking through social media on her tablet. Carl took a sip of his whiskey and started the conversation.

"Not seen Ryan for a bit. How long has he been in Bristol now, a couple of months? He worries me. The booze and coke make him a liability."

Jason's ears pricked up, he gave Wayne a knowing look. Wayne raised his eyebrows in recognition.

"The Dam trip," laughed Wayne, "I can't remember much about that."

They all laughed.

This got Jason thinking about Ryan. He felt worried and didn't like the distance between them. The money wasn't a problem but what was Ryan up to?

"You look miles away, Jason, you okay?" asked Wayne.

"I'm good, did you get chance to talk much to Lee? Top fella that one, hard as nails, ex- para."

Carl stood up to get another drink. "Yeah, sounds like he was living in a shitstorm in Iraq, fair play to him."

"When me and Carl met him at the arches, the fellas he was with were from the world of security, ex-SAS types. I could have listened to them all day. Kirsty sees him and Samantha in the gym, too. I think she has a bit of crush on him, strong silent type, and all that," Jason said.

"Are you sure it's not you who has a man-crush? Bit of bro-love going on there?" Wayne said. Spontaneous laughter followed between all of them.

Jason could take the stick, but only so far. He didn't accept newcomers into the fold that easily. He had been to school with Wayne and Ryan and they had stuck together ever since. Ryan was the youngest of them. Jason took pity on him for being in care and not having all the latest gear. Carl had been the exception. He had been in the firm for about five years. A fella pulled a knife on Jason in a club in Manchester. Carl had stepped in and floored him with one punch. Their association and friendship developed from there.

“I bet there’s some money in guarding VIP’s these days. Those premiership football players are forking out loads to be safe. They even have attack dogs roaming in their gardens,” Jason said.

“There might be some business opportunities coming then, nice sector to get into,” commented Wayne.

“You’ve got your military experience under your belt, Wayne, maybe we can diversify. You need to network with Lee. Having said that, not sure if the Army Catering Corps will impress him,” Jason laughed.

“Didn’t the Catering Corps knock you back when you tried to sign up?” Wayne retorted.

“In all seriousness, I think Lee could open doors for us in that world. They are probably involved in arms dealing too. And you’d be our man, Wayne. Start testing the water with him.”

Carl changed the subject as he sat back down.

“I’m going down to Bristol next week, hooking up with Ryan. Hope my liver is up for it. Anyone fancy a jolly?”

“Wish I had the time, pal,” answered Jason, secretly glad he was busy. *I’m too old for all that shit now, bigger fish to fry,* he thought.

“How about you, Wayne?” asked Carl.

“I fancy it, but need to make sure the bucks in Liverpool are boxed off with the ties to Smethurst from Chester. Anyway, I thought he was your number one suspect for grassing?” Wayne said.

“It’s just me then. Listen, fellas, you’ve known Ryan a hell of a lot longer than me. How concerned should we be getting here?”

“Over the last few years he’s taken too much of a liking for charlie and booze, as you know. Since then he's up and down all the time. One minute he's on top of the world then he's on a downer. That's what concerns me. He gets a bit reckless. I suspect he's instrumental in causing the problems with the gangs in Bristol. I don't think he'd intentionally cause us any grief, but he's got a bit of a self-destruct button. He's become paranoid that I don't respect him. Just keep an eye on him for now, massage his ego a bit. He was dragged up as a kid, and it looks like it's fucked his head up a bit. Just keep an eye on him, that's all," Jason advised.

Jason hadn't clocked the care home connection with Ryan and the exploited kids he tried to protect from the county lines dealing. If he had, he would understand Ryan's predicament more. But maybe it was best for Ryan that he didn't find out. The teenager's welfare wasn't on Jason's priority list, just the money they earned him.

Chapter Ten

Ryan sprinted the last straight to Lisa's flat. He leant forward with his hands on his knees, breathing heavily. He had been for a run around the docks. Lisa was working away. She was cabin crew on a long-haul flight from Heathrow, doing the job she loved. He hoped her company would force him to slow down on the booze and charlie. He'd been here before and didn't like the fallout. But he also knew they alleviated the pressure he put himself under, risking Jason's dealing operations, protecting the vulnerable care home kids from harm. He felt a strong sense of affinity with the kids having been there himself. But his interventions had come at a financial loss for Jason.

He entered the flat and walked into the bedroom, where the smell of her perfume lingered. He felt comfortable and at home here. *Is it time to move on from the Manchester scene and stand on my own two feet? But now I've complicated matters getting involved with Kirsty, I need to get a grip* he mused, as he stripped off his sweats and got into the shower. He also knew if it came to a choice between the two of the women, there was only one winner.

Ryan was looking forward to Carl arriving later, and to a few beers out, with some food to follow. Carl had been a breath of fresh air when he joined the firm. No doubt Carl would share the stories from Amsterdam. He wished he had been out there with them, but whether he liked it or not, he was lowest in the pecking order, which usually meant staying back and keeping an eye on things. *Maybe it is time to leave Manchester and start a new life in Bristol. Kirsty is not going to leave Jason, and if we carry on, Jason will no doubt find out.*

Later that day, Ryan walked into the Axe and Cleaver to meet Carl. They'd drank there together in the past. It now had some enjoyable familiarity about it. Ryan got a pint at the bar, grabbed a copy of the Mail, and took a seat. He started at the back as usual, studying the league tables. It was cathartic these days, looking for City at the top rather than lower down the league table.

Ryan was halfway through his pint when Carl approached his table. He jumped up, chuffed to see him. The feeling looked mutual. They had a big man-hug then gravitated towards the bar. Carl got the drinks and they remained standing. It was a typical town-centre pub. A long bar with insufficient staff behind it, televisions on the walls showing the news muted and menus offering microwaved pub food.

They were never short of conversation, especially with a pint in hand. Girlfriends were discussed, followed by City.

"We've got a shipment of H coming in on Monday, so it's going to be busy. It's going to be kept at the unit to help us move it on to Scotland quicker. I could do with a lift if you're about?"

"Lisa's first day back, sorry, mate," Ryan replied.

"Wouldn't want to put you out, Ryan, leave it with me then." Carl looked a bit put out.

"Sorry, mate, I'm not being funny but I'm going to be spending more time down here. I need to get my shit together," Ryan said.

"No worries, did you hear about Jason decking that punter in Amsterdam?"

"No. He can't help himself, can he?" Carl related the story, with a bit of artistic licence for better effect.

"It's what he enjoys. Psycho." Ryan was no longer impressed by Jason's violence and not interested in the stories. He changed the subject back to City and finished his pint.

"Come on, mate, let's go for a curry, I'm starving," Carl said.

They'd had quite a few pints and time was knocking on. The clientele in the pub was changing from the afternoon shoppers to the early evening crowd.

"Usual place?" Ryan replied. "We know the food's good there."

Ryan hadn't even thought about charlie. He enjoyed being with Carl, who was a quiet-spoken, unassuming, laid back type of guy. He wasn't on an ego trip like Jason and Wayne. At the restaurant they went down the stairs and were seated at a table. The place was pretty full. The sound of chatter made for a good, friendly atmosphere, and the smells of delicious spices left Ryan feeling ready for some dinner.

They got stuck into the poppadums right away, a perfect accompaniment to their beer. Their mood was good, but the banter, chatter and beer-supping had given way to their hunger and the feast ahead. The main courses arrived quickly, but they weren't complaining on this occasion. Carl had gone for his usual chicken madras, and Ryan Special biryani, both of them creatures of habit.

Ryan forked the last of his curry into his mouth. He was full, now feeling the taste for another beer.

"Shall we do Irish coffees and beers here or move on?" he asked.

"Let's go and have some proper beer and ogle at some women," Carl replied, "might even get lucky."

They asked for the bill, which came straightaway. The table was obviously booked and ready to go again. Carl left some cash on the plate.

They left the curry house and walked over to the pub, which was a lot busier now. They ordered two beers and found two seats at a table. Ryan knew the first beer would be a struggle after a curry, but he also knew it was only a temporary slowing of proceedings.

"Jason's looking at getting out of the business and focusing on his legit stuff. I'm not sure if the shooting on the canal has influenced him, or Kirsty, but he's good to go. He wants Wayne to take the reins."

Ryan felt his blood boil and a feeling of anger take over him. He'd been overlooked again, taken for granted again, ignored again. Without even thinking it through he spat out, "Well that's two of us good to go, mate. I'm obviously persona non-grata these days, not in the inner-circle, just making up the numbers."

Carl looked surprised.

"Bit of an overreaction, mate, you're one of us and always will be. You were never going to be the next boss, you know that," Carl said, a bit taken aback.

"No, but I'm trusted with the shit end of the stick, like the stuff from the canal which I've still got tucked away."

Ryan realised he'd said what he was thinking out loud. He also knew the amount of coke he was taking wasn't helping, his paranoia and irritability was taking over.

"Take a chill pill, Ryan. I'll go and get the beers in."

Carl left the table for the sanctuary of the bar.

Whilst Carl was away, Ryan brooded darkly, contemplating his exit. He didn't deserve this treatment anymore. If anything, Jason owed him big time. And to complicate matters he had slept with Kirsty. He felt paranoid and anxious.

Carl returned to the table with two pints.

"Have you calmed down, Ryan? You sounded like you needed to get that off your chest. I didn't know you were so pissed off?"

"Jason knows how to press my buttons."

"He's rattled your cage for sure. I hope you've not still got the stuff from the canal. That should be destroyed by now. You could be in big shit over that."

"I'm out of here. I'm fucking sick of all this, I'm out. Good to see you, pal."

Ryan necked his pint and walked out of the pub. He could see Carl looked gob-smacked. He walked back to the flat and collapsed on the bed. *What the hell did I kick off for, I don't even want to be involved anymore, let alone put in charge.* He knew it was the beer and his growing loathing of Jason which had caused him to spill into an emotional rant.

The following morning, Carl was up early and enjoying the 'eat all you can' breakfast at his hotel. He had phoned Ryan but got no reply. He was worried that Ryan was in a bad place. He hadn't seen him kick off like that before. The bigger issue was the uncertainty of whether he had destroyed the incriminating evidence, a matter he couldn't ignore. Carl left the restaurant and went outside for a cigarette. The suspicions of Ryan being a grass had been amplified, this wasn't good for Ryan, but it kept Carl out of the spotlight of Jason's critical glare.

Back in Manchester, Jason was also having breakfast when his phone rang. He looked at the screen, it was Carl.

"Morning, Carl. You okay, pal?"

"I've been better. I was out with Ryan last night. He's definitely off the rails again. His head is all over the place."

"I suspected as much but hoped I was wrong."

"I'm worried, I don't know if it's paranoia but he took news of the handover badly. I think he felt passed by and disrespected, he thinks you owe him better than that. The worse bit though, he said he still has the stuff from the canal almost by way of a bargaining chip."

Jason couldn't believe what he had just heard. This was serious. Was Ryan taking him on, or was he bluffing in the paranoia of coke?

"We need to get to the bottom of this, Carl. Can you and Wayne bring him back up to Manchester? I need to speak to him face to face. And locate the pistol and stuff too."

"Leave it with me. Before I forget, I've told him a shipment will be at the yard on Monday. So, if the cops raid our yard, he's the grass, only me, you and him are in the loop."

Jason ended the call and placed his mobile on the table. His mood suddenly darkened, but he tried to put on a calm appearance for Kirsty. He grabbed another piece of toast and began munching, but he couldn't stop his mind from ruminating through the potential problems. *If Ryan started talking, and could back up his story by producing the pistol, cctv footage, and clothing, he was looking at prison time courtesy of DS Higgs. Or even worse, was he grassing already?*

Kirsty broke his thoughts, "You okay? What was all that about?"

She had been with him long enough to know when he'd been rattled by someone.

"Ryan's going off the rails again. He's hitting the charlie big time. It's built up his inferiority complex again. We don't need this, not now."

Jason was looking at Kirsty. She looked shell-shocked. *Bit of an overreaction,* he thought.

"He'll sort himself out, he always does. There's no malice in Ryan, he just wears his heart on his sleeve. You should wrap an arm around him, he's been a good mate to you over the years." she replied.

After speaking to Jason, Carl phoned Wayne and explained what had gone on the night before. Wayne wasn't surprised, he knew Ryan well.

"I'll get the train down to Bristol. Can you pick me up at the station?"

"Yes, mate. No worries. What do you think Jason's got in mind for Ryan?"

"Whatever it is, it won't be pleasant. I can't believe he's still got the pistol, this is serious. You need to get that stuff back asap," Wayne said.

"I know, I'm just trying to keep him on-side, so he doesn't do anything stupid."

Carl tried Ryan on the mobile again. This time, Ryan answered.

"Morning, Carl, sorry about the drama last night, it's not your issue."

"No worries, pal, think it through, you said some heavy shit, you had me worried."

"You fancy meeting up for something to eat and a few beers later on?" Ryan asked.

"Sounds good, listen, give some thought to coming back up to Manchester. It sounds like you need your friends wrapped around you."

Carl was relieved Ryan hadn't gone missing, and planted the seed to normalise the Manchester request.

Ryan felt disenfranchised. For the first time in his adult life, he didn't feel as thick as thieves with the others anymore. He took a few lines of coke from the table. His stash was almost gone, he needed more. Confidence returned to his veins. *Did I say too much last night? Probably*, he thought. He regretted kicking off. Even if he did want out of the firm, he had probably gone about it the wrong way as usual. He knew he was sometimes his own worst enemy, saying out loud what he should just be thinking, which was sometimes akin to pressing a self-destruct button in this game. He knew he would never grass Jason and the fellas unless they pushed him to it, but maybe kicking off would prick their ears up to giving him a bit more respect. He'd made complaints to social services about practices at the care home and fed information when the care home lads were getting in trouble, all anonymous. But he was careful not to leave bread crumbs leading to Jason. It was a delicate situation that stressed him out. But he couldn't stand by and see these lads exploited. Jason could easily run the dealing without them.

As planned, Ryan turned up at the pub to meet Carl. As soon as he approached the bar, he noticed Carl and Wayne standing at the end. Carl waved him over. Wayne smiled, looking glad to see him.

"What are you doing here, Wayne?"

"It was the plan to come down for a beer, but now Carl tells me we're going back up to Manchester tonight," Wayne said.

"I don't remember agreeing to that," Ryan said and looked at Carl.

As they sat down at a table, Carl got straight to the point.

"Ryan, you opened my eyes last night. I didn't know how pissed off you were, we need to get this sorted. Jason is going hands-off to work on his property empire and he wants Wayne to take over. We need a smooth transition, and you're part of that."

Wayne filled the pause, "We need a smooth transition, and everyone needs to be happy. Come back to Manchester with us tonight, the four of us need to sit down and thrash this out. We can discuss your position and what you want."

"Lisa's back on Monday, fellas, no can do." He sensed that Wayne was getting agitated. "It's a needs must, mate," Carl said. "It won't wait. Jason wants to walk away, but it needs to be right for him. It won't take long. You can be back down here before Lisa gets back. It's not the right time to wind Jason up."

Ryan realised this wasn't a polite invitation. Wayne's agitation worried him.

"Fellas, the stuff I had to get rid of is gone. I was just mouthing off last night. I'm pissed off with it all."

"We know, mate, no worries."

They finished their beers and headed for Carl's car. Ryan was beginning to feel a little apprehensive. *Have I overstepped the mark?* It wouldn't be the first time, and differences had been ironed out before, but he had a nagging thought. This felt different. Or was he being paranoid?

They got into the car. Carl was driving, Wayne front passenger and Ryan was in the back. It was only 7.00pm, with Carl's heavy right foot and a clear run they could be in Manchester by just after 10pm. Ryan felt more reassured when the banter got flowing. The fellas seemed fairly normal now. Maybe he had just put the wind up everybody when he gobbed off. What did they expect though? He thought he had good reason to be pissed off. Surely, they could see that.

Then his thinking took another turn. *Shit, has Jason found out about the other night with Kirsty, has she told him? Has he got other hidden cameras?* Ryan's anxiety and paranoia levels went into overdrive again. He felt a hot flush of panic. He began to think he'd messed up getting into the car. Would he have been better just disappearing?

His attention was re-focussed when he tuned into Carl and Wayne's conversation. They were discussing the way forward once Wayne was in charge. Wayne was satisfied the shooting on the canal was now sorted. The cops appeared to be getting nowhere with the investigation. Maybe Wayne and Carl would continue to look after him. It was only Jason who he had a problem with.

Ryan's head was starting to feel overloaded. He couldn't think straight. He concluded that this wasn't good. It was probably not going to end well. He needed a plan B.

Whilst the car was progressing up the M6 through Cheshire, Jason was in his office. To say he wasn't happy was a significant understatement. Everything had been coming together nicely. He was comfortable in his new role and looking forward to focusing more on his property. And therefore, untouchable as far as the cops were concerned. What was Ryan playing at? He had looked after Ryan, and now Ryan was taking liberties. Jason questioned whether he should have seen this coming. Had he let his guard down? Ryan's descent to becoming a cokehead had gone under all of their radars. *One thing is for certain, Ryan isn't going to fuck things up.*

This had to be stamped on. There wouldn't be a second chance, and he certainly didn't want to sort it from a prison cell. Jason was fuming. He was slowly stepping into old territory, when he had been a hands on enforcer. Emotional and friendship ties had been diluting in his mindset, this was critical business, with one focus, coming out on top.

How he played this depended on the way Ryan responded. What was Ryan after? Did Ryan still have the evidence? Would he go to the cops with it? Jason would have thought the answer was a definite 'no' not so long ago, but now he wasn't too sure, doubt was creeping in. Ryan had allowed himself to fall into a bad place but he wasn't taking Jason and the others with him.

He would play it by ear. This wasn't the first time he'd been in a tricky situation, but hopefully the last. It was self-preservation time, sentiment and emotion had just left the room. He took his pistol out of his stronghold, quietly hoping he wouldn't need it. He left the house, got in his car and set off for the meeting. He was in the zone; survival instinct was his priority.

As Jason left his driveway, Carl was bringing his car to a halt at the Manchester Ship Canal near Urmston. Ryan was fighting to keep focused. His thinking was slow, he needed to concentrate. He felt anxious and restless. He knew what he needed.

"Fellas, you got any charlie on you?"

Carl and Wayne shook their heads and mumbled apologies. Ryan was not in a good place and it didn't feel like it was going to get better. He looked out of the car window into the black darkness. It made him feel claustrophobic and isolated.

"What's the score, fellas? Why have we stopped here, why not at the unit or boozer?" Ryan could feel panic swelling inside him. He felt light headed. He looked at the door handle. He wanted out of here, but he knew it would be locked.

"Mate, you know you've pissed Jason off. What were you thinking, not getting rid of the stuff, and then thinking you've got an ace up your sleeve to bargain with?"

"Of course, I got rid of the stuff. I'd had a skin-full of ale and was angry, give me a break," Ryan pleaded.

"Jason can't take that risk and watch you take us all down. You've let yourself go. Pull yourself together and dig yourself out of this hole."

Their attention was taken by car headlights sweeping across the car park. They lit up the woodland. Ryan clocked where the nearest woodland was, should he get the chance to break free. He felt nauseous and physically sick.

Jason drove onto the car park and saw Carl's car in his headlights. He parked on the opposite side and walked over. The beep-beep accompanied the indicator's orange flashing, as the doors were unlocked from within. He opened the back door and slid onto the back seat next to Ryan. He felt in control and focused, the way he dealt with this would reflect his status and reputation.

"So, you thought you'd do me over," Jason said.

"No, that's total bollocks. I was pissed up, on the lash, gobbing off, no way am I trying to turn you over." Ryan sounded desperate. "Fucking hell what's up with you three." He sounded desperate.

"Where's the pistol, where's the cctv, where's the clothes? Where's the van?" Jason demanded. He looked straight forward as he spoke, unemotional and matter of fact.

"I've got rid of them. They're in the water at Bristol docks."

"I wish I could believe you, Ryan. I've looked after you. Look at you now, a rattling cokehead that can't be trusted."

Ryan was in total fear, flight or fight was kicking in.

"Bollocks, what's with the overreaction here? I've always got the shit end of the stick, I've been a running boy at best, and now I'm not even in on the handover."

Ryan had clocked that the central locking had not been re-activated. He had one chance. His hand flicked the door catch. He was falling out of the car before the door was fully open, onto all fours, and into a sprint. Within seconds he was gone into the darkness of the woodland.

Wayne, Carl, and Jason had been taken by surprise. They jumped out of the car, scanning the area frantically. It was almost a token gesture of effort. Ryan was already gone, on his toes. Wayne sprinted in the most likely direction towards the undergrowth and trees. He could hear the snapping of twigs and rustling of undergrowth, but couldn't pinpoint it. Reluctantly, he returned to the car. Jason was fuming. His hands on his hips, staring at the floor.

"See you back at my place. What a fucking shambles," Jason said. He got into his car and left.

Wayne and Carl got back into their car. A stunned silence remained. They both knew they'd let their guard down, they should have seen that coming. Carl drove from the car park and headed to Jason's house.

Ryan remained still, lying flat in the undergrowth. He was fighting to get his breath back, although he was well experienced at this from evading the plod on many occasions. His heart felt like it was going to beat out of chest. His evasion was practiced almost with military precision. For now, he stayed put, still and quiet, just watching and listening. The smell of soil and vegetation gave him a weird sense of freedom and comfort in such hostile circumstances.

When Jason arrived back home the house was empty. Probably for the best, he didn't like Kirsty around when he was in a foul mood. He was trying to remain focused and not let emotions get in the way of the right decisions being made. *I can't believe he hadn't locked the car. Fucking basics*. It was pointless going over the events at the car park. That was now history. He focused on the way forward.

His thoughts were interrupted by the doorbell.

"Hi, fellas, come in."

Wayne and Carl entered the house shamefaced. They followed Jason into the kitchen. Jason took three bottles of beer from the fridge and opened them. Each took a bottle and had a swig. Jason broke the silence.

"Well, how stupid do we look?"

Carl and Wayne shook their heads. The mood was low.

Jason's mobile started to ring. He picked it up and looked at the screen.

"It's him," he spat out with contempt and picked the phone up. "Speak."

"It shouldn't have come to this. At least I know the score now. You were going to kill me back there. Fuck me. We have known each other since we were kids. I just want to walk away. We can draw a line in the sand. You can trust me, let me walk away and you won't hear a peep from me."

"You should have destroyed the stuff, what are you playing at?" Jason said.

"Good job I didn't then. I'd be knackered now without an insurance policy."

"You know you're playing with fire don't you, Ryan?"

"If I didn't, I do now. I think I'm due some redundancy money, if I'm leaving quietly. Transfer it to the usual account and I disappear, not causing you any grief. You've treated me like shit over the years and I was supposedly your mate. You owe me the respect of letting me walk away quietly, you'll never hear from me again."

"You been talking to the cops, Ryan?" Jason asked menacingly.

"Fuck off…you're having a laugh now. What next? You sure you're not on the gear? And I thought It was me who was paranoid."

"Watch you don't burn your fingers, Ryan, probably best for you if you get the pistol and stuff to

Wayne or Carl sharpish. I'll be seeing you then. I'd better get some wire ties and electrodes for next time," Jason said, and then terminated the call.

"I caught most of it, what does he want?" Wayne asked.

"Cheeky bastard wants a last payment, to walk away. He's still got the stuff as insurance."

"Jeez, I thought he'd be trying to mend fences, not smash them down. He's going to cause us some problems if we don't get a grip of him," Carl said.

"He must know by the meeting, it's serious," Jason said. "He took off as if is life depended on it. I think he's passed the point of no return for sure. I still need to take care of him."

Jason suddenly noticed Kirsty standing at the door.

"Wow, you made me jump, Kirsty. I thought you were out?"

"I've just had a bath. You three okay? You look like you've just had your fingers in the cookie jar."

Kirsty laughed at her own wit and headed back upstairs to do her hair.

Her visit lightened the mood momentarily.

"We'll get it sorted," Wayne said. "I don't think he'd take you on, it's all talk. I'm guessing he's got rid of the stuff anyway."

"It's a risk I'm not going to take. You two try and keep tabs on him. If you want to drop him a few quid, try and keep him sweet for now. Remember, keep your friends close, but your enemies closer. Carl, you seem to get on well with him these days, you could play the intermediary. Show him some empathy."

"It must be the cocaine and booze. He isn't thinking straight, we'll keep tabs on him," said Wayne.

"What did you actually have planned for him, Jason?" Carl asked.

"Pain," Jason replied.

Carl and Wayne finished their beers and headed for home. Jason returned to his office and returned his pistol to the strong-hold. He left it loaded as always in case he needed it in a hurry. He sat down in his chair and put his head in his hands. He accepted to himself that he could have shot Ryan without hesitation. Business was business.

Chapter Eleven

Ryan put his mobile phone back in his pocket. *Well, that went well.* He hadn't moved for over an hour. He was getting cold, but he needed to be sure the coast was clear before he made his exit.

He found a path and followed it carefully towards the lights of a housing estate. Jason looked like he meant business in the car, and the phone call confirmed it. Ryan couldn't risk them picking him up again. When he reached civilisation, he clocked the street name and called a taxi. He needed to get to one of the lads and collect some cash 'for Jason' before word was put out that he was no longer part of the business.

Whilst he was waiting for the taxi, he put a call in to one of their fellas, Eddie, to tell him he was on his way to collect the takings and some coke for his personal use. Ten minutes later the taxi arrived and Ryan was on his way. He found himself studying the driver. *He's not one of Jason's men, is he? Shit, I need to get a grip.*

Ryan got the taxi to stop by a telephone kiosk outside a row of run-down shops. The street was in almost total darkness, just one street light still working. No sooner had they stopped, a lad on a BMX bike wearing a hoodie rode over from out of the shadows. Ryan wound the window down. The lad approached the taxi and handed him a carrier bag. Inside, Ryan could see a bundle of tens and twenties and a bag of white powder.

"Nice one, tell Eddie I'll phone him later," he said.

The lad rode off back into the shadows. Ryan directed the taxi driver to the centre of Manchester. *So far so good*, he thought. He got dropped off a few blocks away from the budget hotel and gave the driver a twenty. He stood still and watched whilst the driver disappeared down the road and out of sight. Then he walked to the hotel, keeping to the shadows. He checked in and took the lift to the thirteenth floor. *Good job I'm not superstitious.*

He entered the room. Open wardrobe, desk, and chair on the left, and a bed on the right next to the bathroom. He could see the lights of the city through the net curtains. He felt safe, for now. Ryan put the telly on and sniffed a few lines from the desk, then he lay on the bed. The world felt like a better place already.

The following morning Ryan was up at the crack of dawn. He took a taxi to his flat and got the driver to do an initial drive past around the block. He needed to check if anyone was watching his flat. He didn't see anything of concern, so he got the driver to pull over next to his car. Within minutes he was driving his 4x4 towards the M60, Bristol bound.

As the distance from Manchester increased he felt safer and more confident. Jason needed to leave him be and all would be fine. In the back of his mind he knew he was kidding himself. That was never going to happen. He had overstepped the mark and Jason had a fearsome reputation to keep. In this game his reputation was everything. If Jason showed weaknesses the challengers would form a queue to get a piece of him. Even Wayne and Carl needed to be reminded of his ruthlessness.

Ryan exited the M6 and pulled into Sandbach Services. He had one last task to complete. He parked his car up and gave it a close inspection, looking for a tracking device. He was in no doubt that Jason would have some lads on with finding him already, and Ryan wasn't going to make it easy for them. He walked through the car park to the toilets, took a few lines of coke, and then walked around to the shops. He bought a steak pie and an americano coffee. As he walked back to the car the sun felt warm on his face. It could have been much different and he knew it.

He made good time and was in St. Pauls, Bristol by lunchtime. He found a car sales pitch and parked up. He liked his car but didn't want it to be his undoing. An hour later, following a hard luck story and some serious haggling, he handed over the car keys and left with a wad of cash. Already Manchester was feeling like history, he was looking forward to hooking up with Lisa. But the shadow of Kirsty was still hanging over him. His loyalties had been thrown in the mix. He gave her a bell and arranged to meet at their local. His new start in life was about to begin.

Whilst Ryan was ordering his first pint, waiting for Lisa to arrive, Jason was still seething back in Manchester. His mood had been black ever since Ryan started to take the piss. He was taking this very personally.

It had all started with Smethurst at the canal, then the break-in at the house, and rounded off with a visit from DS Higgs. And now Ryan could do some serious damage, if he hadn't already done so. *I can't take any chances. I need to move fast on this one, damage limitation.* He had always been one step ahead of the cops. There was no way on this earth he was going to let Ryan ruin everything. He knew tough measures were now called for. He would shed no tears. He had taken care of Ryan over the years, now Ryan had made his bed, he was about to lay in it.

Jason knew he couldn't ask Carl and Wayne to be involved in what he was planning, which was to kill Ryan. They probably wouldn't agree with it and wouldn't want to be part of it. Jason was different. He hadn't got to the top by dodging the tough decisions. Ryan was now a threat to him, the threat needed to be eliminated. Jason also knew that the fewer people who were involved in his plan, the better.

Jason heard the doorbell. He heard the door open, followed by chatter. Kirsty entered the kitchen followed by Lee, who was carrying a pack of lager.

"Thought these would settle the pre-match nerves," Lee joked, placing the cans on the island worktop.

"No nerves today, mate. It's three points in the bag, champions in waiting," Jason said.

They cracked a can each then settled on the sofas. The pundits were in full flow with their predictions, analysis and opinions.

"These fellas could bore the hind legs off a donkey. How's work been?" Jason asked.

"Routine this week. Been down in the smoke, looking after a Prince and his mates from the Middle East. You want to see the motors they're driving around in. They just ditch them anywhere. We get tasked to pick them up, the windscreens are usually covered in parking tickets," Lee said.

Jason continued quizzing Lee about his work, old and new. He was impressed, especially with the Special Forces tales. The booze and chatter was flowing nicely, the football match had almost become a secondary interest.

"So, with all your contacts and background, do you get involved in any dodgy stuff? You know, mercenary jobs?" Jason asked.

"Depends if the money is good. There is a dark market in our game, of course there is."

"It's something I'd be interested in getting involved in. You know Wayne's ex-forces?" Jason said.

"Yes. Catering Corps, wasn't it?" Lee joked.

"He was actually in the Guards but we've got to keep him reigned in, it would be exaggerated to ex SAS before you knew it."

"Did he get any active service under his belt?"

"He was in Northern Ireland for a tour but I think that was it. I'd have never heard the last of it if he'd served in the middle east."

"He would get on well with our firm, it's a brotherhood of vets."

Kirsty approached them with a tray of pizza.

"These should keep you going for now, boys."

She noticed Lee's arms looked pumped-up and guessed he'd just been to the gym. They delved into the food straight away. At half time Jason paid a visit to the toilet. Kirsty walked in with two more cans for them.

"Lee, I need you to keep an eye on Jason and look out for him. He's really angry at the minute. He's had a dispute with his pal Ryan. He's overacted and took it really personally. I don't want Jason doing anything stupid in revenge. Ryan's a decent lad, they've been mates since they were kids."

Lee's ears pricked up straight way.

"No worries, Kirsty, it just takes a bit of time to cool down with things like that. I'll keep an eye on him. Let me know if things are heading downhill."

Jason returned and opened his can, "I think we'll nail this in the second half, we're all over them like a rash."

"Men versus boys, mate," Lee said.

"You've dealt with some right shit out there in the Middle East, how do you cope with the fallout?" Jason asked, genuinely curious.

"It's second nature. We've done all the training, so you just follow the drill. You don't want to let your pals down, so it becomes routine, watching each other's back and getting the job done."

"So, hypothetically speaking, if I needed someone to disappear, would you know any operators out there who could get it sorted?"

"You taking the piss?" Lee replied, and took a swig of his beer. He looked Jason eye to eye, as if weighing him up.

"No, seriously, would you know the right associates? If I'm out of order asking, tell me and we move on."

Jason was in the zone, business mode, problem solving. Kirsty had paused, listening at the other side of the door.

Lee opened another can, took another swig then put his game face on.

"That's some enquiry, mate, it's something I wouldn't recommend you to get involved in. But obviously I know fellas who would. It's serious shit that, surely there are other ways of sorting it?"

Their attention was grabbed by the football. City had scored straight from the restart, one – nil. Jason celebrated and watched the replays.

"I wouldn't go down that road if I were you, no matter what this geezer's done, it's not worth the risk," Lee said.

"I might have to, self-preservation." Jason thought the conversation had gone well. He knew it was a game of poker, neither wanted to give too much away, and he knew not too ask too much or push too hard. But he had established that it was feasible, the ball was starting to roll.

"Don't go there, Jason, it's not worth it, will a beating not suffice."

"No that would probably make matters worse." The match finished with a comfortable win for City. Both Jason and Lee were feeling good on the back of the performance. Their mood was helped by the beer.

"I'm meeting Carl and Wayne in town for a few beers and probably some food, do you fancy joining us?"

"I'd love to, but I've got an early start, back down to the smoke in the morning. I'd better get off and get my shit together," Lee replied.

"No worries, great to see you, give me a shout next time you're back."

Lee said goodbye to Kirsty and went on his way. Samantha was waiting outside to give him a lift to the flat. He got into the car.

"How did it go?" Samantha asked.

"It's going well. He gets on well with me and trusts me. He started talking business, which is good. The match was a corker too. I declined a night out tonight, can't be seen as too keen, can I?"

"Fancy something to eat on the way back? I'm starving."

"Good call. I don't know if he is testing me out, or talking bull, but he has sounded me out for a contract kill. He's had a fall out with one of his boys."

"Really, he's only just met you," Samantha gave him a knowing look.

"It might be a test, let's see how it develops."

Samantha headed for the local take away.

Carl and Wayne were sitting in the corner when Jason entered The Crown on Oldham Street in the Northern Quarter. He loved this pub, which was a proper boozer. It still had the old-fashioned design and tiled décor from the years ago. Jason went straight to the bar and bought three pints. Carl necked the last of his pint as Jason approached the table.

"Did you see the game?" Wayne asked.

"Yeah, it was always going to be three points. In fact, Lee came around to watch it. He wanted to join us tonight but he's back down south on business tomorrow. I mentioned our interest in getting involved in the close protection stuff. I reckon it would open a whole new network for us, possibly military hardware too."

"We might need military hardware sooner if Ryan doesn't behave himself," Carl said. There was a quiet pause. Jason clocked that Carl never missed an opportunity to have a dig at Ryan, he found it was getting a bit tiresome.

"How's it going with Lee?" Wayne asked, changing the subject.

"He's a good lad, not heard anything to the contrary. His story stacks up and I wouldn't mind venturing into his business at some stage. I don't think he's told me the half of it yet. It wouldn't be a surprise if they're involved in arms deals themselves."

"He seems to have impressed you," Wayne said. "Are you keeping him at arm's length with our business? Early days yet, need to get his full story and pics."

"Yeah, defo, as far as he's concerned I'm a property developer. No doubt he suspects I've been involved in some moody stuff over the years, but he doesn't need to know that for now."

"Nice one, we need a tight ship especially at the moment," Carl said in approval.

"Have you two heard from Ryan?" Jason said

"No, I'm letting him sweat," replied Carl. "He'll have realised what a prick he's been by now. I'll contact him soon and pretend to put an arm around him. A friendly understanding face and all of that stuff. If you're okay with it, Jason, I think I can tidy him up and get this mess sorted."

"I'm not too sure. He could do us some serious damage."

"We can sort it, Jason," Wayne chipped in. "He hasn't got it in him. I think he was bluffing anyway. It was the charlie talking. You know he becomes 'The Big I Am' when he's off his head."

"That's what worries me. He's gone reckless again, which makes him unpredictable, and he sounds paranoid. We've always had his back, but he doesn't see it like that."

"Leave it with us, there'll be no dramas," Wayne insisted.

"Carl, you were with him when he was spouting off. What do you really think?" Jason asked.

"I think he's ditched the pistol and stuff. He's talking bollocks, but he does worry me. He knows a lot of stuff that could do us serious damage if he decides to talk to the cops."

"For me it's no coincidence that the cops are all over us and he's in meltdown. I'll leave it with you then, fellas, but seriously, I don't want any shit-storms heading my way."

Jason agreed to let his boys handle it, but that didn't mean they'd convinced him. *Ryan has to go, he's brought it upon himself, he's crossed the line, there are no margins for error in this game.*

"There's one positive," Carl said, chirping up as though something had just occurred to him. "That misinformation I gave him about the shipment at the yard didn't result in us getting raided. So that goes in his favour. I may feed him some more misinformation and see how it goes."

Jason mulled this over but decided not to comment. Instead he said, "Come on, fellas, curry time."

They all knocked back their beers and headed out for a curry in Rusholme. Ryan was forgotten, for now.

Chapter Twelve

The following day, Jason was driving along the M62 back to Manchester after viewing some apartments on the docks in Liverpool. They looked like a good investment and he was eager to make a bid, but he didn't want to look too keen. There was still room for negotiation. Yet the issue of what to do with Ryan was still pawing away at his subconscious. *Time to get on with this,* he thought. He dialled Lee on the voice-activated phone book.

"Jason, how are you doing, mate? I was going to bell you today."

"I'm not bad, pal. You still down in the smoke?"

"Yeah, I'm back at the end of the week. I'm going to take a few days off with Samantha. This job is good money but we're babysitting some right arrogant wets at the minute. They treat us like dirt and we have to smile and take it on the chin."

"Listen, mate," Jason said, cutting to the chase. "You know the business I mentioned last time I saw you? I'm going to need it sorting."

"Okay, but you need to be one hundred percent sure. These guys are moody. They don't get messed about by anyone. These are proper psychos, mate, they enjoy their work. I can test the water for you, but are you sure? This is serious shit."

Jason was amused by Lee's words of caution. It was sort of adorable. Lee had no idea that he was talking to a guy who had been described as a psycho himself on more than one occasion.

"Yes, it needs sorting. There's no other way really. He could cause me major problems." "I'll make a few calls for you, but it will be your gig. It's not my scene. I'll do the introductions then I'm out."

"Okay, pal. Give me a bell for a beer when you're back."

Ryan was out running. Life was good. Lisa was on downtime and he had spent the last four days with her. His only problem was money. He had been living on the proceeds from selling his car. It brought home the reality that his income from Jason had come to an end. Ryan really didn't want to go back to thieving or dealing, but he didn't want to get desperate for cash either. He just needed a few handouts until the sale on his flat went through. If he did get desperate he could move in on the local door security scene or even the drug scene. It wouldn't take long to make some contacts that would be keen to take advantage of his skills. But that was a last resort.

Then the idea hit him. Ryan found a bench and took a breather. He retrieved the new burner phone from his pocket and called Kirsty. She answered on the first ring, although she didn't sound overly thrilled to be hearing from him.

"Hi, Ryan, for what do I owe this pleasure?"

"Kirsty, I'll get to the point. I doubt you've heard, but me and Jason have gone our separate ways. I was sick of being the errand boy. It's time to stand on my own two feet. In the process I've pissed him off. I'm persona non grata. My problem is, I've got cash flow problems until I get sorted out."

"Give him a bell, Ryan. You've fallen out before but it's always got sorted. You know what he's like. Just stroke his ego and eat some humble pie, it will all be forgotten. I overheard him talking to Lee the other day, he's really pissed off with you, I'm worried for you. Ring him and sort it out before he does something stupid."

"I think I've burned my bridges this time. Can you help me out? I wouldn't ask if I wasn't desperate. I'll pay you back as soon as I can."

"I haven't got that kind of money. I've got a hairdressing business, not a Central Bank. Jason's the one with the money and he would clock it right away. You know that, Ryan. It would be easier for Carl or Wayne to sort you out."

"I know, I just thought I'd ask, let me know if you hear anything more. I'm going to keep my head down in Bristol for now."

"Okay I'll try and pull a few quid together for you, but it won't be a lot. You need to get a proper job down there, get yourself back on track. And quit the coke, it's doing you no favours from what I hear."

"That's my plan, it's a fresh start, something worthwhile. I've been helping out at a boxing club, coaching the kids in Manchester. I'll see if there's anything similar down here."

"Fantastic Ryan, this is like talking to the old you, you can turn this around. Let me know if you're back in town. Maybe we can meet up."

There was only one person Kirsty trusted to help her with this. She picked her phone up. "Hi, Kirsty, how are you doing?" Lee said, as he answered her call.

"Lee, I need some help. I mentioned to you that Jason was in a dispute with one of his mates, Ryan. Well, I overheard you and Jason talking, when you were at our's watching the football. This needs nipping in the bud right now."

"I'm with you one hundred per cent, Kirsty. That kind of stuff is for the movies, not here. I was just humouring him for a few days, by which time he'll have calmed down and seen sense."

"I hope so, but I'm not confident, I'm really worried about this. All is not what you see with Jason. I don't know what to do."

"Listen, I will sort this, don't worry. No one will get hurt. You have to trust me, I can sort it. I will keep Jason busy with some business ideas and make sure Ryan is safe, I have the contacts. Do you trust me to sort it out?"

"Yes, of course, that's why I called you."

"Right then, leave it with me. Don't do anything without speaking to me first. Let me know if he causes you more concern. Are you okay?"

"I feel a bit better now. Thanks, Lee."

"No problem. I'll keep in touch. Give me a bell if there are any updates. See you at the gym soon."

It was such a strange thought, her two worlds finally colliding, that Kirsty laughed as Lee ended the call.

Ryan arrived back at the flat and took a shower, then checked his coke stash. It was almost gone. Was it worth a drive back to Manchester? Probably not. Word was probably out by now that he was persona non grata. The optimism brought about by his morning run had drained away. Now he was feeling paranoid and anxious. He felt isolated, although he knew the isolation gave him safety, for now. But he also wanted to quit the coke, he willed himself to be strong.

He reflected on his call with Kirsty. *Should I present myself to Jason and take my medicine? What would his punishment be?* He knew Jason was ruthless, and their last meeting had scared the shit out of him. Would Jason do him serious harm? Probably. He had a reputation to maintain. Ryan wouldn't be the first to be made an example of. His only hope now was for Carl or Wayne to give him some support.

Out of the two of them, Ryan felt more of a bond with Carl. He had always got on well with him. They had shared a few scrapes together on nights out. But he wasn't oblivious to the situation. Ryan understood that Carl's loyalty was with Jason. The best Ryan could hope for was to be thrown a few scraps, and perhaps to be given the benefit of the doubt by Carl.

Out of options, he dialled Carl up, not sure of what he was going to say. But he knew what he needed, money or charlie.

"Ryan, I wasn't expecting a call from you. Have you got your head straight yet?"

"I just want to know where we stand, mate. I know I'm cut adrift and that Jason wants to do me some damage. It leaves me in the lurch until I get sorted."

"This is easy to sort, Ryan. Where is the gear you should have disposed of? Get it to me and that's a start."

"You know I can't do that, it's insurance. If Jason backs off it will never see the light of day."

"There's no helping some people, all of that charlie has pickled your brain. You're not thinking straight, this isn't going to go away. I can help you, but you need to help yourself."

"Can you transfer me a few quid?"

Ryan knew it was shit or bust and the answer would probably be laughter.

"I will but it's the last time, and it's an act of goodwill. Think about it. Give me a bell when you've got your head sorted."

It was Carl who terminated the call.

Well, that's a bonus, Ryan thought. *Cash flow problem sorted.*

Chapter Thirteen

Whilst Ryan was on the phone with Kirsty, Jason was down at the gym with Wayne. They had just finished their weights session. Wayne returned to the table with two protein shakes. They were sitting in the café, in the corner of the gym. Jason thought that 'café' was a loose description. There was a bar knocked together from timber and plywood, surrounded by white plastic garden furniture. It was very cheap and cheerful in appearance, in contrast to the products, which were actually of good quality.

Wayne was assuring Jason that business was running smoothly and that Jason's cut would be laundered in the same way as usual, through Amsterdam and Dubai, leaving no trace for the authorities to link them to.

"That's not a bad pension," Jason said. "I deserve it though. I got us all to a good place. Are you looking at changing much?"

"We need to grow to keep our competitors on their toes. Core business will always be Liverpool, Manchester, Edinburgh and Glasgow. I need to keep an eye on Ryan. I'll sort things out, he's one of us, he won't be a problem. Bristol might be worth another try. Geordie land is probably still a no-go, after our last scrape up there."

"Sounds good to me. How's the business going in Cheshire and Wales?"

"Good, the Smethurst thing opened our eyes a bit, which isn't a bad thing. The kids we had dealing there are proving to be high maintenance. And they seem to be getting a lot of attention from social services. That's a worry."

They were interrupted by Jason's mobile ringing. It was an unknown number. Jason declined the call. The phone rang again immediately. Curious, Jason decided to answer.

"Jason, it's Lee. I'm on a burner, mate."

"Business, I take it?" Jason asked.

"It is, mate, I'll be back in Manchester in about an hour. I've got a contact who is interested in sorting your issue for you. He wants me to meet you later, with the possibility of you two hooking up after that. Are you free today?"

"Yeah, I'm just finishing off at the gym, sounds great."

"Okay, pal, see you at Burtonwood Services, Westbound, at three o'clock."

"Nice one, see you then."

That's good. Let's get this show on the road. If we get a move on we can still manage some damage limitation.

"That was Lee," Jason said.

"You seem to be seeing more of him, you still impressed by his who dares wins adventures in the desert?" Wayne said mockingly.

"It beats making army bully beef in the Catering Corps! He's a top fella, and he might open some doors for me in new business ventures. He has some tasty contacts too. I told him about your time in the Grenadiers. That army brotherhood bond goes a long way."

"Some new lines of business would be nice, especially with the attention we're getting from the cops at the moment."

Jason was not about to share the real reason for the meeting. The fewer who knew about his plan the better, and that included Carl and Wayne. He'd not got this far to be undone by Ryan. Business was business. Jason knew when he had to be ruthless and clinical, and it didn't bother him. He had always been the psycho of the group. Yet he did sometimes wonder whether Carl and Wayne could match his ruthless streak. Maybe he enjoyed it too much?

They left the gym and headed off separately. Jason needed to focus.

Shortly before three, Jason drove onto the services car park. He parked at the far end, away from the cameras and busy bodies. His plan was to stay in the car and be discreet. If anyone did see him, he looked like a sales rep having a break before his next appointment. The burner number started to ring on his phone.

"Hi, Lee, I'm at the services," Jason said.

"I'm just turning off now. Where are you parked?" Lee replied.

"Towards the HGV area. Keep it low-key."

"See you in a minute."

A black saloon pulled up alongside him. Lee was driving what looked like a hire car. So far Lee was ticking all the boxes, he knew the script. This piece of business would hopefully cement the bond of trust between them and open doors. Jason left his car and got into the front passenger seat of the hire car. His initial impression was confirmed by its immaculate state of cleanliness and the pungent new air-freshener hanging from the rear-view mirror.

Jason noticed that Lee had a serious, business persona about him. At least he understood that this wasn't a time for pleasantries or football talk.

"Jason, Vinny has asked me to meet up with you to ensure you know what you're getting into. He wanted me to make it clear you can still back out of this, here and now, because once the ball starts to roll there is no turning back. He is a professional and will not be messed about."

"I understand," Jason replied, hiding his amusement with his own game face.

"Right, this will be my last involvement. It's not my area of expertise."

"No worries, I appreciate the contact."

"He's expensive, but you pay for what you get in this game. This isn't some kid on a BMX with a used gang pistol. This is premium service, with no comebacks to you, whatever the outcome."

"How much?" Jason asked.

"In total, £25,000, £10,000 up front in used twenties."

Jason winced. That was above the going rate, he had been expecting a much lower figure.

Lee asked, "You still want to go ahead?"

"Yeah, it's an inflated price, so it needs to be spot on."

There was a silence whilst Lee dug into his pockets.

"Take this burner phone. Vinny will call you on this. No other means of communication. You need to pull the money together by tonight, is that okay?"

"Yeah, that's not a problem," Jason said.

"Mate, don't fuck him about, he's a proper nasty piece of work. I'm back down south next week so I'll catch up for a beer when I'm back."

"See you then, pal. Thanks for the introduction."

Jason returned to his car. As he drove away, he could see that Lee was talking on his phone. He pulled into a lay-by on the way back home and speed-dialled Wayne.

"Hi, Jason. I can't speak for too long. I'm in Liverpool meeting the fellas over here."

"No worries, pal, this isn't a social call. I need £25k for tonight, can you sort it?"

"Yeah, you want me to drop by yours?"

"No, we'll meet somewhere quiet."

Like he had told Lee, Jason knew it was an inflated price. There were kids in town who would sort it for next to nothing. He also knew you tended to get what you paid for. Lee mixed in some tasty circles. These guys were ex-military. The job would be tidy with no comebacks. They too had a reputation to keep. It also embedded him in their circle of trust.

Jason's next call was to Carl.

"Hi, mate. Were you planning on paying Ryan a visit any time soon?"

"Yeah, it's on my to-do list," Carl replied. "I've thrown him a few quid, he's been quiet since."

"Good man, I was thinking it's been a while, can you get down there today or tomorrow? I'd like to know the crack. I don't want any dramas. We've too much at stake."

"I'll have a drive down tomorrow and keep you up to speed."

The new burner phone started to ring, Jason was taken by surprise. He didn't think the call would come so quick.

"Got to go."

Jason tossed his phone on the passenger seat and picked up the burner.

"Hello."

"What's the name of the guy who gave you this phone?" Vinny asked.

"Lee."

"You still want our services?"

"Yes, Definitely."

"Tonight at 9pm, in your own car, on your own. Park up on Burtonwood Services, same place as before. I'll be in touch."

"Okay."

Vinny, not the most talkative of fellas, ended the call.

This left Jason with three hours to kill. Things were moving faster than he expected. He ran through his checklist. There was only himself in the know, for damage limitation; the money was on route to him with Wayne; Carl was set to provide a location for Ryan at the set time. The job was running smoothly. Ryan would be eliminated sooner than later, which meant problem solved. Jason drove onto the Retail Park, near to the M62 at Winwick. He saw Wayne's car, parked up. He parked next to him and walked over. Wayne saw him approaching and jumped out of the car.

"Cheers for this, Wayne, I know it was short notice. I need to grease some wheels tonight for the Liverpool apartments. The bent bastards always require back-handers at the last minute."

"No worries, mate, I was nearly finished over there anyway."

Wayne passed a sports holdall to Jason. They chatted over some day to day stuff. Jason knew his mind was elsewhere, but he concentrated on giving

Wayne his attention whilst he was standing in front of him.

"Right, I've got to get going. Catch up with you later in the week," Jason said.

Jason got back into his car and looked into the bag. The money was there. He split it into two carrier bags and placed them back in the bag, before placing the lot into the boot. He was good to go and headed to Burtonwood services on the M62.

He had been parked up for about ten minutes, weighing up other drivers parking near him, when his phone rang.

"Get on the M62. Pick up the M6 North. I'll see you on Charnock Richard Services."

Jason was about to say 'okay' but the line was already dead. He started the car and set off, keeping an eye out to clock any cars that might be following him. This run-around was probably to make sure he was on his own. In all fairness, he had expected it. It gave the reassuring impression of professionalism.

About thirty minutes later, Jason exited the M6 into Charnock Richard Services. He found a parking place and switched the engine off. He had not clocked any cars following him. Again, the phone rang.

"Who was that you spoke to at Burtonwood?" Vinny said.

"I didn't speak with anyone."

"No worries, just messing with you. Stick BL7 0LU in your sat-nav and call me when you get there. It's a car park next to a reservoir."

Again, Jason started the car and headed for the exit. The run-around was getting a little tiresome for him now. The sat-nav estimated another thirty minutes. *It could be worse*, he thought.

It was getting dark. The route brought him off the motorway, through a small former mill town called Darwen and into the sticks along country roads. By the time he arrived it was pitch black. Jason left the road and drove down a gravel track. The car park opened up in front of him.

As Jason parked up, he felt vulnerable for the first time. The shadows from the trees played tricks on his eyes. He couldn't see who was out there, but they were probably watching him.

There was a bang on his driver's window which made him jump. As he opened the door a voice said, "Get the £10k and follow me."

This was the same voice from the telephone calls. Jason couldn't place the accent. The guy was about 5'10, with an athletic build, wearing a flat-cap and a scarf over the lower half of his face. His waxed jacket looked old and tired. He definitely had a menacing presence about him.

Jason followed him along a footpath by the reservoir. The guy calling himself 'Vinny' had a border terrier on a lead. The area was isolated, with woodland on one side and the reservoir on the other. This situation felt surreal. If he didn't have such trust in Lee he'd be asking himself 'What the fuck'. The fella stopped.

"Stand still. Put your arms in the air."

Jason was then searched. Not just a pat-down, under his clothing too. He knew he was being checked for a wire.

"I'm Vinny. You understand I had to check you were on your own, is that the 10k?"

Jason handed him the carrier bag. Vinny didn't look inside, he just stuffed it into his man bag and carried on talking.

"I need you to text me a photo of your target, with a few details of where I will find him. Get one of your own lads to place him and I will sort it from there. I'll need a photo of your lad as well. Afterwards, your burner phone comes back to me with the outstanding £15k."

"I've got a tracker on one of my lad's phone to place the target. He will be unaware of the set up. What proof will you send me for confirmation?" Jason asked.

"You've been watching too many gangster movies, son. We don't fuck about. When I tell you it's done, it's done."

This didn't sit well with Jason. It made him uneasy, not feeling in control. And he wasn't used to being spoken to like a wet-behind-the-ears punk.

"Any more questions?" Vinny asked.

Jason knew it was said with an expectation that there wouldn't be any more questions.

"No, I'll text you the info."

"Good, that's what I like."

Vinny walked off into the darkness, in the opposite direction of the car park.

Jason wasn't enjoying this, not due to any lingering affection for Ryan, but because he was used to being top dog and giving the orders. This task was a needs-must though. It also provided him with an opportunity to develop trust and business interests with Lee. The inflated price didn't bother him, either. As far as Jason was concerned it was small change. Ryan had to go. Jason knew such a display of ruthlessness would create the fear he needed to keep the wolves away from his door.

So far so good, he thought, as he walked back to the car. As he opened the driver-side door, another vehicle had parked up opposite his car. Its headlights flashed on and off. *Great, that's just what I need, a clandestine meeting at a dogging site.* He didn't hang about to confirm his suspicion.

Chapter Fourteen

The next morning, Carl set off on his drive down the M6 to Bristol. It felt different this time. Ryan had overstepped the mark. He had challenged Jason and should have known better. Carl was in no doubt that Jason would make an example of him. If Jason let stuff like that pass by, others would see it as a weakness. Carl also felt a little relieved. Whilst the spotlight was on Ryan, it wasn't on him. The hands-free started to ring. The caller display told him it was Wayne. Carl pressed the green telephone icon on the steering wheel.

"Morning, Wayne, thought you'd still be in bed."

"Nah, there's too much to do. I'm meeting with the weed grafters today. We can't keep up with them. We've already doubled the number of house farms we're growing at since Jason handed over."

"Sounds good, I'm on my way to Bristol. I'll see what state Ryan's in. It's in our interests to sort this quietly. I think he will still do a decent job for us, if and when we establish that the stuff has been destroyed. Jason's not going to let this one go. I'm surprised he's not asked us to straighten him out."

"He'll have the punishment up his sleeve. Remember, Jason's had people shot for less than that. Ryan's not helped himself here, Carl. Business is business and there's nothing we can do. He's made himself a liability."

"I'll just try and get to the truth of where the stuff is. I still think he's got rid of it already, which makes it harder to know for sure. If he disappears to Spain and keeps his mouth shut, I'm happy either way."

"That's a big 'if' mate. We need to keep him on a short leash. We're running the show now, we've got to be more ruthless than Jason was."

Carl understood what Wayne was saying and he was right. They needed to build a fearsome reputation post-Jason. Even so, Carl was content to be the thinker, and to let Wayne be the tyrant.

Ryan was just out of the shower when his mobile rang. He checked the display. It was Carl. He was about to toss the phone onto the bed, but decided he couldn't avoid the inevitable. *I'd better answer it*, he thought.

"Carl, what can I do for you?"

"I'm on my way down the M6 to see you, Ryan. We need a talk over a few beers."

"Get out of town. I know the score. It's not beers you're coming down for. Who's with you?"

"The charlies making you paranoid, fella. Would I give you a courtesy call if I was coming down to straighten you out?"

Ryan felt anxious, and he had good reason to be. He knew he had it coming. Maybe his insurance policy was keeping Jason at bay for now, but for how long? He regretted answering the call.

"Carl, I have no axe to grind with you, you know that. I'll meet in a city centre boozer, just as a safety precaution. I know I'm persona non grata now but you can trust me. If Jason leaves me be, I won't be creating any drama."

"I know that, I just want everyone coming out of this okay. If you trust me I can sort it and get Jason to back off. I'll phone you when I reach Bristol."

"Have you got some charlie with you"?

"No, mate, it sounds like you need a break from it," Carl laughed out loud, "Jeez you need to get a grip of yourself."

Ryan ended the call. He felt vulnerable. Could he trust Carl? Or should he just do a runner? In truth, he now didn't know which way to turn. The situation was making him feel battle weary.

Ryan was already in the city centre when he received a text from Carl. He had just scored some charlie to settle his nerves, and it had done the trick. His confidence was back. *Bring it on*, he thought. They were both familiar with the Rope and Anchor, which was probably the reason Carl had chosen it. Ryan knew which way Carl would approach from, so he entered an outdoors activity shop. He climbed the stairs to get a good view from the window next to the tent display. Almost straight away, he saw Carl walking down the shopping precinct towards the pub. *That's good, he's on his own. Let's find out what he wants.*

When Ryan entered the pub, it was full of customers, families dining, and drinkers propping up the bar. It was what he wanted. No way was he going to get turned over in here. He looked around, taking in the historical Bristol seaport theme of the décor, and spotted Carl at a small table. He went to the bar, ordered two pints and made his way over. As he sat down, Ryan looked Carl in the eyes and said, "Go on then, what's the score?"

"You know damn well, Ryan. Where is the stuff? You know Jason will want his pound of flesh. You've pissed on your chips big style. But work with me and I can sort it."

"The stuff is safe. It will never see the light of day. As for Jason, that's down to him. I'm not going to be taken back into the fold whatever happens, I know that."

"The way I see it, you have two choices. Disappear abroad, or face it out, take your medicine and move on. Either way we need the stuff back. Make Jason happy and you have a new start with Wayne... clean slate."

The conversation continued. Carl was working hard to reach some kind of compromise, and it was working. Ryan was tired of the Mexican stand-off.

Vinny had been following Carl's phone location since he left Manchester. Vinny had trailed him to Bristol and followed him on foot to Corn Street. He watched as Carl entered the pub and nearly walked into Ryan as he walked out of the camping shop. *Shit, that was too close for comfort ... good vantage point though.* The close proximity had made positive identification of Ryan even easier. Vinny entered the camping shop and started looking through the racks of gortex jackets near to the display window. *That's them both in the pub and it looks like only one exit.* Vinny could not see them inside the pub so he had to focus on the exit, whilst looking at jackets.

"Is it particularly gortex you're interested in?"

Vinny looked around and saw a teenage sales assistant had approached him. He was a slip of a lad with long hair. Vinny guessed he was probably a student at the University.

"No, I'm going to have a good look through all of your jackets. It's got to be the right one, I'm very particular."

Now do me a favour and piss off, I've got work to do.

"Can I recommend this one to you, it's on special offer, a real bargain" the lad said, removing a blue jacket from the rail. This sales assistant was persistent. Vinny was doing his utmost to concentrate on the pub exit. "Thanks pal but just leave me to browse, I'm more likely to buy one." The lad looked disappointed. He obviously got the message and resumed tidying up the walking boots.

Back across the road, Carl suggested a plan.

"You can give me the stuff. We can drive back to Manchester. You're probably going to have to take a beating, and then it's over. It's got to be better than looking over your shoulder for years to come. You know Jason won't let it rest. You know that."

Ryan felt weary with it all. He knew his head had gone. He wasn't in a good place.

"Okay, I'll get the stuff and come back with you," he said. *Like hell I'm coming back with you. You can have the stuff but I'm not being the lamb to the slaughter. Last time was close enough.*

They left the pub and walked to Ryan's local. Ryan veered off and headed to the flat for the rucksack. He was constantly checking behind him, to ensure Carl wasn't following him. Carl went inside the pub and ordered two pints.

A short time later, Ryan approached the table and sat down.

"Everything's in the rucksack, except the pistol. That's in pieces in the docks, which is the truth. I wasn't keeping hold of a murder weapon, it's gone."

He thought that Carl looked disappointed.

"I've no reason to lie, have I? I didn't want to get caught in possession of a pistol, did I? That would be a long stretch inside. So, I got rid as soon as I arrived here."

"You don't make life easy, Ryan. It just doesn't sit well in the drama so far. Anyway, let's have a beer and head back to Manchester in a bit."

Ryan's thoughts were caught in a loop. *Yeah, seriously, no chance I'm going anywhere near Manchester, you can ride back on your own, then if Jason still needs to beat on somebody it can be you.*

Carl rummaged in the rucksack.

"Where are the burner phones that Jason gave you?" he asked.

"In the water at Castlefields. I ditched them after I dropped you at the airport."

Carl raised his eyebrows and gave him a knowing look. Again, he didn't look convinced.

Vinny had followed Ryan back to his flat and established a potential start point for following him later, if needed. When Ryan came out he was carrying a small rucksack. Vinny followed him at a distance, back to The Fusilier Pub. He watched him go inside. Vinny was having a cigarette in the shadows when his attention was caught by Carl and Ryan leaving the pub not long after he went in. Ryan lit up a cigarette, looking uneasy. Carl took a mobile phone out of his jacket and put it to his ear. As he talked, he started to pace around. It looked like he was putting distance between himself and Ryan. Vinny watched as Carl ended his conversation. Not a minute later, his own mobile began to vibrate in his pocket. He knew who it was from the display.

"Speak."

He didn't like being disturbed when he was working.

"I've just spoken to Carl. He's going to get Ryan to take him to the van. It's in a quiet location, out of the way, sounds just like the place you're looking for. Carl isn't aware of the plan, he is taking Ryan to the van to search it."

"Okay, leave it with me."

Vinny's eyes never left the two men across the street. Carl now had the rucksack. *Wonder what's in there. It looks like a handover has taken place. I'll have that later.* His hand involuntarily felt the outside of his jacket pocket, by force of habit. The pistol was still there.

Vinny made a quick phone call of his own.

"Go on, pal," said the male voice at the other end.

"Change of plan, we are going to a new location. They're going to a white van nearby. It's parked up in a quiet area on the edge of an industrial estate called the Waterside, see if you can locate it. I'll update you with where we're heading," Vinny said, then slipped the phone away.

Carl and Ryan walked away from the pub. Both were now smoking new tabs, and were in conversation. Vinny followed at a safe distance. They weren't surveillance conscious. They were making his follow easy. *Perhaps they let their guard down when they left Manchester?*

They stopped suddenly by a multi storey car park. Vinny managed to conceal himself in a doorway and watched. Carl entered the car park and went out of view, whilst Ryan sat waiting on a small wall. A few minutes later, Carl returned with the empty rucksack, and the two of them continued walking. Vinny followed for about ten minutes. The area was mostly warehousing and industrial units, rougher than the city centre they had just left. They turned left into a road. It was starting to get dark and the street lighting was poor. The road was surrounded by wasteland, rough grass, builders' waste, and litter from fly tipping. They were on the edge of an industrial estate. It looked like it was a phase two plan, but the developers had run out of money, or made enough already to call it quits.

Vinny made a quick assessment. He could see a white van parked further down the road. It was too far away to keep following in the open, and he needed some dead ground for cover. His adrenalin kicked in, making him hyper-vigilant. These two hadn't looked behind them once yet, it shouldn't be too hard. He headed for a parked car. This move left him a bit vulnerable to being clocked, as it meant he would have to walk into the open, where they might see him. But he had a contingency plan and was prepared to portray himself as the car owner. His pace quickened, as did his breathing. He reached the car and crouched down behind it. He took his phone out. The same male answered, "I'm on Rope Drive, I can see the white van at the other end. They will be there any time." Vinny warned.

"Sorted, I'm concealed in the building debris about forty metres from it. I've got eyes on the three of you, same plan?"

"Yes, I'll make an approach now, stand by." Vinny ended the call.

Carl and Ryan reached the van. Ryan opened the back doors and Carl climbed inside.

"Is there anything in here, Ryan? If you just tell me it will save me searching it."

"No, mate, I told you. The pistol and the burners are long gone if that's what you're looking for. Everything else is in the rucksack."

"Why have you not had it crushed?" Carl asked, as he removed the cover from the bulkhead.

"I was on with it. Then you dragged me back up to Manchester to get shot, remember... mate."

Time to go. Vinny stood up and walked towards them, as fast as he could without drawing their attention. They didn't even look his way. About ten metres away, he whipped out his balaclava and put it on. He took the pistol out of his pocket and sprinted to the rear of the van.

"Get in the van," Vinny shouted at Ryan as he ran at him. He knew he needed to keep the momentum. He gave them no time to think or to regain their composure. Surprise was one of his main advantages to catch them unprepared.

"Both of you empty your pockets and put everything on the floor. Try anything and I'll shoot you."

Both Carl and Ryan looked like rabbits in the headlights. They couldn't empty their pockets fast enough. Vinny pointed the pistol at Ryan.

“Kneel down,” he ordered, “face the bulkhead, hands on your head.”

Ryan was almost in position before Vinny had finished speaking.

Vinny knew he needed to be fast. They would already have some comprehension of their situation and would be switching to survival fight mode. Any breathing room he allowed them to have would enable them to present a greater threat to him.

“You,” he said, waving the pistol dismissively towards Carl. “It’s got nothing to do with you. Get out of the van and start running. If I see you coming back, I’ll kill you.”

Carl didn’t need asking twice. He jumped out of the van and sprinted back the way he had come. With the help of a push in the back from Vinny’s accomplice.

Vinny placed a pair of handcuffs on Ryan’s wrists. He told him that they were police officers, and that he was safe.

“You are under arrest on suspicion of being concerned in the supply of class A drugs,” Vinny informed him, and gave him his rights.

Vinny’s colleague had approached the van from the rough ground. He pointed his blank-firing pistol towards the floor and fired three shots. He was watching Carl running into the distance. Ryan screamed out involuntarily, anticipating the pain of his imminent demise. But neither was forthcoming. He felt nauseous, disoriented and unable to make sense of the situation.

“Fuck you,” he shouted, “The police? What the fuck... are you working for Jason?”

Ryan was in shock and trying to make sense of what was happening. It felt surreal, like an out of body experience.

"You're the police? Drugs? Not got a clue what's going on here, you sure you got the right guy?" he stammered. Ryan was regaining his composure by the second and experiencing a massive shot of elation that he wasn't dead.

The second police officer picked up the keys to the van and got into the driver's seat. It started first time with a splutter. He drove away, ten minutes later, he was turning the van into the Bridewell Police Station. When they had stopped, he said, "Listen to me carefully. I am a police officer. We have just arrived at a police station. We have credible evidence that your life is at risk, and that someone has taken out a contract to have you killed. We will deal with it inside. Are you okay?"

"I'm fine." Ryan was feeling a surge of relief.

For the first time Ryan believed they were genuine police officers and he was safe. The back doors of the van opened. Three plain clothes police officers were looking inside.

"These officers are going to take you into the station," one of them said, as he helped Ryan out of the van. He was then led into the police station custody office.

Chapter Fifteen

Carl had finally stopped running and was making his way towards the city centre. Adrenaline was surging through his body and he was coming to terms with what had just happened. *Christ, Ryan's been shot, he's pissed someone off down here big time.* These thoughts were barely formed before an alternative explanation hit him. *Fucking hell, was it Jason who's had him killed? Is that why he sent me down here?* He reached into his pocket for his mobile. Luckily, he hadn't dropped it in the van, totally unintentional, just out of sheer panic. He dialled Jason's number.

"Hello."

"It's Carl. Ryan's just been shot. We were at the van and a bloke in a balaclava came out of nowhere. He told me to do one and shot Ryan. There was nothing I could do, there were two of them with pistols."

A pang of guilt struck Carl for the first time since the shooting. *Could I have done more to help Ryan?*

"Chill out, Carl, I had no other options. I was tracking your mobile. He had backed me into a corner. Ryan was a liability and had to go. He should have known better. Have you got the stuff back from him?" Jason sounded smug.

"Yes. I've got the clothing and the hard drive. I'm satisfied that he got shut of the pistol and the burner phones, there was nothing else in the van."

"Excellent, get shut of it down there and get back up to Manchester, job done."

Carl placed his phone back into his pocket. The reality of the situation didn't sit well with him, he reached his car and got in. Not wanting to hang around, he drove from the car park and sped off. He remembered the hard drive and clothes on the back seat. It was a good job he emptied the rucksack. He stopped at the rear of an industrial unit and threw the clothing into a bin, got back into the car and set the sat-nav for Manchester. After lighting a cigarette, he set off again.

There was a sign indicating the River Avon was ahead, as he approached a bridge. *Perfect, I need to get rid of the hard drive.* He stopped at the side of the road, got out of the car and placed the hard drive against the front tyre. After roughly driving over it several times he threw the bits and pieces of plastic and metal off the bridge into the river below. *Time to get out of here.*

Carl needed a piss by the time he turned off into Strensham services on the M5. He locked the car and walked to the toilets. The night air was fresh and cool. Once sorted, he got back into the car and took out his mobile phone. He needed to speak to Wayne.

"Hey, Carl, how's it going in Bristol?" Wayne said.

"Mate, what a nightmare, Jason's had Ryan killed. I'd got the stuff off him. He agreed to come back to Manchester to face it out. We were at the van and two blokes in balaclavas with pistols were on top of us. I was weighing up my options to tackle them, but they were professional. I had a pistol in my face. They'd done this before. I was about to have a go but he ordered me out of the van and told me to do one. I didn't stand a chance. I wasn't close enough to go for him. Next thing, Ryan's shot three times."

"How do you know Jason set it up?"

"I've spoken to him. He sounded chuffed with himself, no regret at all. It was evil mate."

"I can't say I'm surprised, Carl. He was probably going to shoot him before he escaped from us in Manchester. Unfortunately for Ryan he had it coming."

"I don't like it, mate. Was it really necessary to kill him? At the end of the day he was one of us. Jason had been his pal since they were kids."

"Jason's ruthless, mate, you said it yourself. You need to get used to it." Carl felt goose bumps on his body, this wakeup call made him question his decision and rationale for getting involved with Jason. He questioned whether he was out of his depth.

"I'll see you tomorrow," Carl said. He didn't want to be having this conversation any more. "I'm going to drive up to Manchester tonight."

Carl took the SIM out of his phone and dropped it down a drainage grid. He ditched the phone in a bin and continued his drive to Manchester.

Jason walked through to the kitchen and took a can of lager from the fridge. He took a long drink and savoured the moment. He felt ecstatic. Jason thrived on this type of power, controlling who lived and who died, it was like a drug for him. The threat had been eliminated. Ryan was no longer a problem. There was no sadness or emotional regret for Ryan's demise whatsoever. He imagined the shock that Wayne and Carl must be in. This was another reminder for people, of why they shouldn't fuck with Jason Hamilton. He started to laugh at the thought of it.

Shortly after speaking to Carl, Jason's new burner phone rang. He picked it up. It was Lee.

"Lee, how are you doing?"

"The job has been completed, mate. Ryan was shot three times. He's dead. Meet me at the services with the money and the phone."

"Okay, mate, I'll set off now."

Lee had come good. Jason hoped to do more business with him in the future. He took his phone and searched on BBC News Bristol. *Nothing. Probably too early.* He shouted up the stairs, "Nipping out, Kirsty. Do you want me to bring some food back?"

"No, let's go out later, what were you laughing at?" she shouted back.

"Just having a bit of banter with Lee on the phone, see you later."

Jason grabbed his car keys and left the house. About forty minutes later he pulled into the M62 services at Warrington. He saw Lee in the hire car, in the same place as last time, and pulled up alongside him. He grabbed the carrier bag of cash and got out of the car. Lee was already out and standing beside him.

"Let's get a coffee, Jason. I've not stopped all day."

"Good call, do they not do champagne here?"

Lee started to laugh, "You're merciless. No regrets I take it?"

"He crossed the line, Lee, so he paid the ultimate price. Did it go as planned?"

"I assume so. Vinny just told me the job was done and the target was dead."

They walked across the car park towards the cafes and shops.

Jason heard the sound of screeching tyres and saw a black BMW X5 speeding towards them.

"He's going to mow us down," Jason shouted. He turned to run for the cover of the parked cars and saw another X5 screeching to a stop behind them. A sudden surge of adrenaline made his legs go to jelly. Three armed response police officers jumped out of the car pointing MP5 sub-machine guns at him. They looked menacing, like SAS troopers.

All three were yelling, "Armed police officers. Lie face-down on the floor. Keep your hands where we can see them."

Jason knew there was no escape. No sooner than he was on the floor, police officers surrounded him, demands being shouted left, right and centre.

"Legs out."

"Spread your arms out."

"Are you in possession of any weapons?"

It was all happening so fast. Jason felt disorientated. He turned his head back to the left. The rough tarmac grazed his chin. He saw Lee was getting the same treatment. He could feel the hand-cuffs being tightened over his wrists, whilst other officers were manhandling him and patting him down. Just as his composure was returning, an officer leant down towards him.

"You are under arrest for conspiring to murder Ryan Young, and being concerned in the supply of Class A controlled drugs. You do not have to say anything, but it may harm your defence if you do not mention when questioned something which you later rely on in Court. Anything you do say may be given in evidence."

Jason was helped to his feet by two other officers and led to a marked police van that had just pulled up. He stepped through the back doors and sat on the bench in the cage. The door was slammed shut, causing a vibration throughout the cage.

All that he could feel was disbelief. The shock of the arrest was now fading and reality was kicking in.

I've been grassed up, someone's sold me out, he thought. A mental tick-list was forming and being processed. Not Lee, surely… he was getting locked up too, it can't be Carl, definitely not Wayne…but somebody has? Who… Vinny? He realised he should have done more due diligence on the hit-man. His heart sank as the realisation hit home. *Vinny must be a cop. But surely, he can't be. He was Lee's contact? What the fuck have I done?* His thoughts were broken by the need to stay balanced and seated as the van sped off.

Lee was helped to his feet by his colleagues.

"You okay, Lee? Sorry for making you taste the tarmac, but it just helps to keep Hamilton guessing for now. Hopefully until after the interviews."

The Detective retrieved the carrier bag of cash with Jason's burner phone, which were then placed into evidence bags. Samantha appeared once the melee calmed down.

"Nice one, Lee, I think we've got him banged to rights. Let's go and get you something to eat and drink before the debrief and sort the evidence out."

They got into the car and took off from the services.

Whilst Jason was being placed in the back of the police van, Kirsty was sitting in the kitchen with a coffee, pondering which restaurant to book. She heard a knock at the door, *it's probably Wayne or Lee,* she thought, subconsciously hoping it was Lee. *I need to know how he is getting on sorting this mess out, I can't cope with this, I need out.*

When Kirsty opened the door, she saw that it was neither of them. She was confronted by a group of men and women in suits, none of which looked familiar. The one at the front held an ID card out towards her, "DC White, Manchester Police, Serious Crime Division. We have a warrant to search your premises under PACE 1984 and the Misuse of Drugs act 1971."

Another officer then held out a piece of paper towards her.

Kirsty turned and walked back into the kitchen, followed by the group of police officers. It was a situation she had dreaded and feared for a long time, whilst accepting it would be an inevitability sooner or later. She picked up her coffee and took a drink. She felt numb. Inside she had always been prepared for this day. Jason's luck must have run out. *Oh shit, has he killed Ryan?* Her fear put her in a quiet calm trance like disposition.

The cops around her commenced a search of the house. A spaniel dog had been let off the lead, being directed around the room by its handler. A female detective sat next to her at the breakfast bar and started asking Kirsty questions.

The only response that Kirsty gave was, "I've nothing to say."

And this was the truth, she was dreading being arrested.

"You need to have a good hard think about this. Do you want to risk prison with the bad guys, or do the right thing and assist with our enquiries? This is serious shit Kirsty."

Kirsty was scared to death that she would soon be sitting in a police cell.

At about the same time, Carl was on the M6 headed north. He looked into his rear view mirror. *Shit,* he thought, *blue flashing lights.* Carl pulled into the inside lane, hoping the cops would continue and fly past him to another incident. He checked his rear view mirror again. They too had pulled into the inside lane. This was just what he didn't need. Reluctantly, he signalled left and slowed down to a stop on the hard shoulder.

There was no other traffic. The police had initiated a rolling roadblock further back. In his mirrors he saw bodies, emerging from police cars and scurrying around his car.

He climbed out of the car, "Police, kneel on the floor with your hands on your head," being yelled at him from all directions. This was serious. Armed police patrols. He knelt down and placed his hands on his head. Someone was right behind him, placing handcuffs on his wrists.

"You are under arrest on suspicion of conspiracy to murder and conspiracy to supply Class A controlled drugs. You do not have to say anything, but it may harm your defence if you do not mention when questioned something which you later rely on in Court. Anything you do say may be given in evidence."

He was pulled to his feet, pushed against the side of his car and patted down. *Jason, what have you done? We could have handled Ryan, no problem. What was I thinking when I got involved in this shit?* He felt anger towards Jason. There was no need to kill Ryan. Why hadn't he left them to it?

The police placed Carl into the secure cage in the back of a van, and arranged for a full lift to recover his car. As the van started to move off, Carl sat in disbelief. What had Jason done? How had the cops got onto him? Ryan was dead. What a mess. *Why did I get into this mess, I should have kept it simple at a lower street level?*

Chapter Sixteen

Andrea Statham was in her office reading the reports from her team of detectives. With each one she filed, it became more apparent that this investigation was going to be a long haul, but she was quietly confident that they were on the right track. Jason Hamilton was their man. Her mobile phone started to ring. She could see from the display that it was DI Dave Ferguson from the force drugs unit.

"Hey, How you doing, Dave?"

"All the better for speaking to you, Andrea. Just a quick update for you. Hopefully you'll forgive me for not including you in the information loop earlier, but you know the score with these things, need to know sketch and all that. We infiltrated Hamilton with undercover officers from the Covert Operations Unit. Obviously, our primary objective was the drug importation. An unexpected opportunity arose. Hamilton wanted to arrange a contract kill on one of his associates, Ryan Young. The undercover officer took on his request and did a great job for us. Hamilton is now under arrest, sitting in a cell at Longsight. I think we have him bang to rights, so he's not going anywhere for a long time."

"Wow good work, that's excellent, Dave. There's more than one way to skin a cat and you've now got some leverage on him. He may want to talk about those higher up the chain to lessen his jail time, and if he's safely out of the way behind bars, some of his associates may want to talk to us about the canal murder."

"That's why I like talking to you, Andrea, you're always the optimist. I think we'll let him settle into prison life before we make an approach and keep chipping away at his organised crime group. You're welcome to send a couple of your detectives to monitor the interviews if you like. We've got Hamilton, Ryan Young, and Carl Smith in custody. We've not arrested Wayne Davies though. We haven't got much on him yet, so we thought we'd just keep him under surveillance. You never know where he might take us, he will be under pressure and could make mistakes."

"That's great, thank you. I'll get Pete Higgs to liaise with your team. We might pick up a few scraps."

"Excellent. If you and Pete want to come over later, we can run through the events to establish anything that may assist your case. It's probably worth nominating liaison officers now."

"Thanks, Dave, great arrest. Get him charged. See you later."

Andrea rang Pete Higgs to update him about the turn of events, which made things a little more interesting.

Jason was lying on a bench in a police cell in Manchester. He had been booked into custody and given his rights. He had exercised his right to legal advice and requested his usual tried and trusted solicitor, Frank Burton. His clothing had been taken for forensic examination and he had been swabbed to test for traces of controlled drugs. The cops knew it was too late for traces of gunshot residue. Jason was worried about how Kirsty would cope under police interrogation. He knew routine police procedure would include a search of his house, and feared she would be arrested as leverage. This wasn't her world. He'd have to get Burton onto that right away.

Ryan had been through the same custody procedure. Clothes seized, forensic swabs taken, given his rights, and placed in a cell. He had also asked for Frank Burton. The last hour had been mental. Ryan was working his way through the events, trying to make sense of it. Carl must have been in on it? He had led him to the van where the shooter was waiting, and then he'd been told to do one. He probably went reporting back to Jason. Jason was the only one he had pissed off big time, nobody else.

The problem for Jason though, was that he'd hired an undercover cop to do it. Ryan started to laugh out loud. *What a dickhead. What a needless mess. Thank god it was the cops, I thought I was dead.*

A uniform cop appeared at the hatch of his cell door.

"Your brief wants to speak with you on the phone."

He unlocked the cell door and opened it. Ryan followed him to the custody office desk. The smell of sweat and detergent in these places never changed. The custody sergeant spoke into the phone, "He's here now. I'll hand you over."

He gave the handset to Ryan.

"Hello."

"Ryan, it's Frank Burton. Don't talk, just listen. I've got the basics from the custody sergeant. I'm guessing the drugs arrest is a fishing expedition, the attempt on your life obviously isn't. I can't represent you on this one. I'm representing Jason and that would be a conflict of interest. I can't emphasise enough though, everyone must stick together here, and we will all be okay. I'm going to arrange for a trusted solicitor from Bristol, okay?"

"Yeah. No worries," Ryan said, and handed the phone back to the sergeant.

Ryan was escorted back to his cell, where he sat on the wooden bench. The foam mattress in blue PVC barely made it any more comfortable. He leant forward and put his head in his hands. The enormity of the shit-storm was sinking in. Jason had paid to have him shot. Jason was also sitting in a cell and Burton would be up in Manchester representing him. Ryan wasn't on their team any longer. He was on his own. Burton was in Jason's pocket and couldn't be trusted. He'd received Burton's message loud and clear, it was not in his best interests to start grassing.

Ryan pressed the buzzer. The same uniform cop appeared at the hatch in the door.

"The solicitor on the phone said he was going to arrange for a Bristol solicitor. I don't want whoever he suggests, get me the duty solicitor."

The cop nodded and shut the hatch. Ryan knew he had some serious thinking to do. He knew he would never have grassed on Jason. It was just a threat to keep him off his back. But things had changed.

Back at Jason's house, the search was coming to an end. One of the detectives sat down next to Kirsty.

"That's a copy of the warrant. Have a read through it, everything is self-explanatory. There's a list of everything we have seized under the warrant. Do you have any questions?"

"Have you arrested Jason?" Kirsty asked, suspecting she knew the answer already.

"That's something I couldn't discuss with you. If anyone is under arrest, it is up to them as to who is informed, so I can't say either way. There's my card, you really need to give me a call, you don't need to be dragged into this… think it through."

"I really don't know why you are here, I'm not involved in anything."

"We are past playing games Kirsty, we have been watching Jason for a long time, it's not looking good for him. You have a decision to make, don't let him take you down with him. Jail is not a good place for women like you, do you think you could hack it in there?"

The police started to leave the house.

Once she was alone, Kirsty selected Jason from her phone contacts. It went straight to voicemail. She tried Lee next. Straight to voicemail again. Working her way down the list, she called Wayne, and finally got through to someone.

"What's going on, Wayne? Our house has just been searched by the police."

"What? Where's Jason?" He sounded surprised.

"I suspect he's been arrested but they wouldn't tell me."

"First I've heard, Kirsty. Did they question you?"

"No, they tried but I didn't say anything." She felt numb with fear and trepidation. The detective was spot on, Kirsty knew she would struggle with prison life, she felt extremely vulnerable and desperate.

"Right, I'll try and find out what's going on. I think it's best if you disappear to your mum and dad's until I come up with some answers. Don't worry, I'll sort it. I'll be in touch," Wayne said, and ended the call.

Wayne knew he needed to get out of his address sharpish. He couldn't take the risk of the cops having found out where he lived. He threw together some clothes, his computer and other bits and left the house. Within ten minutes of Kirsty's call he was driving out of Manchester towards Wales. Unbeknown to him, followed by a police surveillance team.

He pulled over in a lay-by and called Jason… answering machine, Carl… answering machine, Ryan… answering machine.

It didn't look good, had he been right with his hunch of someone grassing? He was in no doubt; the cops were moving in for the kill. Time to lie low. He knew the drill well.

Carl was sitting in a cell, having been through the same procedures as Jason and Ryan. He felt confident that Jason would keep him out of this. He was of more use to Jason on the outside, not banged up. He wondered how the cops had moved so quickly. Were they all under surveillance? Carl thought back to the break-in at Jason's house.

Or was there a grass? Nobody obvious came to mind other than Ryan. There's no way Wayne would grass, and Jason would have organised the shooting on a need to know basis. Lee? No way, surely Jason wouldn't have Lee in the loop, he hardly knew him. What did the cops have on them?

Carl ran through his involvement in the criminality, he had always sought a peripheral role and been aware of minimising his involvement. He was here to seek revenge, and nothing more. He felt satisfied the cops would struggle to pin anything on him.

Chapter Seventeen

DI Dave Ferguson had finished briefing the Detectives who would be interviewing their three suspects. They were now preparing their disclosure documents and interview strategies under the watchful eye of the tier five trained interview officer. The DI then knocked onto a meeting with Mo, the liaison officer from the Covert Operations Unit.

"Everything went smoothly on the final run. The contract kill went as planned. Hamilton received the call from Lee that the job was done. He turned up with the final payment and his burner phone. It couldn't have gone better, he's banged to rights."

"Great work by your guys, Mo. Please pass on our appreciation," Dave said.

"Will do. They will finish their debriefings and statements later and get them to you tomorrow. Then we'll get the remainder of our evidential package to you. Your tier five officer has my mobile number, in case any issues arise during the interviews."

"Cheers, Mo. Thanks for your efforts so far, I'll be in touch."

When Dave returned to his office, DS Pete Higgs was waiting for him.

"Hi, Boss. DI Statham asked me to come over to act as contact liaison for the Smethurst murder team."

"Right, Pete, get the kettle on, then we can run through what we've got here that may assist you."

A few minutes later DS Higgs returned with two coffees.

"The conspiracy to murder should stick," Dave began. "I think the undercover officers have done us proud. The drugs supply is another matter, but at least we get Hamilton off the streets and maybe progress a divide and conquer operation of the OCG. We've seized mobile phones and computers from Hamilton's place to look at. They're all being fast tracked through for forensic examination. It goes without saying you can have access to everything."

"There's a chance that Ryan might decide to grass on him. He can't be happy that Hamilton tried to kill him."

"I won't hold my breath, Pete, but stranger things have happened I suppose."

"If it's okay with you I'll get some of our team to monitor the interviews of Jason Hamilton and Carl Smith. We'll leave Ryan Young, and speak to your interview team when they get back."

"That's fine. Fill your boots, Pete."

Jason hadn't been asleep for long when he was awoken by the police officer at his cell door.

"Your brief's here."

He couldn't have sounded more disinterested if he tried.

Jason followed him to the consultation room. He was shown in and the officer closed the door. The room was stark and clinical, a desk and two chairs.

"Hello, Jason. How are they treating you?" Frank Burton asked.

"Five stars. But the Jacuzzi's not working, unfortunately," Jason replied.

"Right then." Frank took the hint to get down to business, "They will do a disclosure on tape when we're ready, so we'll listen to that then have a chat about it."

"Have they brought Kirsty in?" Jason asked.

"No, they've searched your place and taken a few bits and pieces. She's fine, I've spoken to her. She's gone to Warrington for a few days."

They were interrupted by a knock at the door.

"I'm DC Murphy. Are you ready to crack on with the pre-interview disclosure?"

Burton agreed and they all made their way to the interview room. DC Murphy read from a pre-prepared typed sheet. The information and evidence that the police were prepared to disclose prior to the interview under caution. A copy was handed to Burton, who was then escorted back to the consultation room with his client.

"It looks like they've infiltrated you. Police intervention contract kill. Who introduced you to the gunman?"

"A guy called Lee. A cop. He was locked up too, but that would have been staged I suppose. I'm seething. How did I not see it coming? He was at the house, flirting with Kirsty and drinking my beer. He's got it coming to him. I need you to start digging on this 'Lee', or whatever his real name is. He had a local accent. I'm sure we can find him."

"Who introduced you to Lee?" Burton asked.

"Me and Carl met him on a night out at the arches at Deansgate, but me and Kirsty had also seen him with his girlfriend in the gym a few times. If he's a cop, there's no way Carl knew. Or did he? Keep an eye on Carl, see how he's behaving. I can't see it myself."

Jason's mind was now racing. Who had set him up here? Had somebody grassed? How had he not clocked the cops? His hatred of Lee was now concrete and growing, his new nemesis had stepped forward. He should have paid more attention to Wayne, who suspected there was a grass amongst their ranks.

"We'll get to the bottom of it. I'll speak to my bent cop, he owes us big time. I can tempt him by letting him walk away from us, debt paid, if he comes up with the goods. It's a worthwhile trade off if he can help to get us out of this mess. Right onto present matters, at the interview make 'no comment' for now." Frank Burton had chosen the word 'us' intentionally. He also had a lot to lose if the cops found out about his criminality. The tumbling down of the house of cards weighed heavily on his mind.

Twenty minutes later the DC appeared at the door. The three of them made their way back to the interview room, where the interviews went on for just over an hour. Jason made no comment to all of the questions. They were more focused on discovering what evidence the police had or didn't have. At the end of the interview Jason was returned to his cell. The door slammed shut behind him.

This wasn't looking good. The interviews carried on for the next few hours, almost like a game of cat and mouse, with the police providing more at each disclosure, prior to each interview.

Back in Bristol, Ryan was going through the same process. Once the police had asked all they wanted to ask about the supply of drugs and about Ryan's relationship with Carl and Jason, they took another break. Ryan and the duty solicitor retired to the consultation room. Ryan had gone with no comment throughout the interviews. The duty solicitor was just a fail-safe, to deter the cops from overstepping the mark. If proceedings followed on from this, he would ditch the duty and instruct one of the Salford or Manchester Firms, which weren't in Jason's pocket.

"Have you got any links with the briefs in Manchester?" Ryan asked.

"No, I've never been there, heard it rains a lot," the duty replied. Ryan thought the bespectacled, quietly spoken man looked more like a librarian than a solicitor.

"Let's keep it that way, there're some dodgy bastards up there. If they contact you about me, say nothing. The last thing you want is for you or your family to get dragged into this mess. No need for me and you to fall out."

The detective knocked at the door and summoned them back to the interview room. They all took a seat on the worn blue fabric-covered chairs. Ryan noticed that the table between them was screwed to the floor. The recording machine made a buzzing noise prior to activating.

The detective made the introductions and gave Ryan his rights.

"There is a copy of the Threat to Life Notice. It's a formal notice to inform you that the police are aware of a legitimate threat to your life. Obviously, you're aware of that already from today's events."

Ryan leaned over and took the duty solicitor's copy from him.

"I'll keep that safe," Ryan said.

The solicitor didn't protest. He looked a little uncomfortable and ready to go home at the earliest opportunity, like he'd lost interest already. He much preferred to be representing juvenile shoplifters.

"So, you are now aware that the two men who staged the shooting at the van are undercover police officers. They were portraying the roles of hit-men and paid by Jason Hamilton to kill you. They have gathered evidence, which will be put to the CPS later for a charging decision. I'll be surprised if Hamilton isn't charged with conspiracy to kill you and remanded in custody."

The detective took a drink of water, and left a pause for reflection.

"Are you willing to make a statement in relation to his prosecution?"

"Piss off. You've seen what I'm up against," Ryan laughed.

"He's going away for a long time. We have a strong evidential case."

"Well you don't need a statement from me then."

The detective paused then continued at a slow, deliberate pace, "So you have some thinking to do. If he is looking like being convicted, which he is, is he going to consider a deal to lessen his sentence? Throw some associates under the bus, so to speak. It's in your interests to keep him in jail. You can do that by assisting us. We will carry out a risk assessment of the threat to you and do what we can to minimise that threat. Do you have any information that will help us to protect you?"

"No. Look mate, I know you're only doing your job, but the best thing I can do is disappear."

"You are also under arrest on suspicion of being concerned in the unlawful supply of class-A controlled drugs. I intend to move onto that in the next interviews, but again you need to think carefully here about what you decide. Our objective is to target the higher echelon of this network, essentially Hamilton and above. I know you have played a minor role, which is reflected in the fact you didn't take part in the recent business meeting in Amsterdam. Should you decide to come across and talk to us, it will be looked upon favourably by the judge in his sentencing. Otherwise you risk a long custodial sentence. There's a lot to think about there, with massive implications for you. From experience, I find these situations quickly develop into every man for himself... loyalties are quickly forgotten."

"The best I'd get is witness protection and looking over my shoulder for the rest of my life. I'm no grass, but more importantly I'm not involved in dealing drugs. No thanks, can I go now?"

Further interviews followed over the next few hours, during which Ryan made 'no comment' to all questions asked of him. He was given police bail after what seemed like an eternity of questions. He made his way back to Lisa's flat, switched on the television and vegetated on the sofa, he was shattered and couldn't fight falling asleep for long.

Carl had been in custody for over nine hours. He had taken legal advice and made no comment to all questions asked of him through a series of interviews. He was represented by a local solicitor, arranged by Frank Burton from Manchester. He was impressed with her. She was switched on and didn't miss a trick. He was in no doubt that the detectives found her to be a real pain in the arse. She questioned and objected to almost everything they did or said. He had been questioned about the conspiracy to murder Ryan and dealing drugs for Hamilton's firm. He had toed the party line, and was in no doubt that the solicitor would report back to Frank Burton and Jason in detail.

When his solicitor had gone to make urgent calls in relation to other business, or more likely to Frank Burton, Carl was approached by a detective delivering his meal. He was given the hard sell on why it was in his best interests to grass on Jason. Carl didn't succumb. That was a decision for another time, not while he was under pressure in custody. He was surprised and relieved when he was informed he was to be given police bail. He'd convinced himself that he was going nowhere and would be charged on the conspiracy to kill.

Maybe they were still going to push him towards a deal. Or did they just want rid of him to shut up his obnoxious solicitor?

Carl left the police station and walked until he found a public phone. He dialled the number which he had committed to memory a long time ago.

"I've been arrested and just released. I need to meet now."

A meeting place was agreed. Carl began the walk. About twenty minutes later he rang the number again. The same voice answered, "Go to the usual pick up point. See you there."

Carl carried on walking. He turned into a quiet street and walked alongside the empty office buildings, where a van drove alongside him. The side door slid open. He stepped in. The door was slammed behind him.

"I've not eaten all day; can we get some food?" Carl said.

The detectives never passed on an invitation to eat. They made their way to a drive-through. Silence prevailed whilst the three of them tucked into their burgers and fries.

Mike and Bob had been Carl's informant handlers now for over three years. They had a good rapport but the trust was always a wafer thin veneer.

Carl relayed the events from when he met up with Ryan in Bristol, to the shooting at the van and his time in custody.

"I didn't have a clue that Ryan was being set up. I'd gone down for a few beers and he needed to get his gym stuff from the van." Carl hadn't decided whether to talk about the Smethurst murder yet. "The next thing I knew, it all kicked off. Two guys in balaclavas appeared and shot him. I thought he was dead, but the shooter was an undercover cop, obviously using a blank firing pistol. I've done nothing wrong. You men have got to help me here. I've been police bailed for now."

"We've got a lot to think about here, Carl. It sounds like they could charge you on the conspiracy to kill. It could be interpreted that you delivered him to the execution site for Hamilton," Bob said.

"We need to think this through, but my first impression is that you have two choices. Either face up to whatever charges come your way or give us some more evidence against Hamilton and his firm. At least if you come across the CPS may put a text forward to the judge in your mitigation," Mike added.

"I started grassing for you to get some drug dealers off the street in revenge for my girlfriend's overdose. Now I'm up to my neck in it, looking at doing time myself, or looking over my shoulder for the rest of my life if I give evidence against Hamilton."

"I'll have to speak with the investigation team, they may apply for public interest immunity to introduce your evidence. That will give you anonymity at the trial. It was your intelligence that allowed the undercover officer to be introduced. We have a problem if Hamilton discovers that's what happened."

"You've always rattled on about risk assessments and your duty of care to me, it's time for you to do your bit. I've kept to my end of the deal." Carl felt a feeling of isolation and panic, *are they going to hang me out to dry?*

"You've got to make sure your next move is the right move," Bob said.

"We'll get the new informant use and conduct authorities and risk assessments done. Are you hooking up with Wayne whilst you make your mind up?" Mike asked.

"Yeah, I'll see how the land lies. I think he'll be busy running around for Jason at the minute. I don't think they suspect me of grassing at all. The spotlight as always been on Ryan."

"There's your new phone. We'll be in touch after we have spoken with the investigation team." Bob concluded.

Carl got out of the van and made his way home. He never expected it to come to this. *I need to keep the cops onside, they owe me a duty of care, I can't give them any excuses to ditch me.*

Lee and Samantha had just finished their debriefing with Mo, their support officer. They had typed their statements of evidence; which Mo would now pass onto the investigation team.

"The Senior Investigating Officer, Dave Ferguson passes his gratitude. He is made up with your work, he was struggling to convict Hamilton." Mo said.

"Got to be honest, Hamilton made it easy for me surprisingly. He let his guard down, so much so, I feared he knew we were cops and was creating a trap for us." Lee said.

"Well done anyway, great result. I'll take the evidential package over to Dave Ferguson and see you back at the Unit."

"Shall we go and get a drink? I fancy a hot chocolate." Samantha said.

"Yes, it's your round."

They arrived at the café and found a quiet seat near the window.

"What are your plans after this?" Samantha asked.

"I think it's a good time to move on back to the CID. I've been here six years now and need to start thinking about promotion. I passed my exams last year so it makes sense."

"It will be a shame to lose you, I've enjoyed working with you."

"I must admit, it does feel like the right time. Nice way to finish though, helping put Hamilton away, nasty piece of work that one."

Chapter Eighteen

Jason woke up in his cell the following morning, his back was aching from a night spent on the piece of foam they laughingly called a mattress. A uniform cop appeared at the hatch and said, "Your brief is here."

Jason followed the uniform cop to the consultation room where he found Frank Burton, looking refreshed in his new clean shirt and suit. Jason noticed his aftershave too. It was a welcome smell in contrast to the aroma of stale sweat in the cell area. It made Jason feel grotty. The sweaty smell of the place hung off him.

"They want one last interview with you. They say it's your last chance to give your version of events," Burton said.

"Well, it's a formality. Quick interview, charged, court and remanded I guess?" Jason said.

"Yeah, I'd be surprised if it's anything other than that. I think we were right about the drugs side. They were on a fishing expedition. Carl and Ryan both went no comment and have been bailed. They tried to get them to grass on you, no surprises there. I'll have to keep my ear to the ground on that one."

The detective arrived and they made their way to the interview room. Further questions and further no comments followed. Afterwards Jason was taken to the custody sergeant and formally charged with conspiring to kill Ryan Young, to which he replied, "No comment."

He was placed back in his cell to await his appearance before the magistrates who would no doubt remand him in custody until his trial at Crown Court.

Jason paced up and down the cell, his fists clenched. Once again, he was trying to make sense of it all. Had he acted in haste with Ryan? If Ryan had behaved himself this wouldn't have happened. He knew he needed to be patient. It would all unfold over the coming months. There was nowhere to hide. The snakes in the grass would be found and dealt with. Number one priority was the undercover cop. *How was I taken in by him? It all seems so bloody obvious now,* Jason thought. He now had to rely on Frank Burton, Carl and Wayne to work for him on the outside. Once he was in prison he would have access to a phone and direct them from there.

Ryan woke up from a good night's sleep. He must have needed it. He looked around at the flat, which was a tip. Clothes on the floor, used cups and glasses everywhere and greasy pizza boxes littering the place. He needed to tidy it up before Lisa got back that afternoon.

But this moment of normality quickly dissipated when his mind took him back to the events of yesterday. He almost struggled to believe that Jason had paid a hit-man to kill him, and as a result was now looking at a long stretch inside. It could be ten years or more. Then on top of that, the cops wanted him to grass, no doubt enter the witness protection scheme, and live the rest of his life looking over his shoulder. He knew Jason would find him. He had access to bent cops, not forgetting Frank Burton, too.

He also knew he would have to leave Lisa behind for a total fresh start, with no links to his old life. The enormity of this clusterfuck was sinking in. The answer was stark and obvious. He needed to move abroad and he needed to keep his head down. He was almost certain none of them knew Lisa's address. That bought him some time, but probably not long.

Ryan made a coffee then picked up his mobile to call Kirsty. He doubted she would answer, but he had to try.

"Hello, Ryan, thank god you're still alive. I called you but couldn't get through."

"I'm sorry, Kirsty, I've really messed up, I should have nipped this in the bud with Jason. But my heads straight now. I'm off the coke and booze for good. Jason paid for an assassin to kill me but the cops infiltrated it. It must have been Lee, he must be a cop."

"Lee's not answered my calls and I've not seen him at the gym. It makes sense. Frank Burton told me he was a cop. I would have thought Jason would have sussed him out, weird." Kirsty said.

"Look, for what it's worth, I just wanted you to know I would never have grassed on Jason. Even though the bastard has tried to have me shot... twice. If he still trusts me, I'm onside for him. But I'm probably going to disappear when the cops cancel my bail. They just wanted to sound me out for grassing him up, but it isn't happening."

"I'm just relieved you're alive, I was getting really worried and concerned for you. Frank's been keeping me up to date. I'm going to see Jason once he's remanded. He's looking at a few years inside. Most of the evidence will be from undercover cops. Frank thinks he's knackered."

"Yeah, it's not looking good, even Burton won't be able to nobble them. Jason let his guard down. He was taken in by Lee. They'll probably offer him a deal for info on the other stuff but that would be like committing suicide, certain death. He isn't going to entertain that. Anyway, I'm here if either of you need me," Ryan said.

"I guess you've got a big debt to pay, Ryan. He knows what you're like."

"That was the old me, but not anymore. See you some time, Kirsty, I'm always here if you need me."

"I hope so Ryan, don't stay away for too long."

Ryan ended the call and sat back into the sofa. That conversation had actually felt cathartic. *Hopefully Kirsty can influence Jason to get him off my back.* He finished his coffee, ready for the next call.

Ryan selected Wayne from his contacts.

"Morning, Ryan, bit of a shit-storm you've created here," Wayne said.

"Wayne, I've got my head sorted. I'm off the charlie for good. This has been a big wake up call. I was never going to grass anybody. My head was up my arse. Me and Jason got into one of our sparring duels, it's not the first time. I'm done with all this shit."

"I believe you, Ryan. Others, including Jason, probably wouldn't. For what it's worth I think Jason went over the top. You deserved a good hiding for sure, but nothing more. Run me through what happened."

Not for the first time, Ryan relived the events of the previous night. He started from Carl arriving, to being taken to the van, and on to the subsequent 'hit'.

"Okay, I need to have a good look at how Lee arrived on the scene. We'd got complacent. The warning was there when the cops got into Jason's house. The good thing is, apart from the conspiracy to kill, they don't seem to have anything else on us. That doesn't help Jason though."

"Where do I stand, Wayne?" Ryan asked.

"I'll have you back on board, Ryan, but for that you owe me big time. No more chances. You've run out of credit, understand? You're in my debt until I tell you otherwise. I'll be in touch."

Ryan's head was spinning. He needed to go for a run. But for now, he felt he was out of the pressure-cooker for the first time in weeks. *Do I disappear to Spain or take Wayne up on his offer? Maybe I can get him to stop using the care home kids for dealing. He thinks they are high maintenance and risky.*

Wayne finished the call, looked across to Carl and said, "Did you get the gist of that?"

"Yeah, I agree. As you know, it was over the top. Was Jason trying to impress Lee?"

"Maybe, he seemed to be taken with him. Ryan's always been reckless but I don't think he'd have grassed on Jason. In his twisted cokehead logic, he thought he could do one with Lisa into the sunset, whilst still on a wage from Jason. He can still do a job for us. We just need to keep him on a tight leash."

"I didn't know Jason was involved in the hit until I called him after. It all looked professional. I thought it was all about some issue Ryan had got involved in with the local dealers in Bristol."

"You must have had an idea. Anyway, the million dollar question is how our boy Lee got into us."

"I think it's simple, Jason let his guard down and was taken in by the SAS crap." Carl knew there was an element of distrust in Wayne's question, and that he had to be careful. "It was at the Arches at Deansgate. We were in the VIP suite and there was a group of fellas on a works do. They slung a bottle of Chablis our way. It looked like they had a bucket-load.

I took it off Lee. He said he recognised Jason from the gym and I started talking to him. It turned out that his group were ex-military. The wine was flowing. Jason joined us and he remembered Lee from the gym. You know the rest. If the cops were looking to bug Jason's house, they probably had us under surveillance too and knew where we went drinking. It wouldn't take a genius to work it out."

Carl felt confident in his answer. It stood up to scrutiny and pointed the breach towards Jason being taken in by them on the back of Special Forces banter.

"But if we had been under surveillance, the cops would be aware of what happened on the canal," Wayne said. They both mulled that over... it was a good point.

Chapter Nineteen

The following morning Jason was driven to the Magistrates Court. He was led down a long corridor and placed in a holding cell. This building was somehow more soulless than the police station. The cells felt grim. Not even a mattress. He felt depersonalised, like something to be processed through the system and moved onto the next stage. As the hours passed Jason tried to sleep, since there was nothing else to do.

Eventually the door to his cell was opened. A security guard who looked like he was ex-military appeared, saying, "Time to go up. I'll just put this handcuff on."

Once handcuffed to the security guard, Jason was led through a series of iron security gates and up a flight of stairs, to a final door that led into the dock of the court room. The feeling of depersonalisation continued. Lawyers and officials were going about their business, chatting. Nobody even appeared to notice he was there.

Jason sat next to the security guard and looked around. It was a modern court room, decked out in expensive-looking pine furniture, with bright lighting, magnolia and beige walls, and the Royal Coat of Arms behind the bench. The plate glass of the dock went floor to ceiling. *I won't be jumping the dock here.*

A court usher commanded, "All stand."

The court fell silent as those present shuffled into position behind their respective desks. *Good of him to come*, Jason thought, as he saw Frank enter the room and take his position. He nodded towards Jason. The three magistrates, made up of two men and one woman, entered the room from a side door and took their seats on the bench. They were all middle-aged, all grey haired, and dressed smart just as they probably did for church on a Sunday morning. None of them looked his way.

Jason was asked to confirm his name and date of birth. The Crown Prosecution solicitor outlined the prosecution case and applied to have him remanded into custody. Burton politely declined to make any representations to the court on behalf of the defence, aside from making himself out to be the most reasonable person ever, for not opposing the prosecution's application. The magistrate remanded Jason into custody and he was returned to his holding cell within minutes.

A while later Jason was led back to the custody reception desk, where he was handcuffed to a private security guard. He followed the guard to the van in the secure area. Jason looked around. He knew this was his last chance to get away, yet he quickly ruled it out as a non-starter. He was handcuffed. He didn't have a tool to chop the guards hand off. And in any case, the brick walls were about twenty feet high and the roller shutter gate was closed.

He followed on, up the steps and into the back of the van, where he was un-cuffed from the guard. The sweat-box door was slammed shut as he sat down on the seat. Claustrophobia hit him right away, as did the stench of cleaning fluid. This was a far cry from his accustomed life. The only way to survive it was to stay strong and hit it head on.

On arrival at Strangeways, HMP Manchester, the door of the sweat-box opened. A mountain of a prison officer with a skinhead and tattooed arms cuffed their wrists together. Jason was led to the prisoner reception area. The cacophony of noise hit him as soon as he walked inside. There was shouting and doors banging. It sounded like bedlam. The heat was oppressive too, increasing the stench of body odour beyond comfort. When his turn came Jason approached the counter and answered all the usual questions politely. He had no issue with the screws, and knew it was better to keep them onside. His photograph was taken and personal belongings placed in a polythene bag.

After he had been booked in, Jason sat in a communal secure room along with some other new prisoners.

"Your first time? I can tell. What you in for, fraud?"

Jason looked over to the interested party. The word gob-shite sprang into his mind to describe the scrawny little weasel with a mouth on him. He was wearing a yellow t shirt that probably started life as white, and grey jogging trousers covered in dubious stains. He looked like he'd never seen a bar of soap. *More than likely one of my customers*, Jason thought, and smiled.

"Nothing serious."

The gob-shite moved his attention elsewhere, allowing Jason to return to his thoughts. Eventually he was escorted into a side room where he was subjected to a strip search. It reminded him of the medical room at school, with its bare white walls, two chairs, weighing scales and not much else. Following the strip search the prison officer beckoned him over to a chair.

"This is a body orifice security scanner. We use it to check for any prohibited hidden items. Sit down please."

Jason did as he was asked. There was nothing to be gained by not acquiescing. It was all procedure and the screw was just doing his job.

"Latest technology, eh? Beats having a poke around, I bet," Jason said.

"Only the best for our clients," the prisoner officer replied. He was an older guy who had probably heard it all and seen it all at this place. Jason laughed. As he was getting dressed there was a knock at the door. A nurse walked into the room carrying a clipboard.

"Nearly done now, just got to take your medical history," he said.

They ran through the usual questions, after which Jason was seated back in the holding room, which was now virtually full of new inmates. The nervousness and tension in the room was palpable. Some blokes were avoiding eye contact, keeping their heads down, and others were nervously talking crap. Jason sat down with his thoughts. *This is worse than I thought. Keep focused, just got to settle into the routine.*

After what seemed like an eternity, but was probably no more than an hour, a prison officer escorted him to the wing. Jason purposely avoided eye contact with the prisoners he passed whilst taking in his surroundings. They arrived at G wing on the fourth landing, which was the induction wing. Another prison officer approached him and gave him a 'welcome pack' Jason smiled at the irony and looked inside; an induction book, tobacco and papers, a bed sheet, a pillow, a rough orange blanket that had seen better days, a toothbrush and toothpaste, a plastic cup, a fork, knife and spoon, shower gel sachets and soap.

The prison officer took his bundle of keys, attached to his utility belt with a chain, and opened the cell door. Jason walked in. His attention was immediately taken by a bloke lying on the bottom bunk. He looked about sixty, had grey hair and seemed to be in need of a good meal. He looked at Jason.

"Welcome to Strangeways. I've only been here a day and I'm definitely booking again for next year."

The man laughed at his own joke, then broke into a smoker's cough. The door slammed shut behind them, which affected Jason even worse than his pad mate's dubious welcome.

"Cheers, pal, I wouldn't want to be anywhere else."

Jason made his bed and lay down, reading his induction book before falling asleep. The wing was unexpectedly quiet.

Jason was awoken by inmates shouting to each other across the wing. He sat up on the edge of the bed for a moment before standing up. It was exercise time. He began his routine, press-ups, sit-ups, dips and burpees, after which the world seemed a better place. His cell door was unlocked at about eleven o'clock.

The prison officer said, "Lunch is ready, gentlemen."

Jason made his way to the hotplates and joined the queue. He selected a tray and held it out to receive the stodge on offer. His cell mate behind him said, "Don't forget to pick up a breakfast pack for tomorrow. That's all we get."

"Cheers, pal. I'm Jason by the way. This just gets better all the time."

"I'm Don. It's my third day, but it feels much longer."

"Not 'The Don' I hope."

Jason carried the mash potato and beef stew to his cell. After the first bite it was obvious that he would have to try and ignore the taste.

Once he had eaten, Jason was led from the wing to the consultation room. Burton was reading a newspaper, looking happy with his lot, which was a bit too happy for Jason's liking. The prison officer left and closed the door behind him.

"Our bent cop reckons there is an informant into you," Burton said.

"Is our boy on the ball or is he telling us what we want to hear, justifying his retainer?"

"Well, he isn't going to mess you about. He won't want to put his family or career in danger, and he knows if we delivered a dossier to police headquarters he'd be looking at a long stretch inside himself."

"So, who is it?"

"We don't know who he is but we have a code name. I know you won't want it to be Carl, but he was with you at the arches when you met Lee. He can't be ruled out yet."

"Okay, but don't forget that Lee had been making inroads at the gym with me and Kirsty as well. Get Wayne on the case. Is Ryan creating any more concerns?"

"Far from it, he's now the prodigal son, in fact. He wants to make amends but doubts you would be interested."

"He's right," Jason said.

"From the initial police disclosure, we are up against it here. It will be compelling evidence so I will focus on any whiff of agent provocateur and procedural blunders. Failing that, we can throw in an early guilty plea for a more lenient sentence. There is one other option though, which I suspect won't interest you."

Burton was interrupted by Jason. "It's not happening. I'm no grass. The Dutch lads would crucify me, never mind the Columbian. There would be nowhere to hide. And once the cops got what they wanted from me, they'd throw me to the wolves."

"I know and I agree. But It would have been remiss of me not to mention it as an option. The approach was made to me at the police station. I'd have been surprised if they hadn't run it by me."

"It's another positive sign that they haven't got any evidence on other matters." There was a silence. Then Jason said, "Have you spoken to Kirsty?"

"Yes, she knows I'm about if she needs anything. As you would expect she seems a bit distant and isn't saying much. She's keeping busy with her salons."

"I don't want her visiting. She doesn't need to see me caged up like this. Not yet anyway."

"She won't like that."

"I know but it makes sense. She was all set for us to leave this stuff behind us and had already had enough of it. Now I'm looking at a long stretch. I need to give her time. She might want to go her own way. Who could blame her?"

They talked further about the prosecution case and about matters that Wayne needed to sort out.

After a knock at the door, Jason left his meeting with Burton and was escorted back onto the wing by the prison officer. It all started to make sense. Burton's bent cop had confirmed there was a police informant into Jason's enterprise. He couldn't come up with the identity, but he had managed to find out the code name of the grass, *Tom Flint*.

Jason had more than enough time on his hands to work this one out. Over the next few days he did a lot of thinking. The first time they came across Lee, other than in the gym, was in the VIP lounge in the bar. Carl walked back from talking with Lee with a bottle of Chablis, saying he was a fellow City fan and recognised Jason from the gym. Thinking it through, Carl's normal behaviour would have been to refuse such an offer. He was suspicious of strangers, an introvert, a loner. Instead he accepted the bottle. With hindsight it looked staged. How often does a stranger present you with a bottle? When Lee walked over and continued to talk about the City match, Jason had let his guard down. The rest was history.

Carl had some explaining to do. *Christ alive*, thought Jason, *Ryan, yes, he is a reckless cokehead with a big red self-destruct button. But Carl, I would never have seen that coming. But was it Carl?*

Wayne finished the phone call with Burton. He had been back in Manchester at his flat for a few days and didn't appear to be on the cops' wanted list. The cops hadn't been through his front door and none of his boys had been bullied into giving up his location. Wayne suspected that the only proper evidence the cops had was in relation to the conspiracy to kill. They were still no closer on the main criminal business.

After all that had happened he wasn't jumping to conclusions about Carl. *Act in haste, repent at leisure, just like Jason*, he thought. He gave Carl a call and arranged to meet at a pub on Oxford Street.

A couple of hours later, Wayne was waiting at the bar. Carl should have been there half an hour ago. Wayne was actually starting to believe Burton might be right. Had he been tipped off and done one?

The pub was quiet. It was traditional, even old fashioned, and was frequented by real ale drinkers. Wayne rang Carl's mobile. It went through to voicemail. Frowning, Wayne put his phone down on the bar. *I don't believe this. It's going from bad to worse,* he thought. *This is unbelievable.*

He took a final swig of his beer and an admiring glance at the woman serving behind the bar. It made him think of better things he could be up to right now.

"Same again?" she asked.

"Why not?" he replied.

"Mucker, sorry I'm late. Traffic was horrendous. What are you having?" Carl said from behind Wayne.

"Same again, mate, I've just ordered. I thought you'd stood me up. I'll get us some seats in the corner."

Wayne walked to the other side of the pub and sat down. He needed to focus and get this right. It was all about watching Carl's reactions for the next half hour or so.

Carl joined him and put the two pints down on the table. Wayne didn't want to hang around. He went straight for the jugular.

"How long have you been Tom Flint?"

Carl took a long drink of his pint, then placed it slowly onto the table, "You what?"

Wayne watched him closely. He maintained intense eye to eye contact. He couldn't see any fear, shock or surprise. And he had known Carl a long time. He knew how he ticked and how to press his buttons.

"You heard me, Carl. The game's up. You've been rumbled, mate. It's all over. Don't insult me."

"Is this a fucking wind up? What are you on about?"

"There's an informant into us and the money's on you, Carl. Let us know what damage you've done and you can walk away, nothing but damage limitation. Why though? I don't get it?"

Wayne snared Carl's eyes with his most intense stare, hoping to intimidate him.

"Fucking great," was Carl's response. "I've been waiting for this one. I get it. I'm there when Jason meets the undercover cop, so I'm the one who set it up. Priceless. Fucking priceless. We know the cops were looking at us. They could have slipped him in anytime. We were in a bar for god's sake. If I was the grass I could have given the cops our whole operation long ago. I'm sure they'd prefer that to a conspiracy to kill."

Carl sat back and took another long drink of his beer. His reaction was what Wayne had hoped for. He looked seriously pissed off with the accusation and genuinely insulted.

"Jason wanted the question asked. You know the score. If the boot was on the other foot, you would have been asking me."

Carl stood up.

"Bollocks to this, Wayne. I need a breather. And don't worry, I'm not running off anywhere."

As Carl turned towards the door, Wayne said, "Point taken. Don't be long. I'll get the beers in."

Wayne knew this wasn't over. Although his gut feeling was to believe Carl, he knew he had to keep close tabs on him. It was still a possibility. He couldn't let his guard down.

Smelling of cigarette smoke, Carl walked back into the bar and sat down with Wayne.

"I know the score, Wayne, but me grassing? Really?"

"Jason wanted it addressing," Wayne said again. "It doesn't matter what I believe. He's got a lot of thinking time on his hands. You'd be the same if you were inside. I'm with you, mate."

"Well, it isn't me, so who is it?"

A silence followed. They both understood the situation. There was now an elephant in the room, and its name was Distrust.

They had a few more pints then went their own ways. Wayne put a call in to Frank Burton and updated him on the meeting. Wayne wasn't taken in either way. He would see how things panned out. Carl was aware of the consequences.

After the drinks with Wayne, Carl stayed in the city. He visited a few more pubs whilst checking his tracks to make sure he wasn't being followed. He had impressed himself with how he handled the accusations from Wayne. He'd always anticipated that the question would come, but hadn't known how well he would cope with the situation. His adrenaline had been going through the roof, but for now he'd kept the wolves at the door. He took out his burner mobile and dialled the number that he had memorised out of necessity.

DC Mike Tate answered, "Hello?"

"It's Tom. I've just had a compromise. I need a meet," Carl said.

"Okay, where are you?"

"I'm in town having a pint on Portland Street, keeping my head down."

"See you at the Chinese Arch at half past,"

Twenty minutes later, Carl was on Faulkner Street. His phone rang, as expected.

"See you in the usual alley."

He made his way and was walking along the alley when he saw the van. The side door opened. He jumped in. DC Bob Nolan was driving and DC Mike Tait was in the passenger seat.

"What's the panic?" Mike asked.

"They've got someone on the inside, deeper than I thought. I knew he had a few bent cops in his pocket but Wayne challenged me with the code name, Tom Flint. They suspect I'm grassing."

Mike suddenly didn't look as complacent about 'the panic.' His game face emerged in seconds.

Carl ran him through the events of the meeting with Wayne.

"They can't be one hundred per cent sure or you wouldn't be here now. At best you'd be at A&E getting stitched up. And it looks like you put on a good, convincing show," Mike said.

"That's no help from you men though, is it? I thought your systems were secure, how the fuck have they got the name Tom Flint?"

"At least we've got the heads up and can now sort it out. We'll put a few things in place to identify the leak. What do you want to do?" Bob said.

"I'm going to take it a day at a time and see how it goes, but you need to tighten things up or else I'm out."

"Leave it with us. We'll have to do the paperwork and risk assessments then run it by the gaffer. We'll change your alias and get you another phone. We'll feed some misinformation about Tom Flint and see who gets to find out. We might be able to flush our leak out too."

"That's just great. I'll need a new life in Australia for definite. Cheers, fellas, it's a fucking omnishambles, not a pleasure to do business with you."

Carl slid the door open and climbed out of the van. He was feeling angry and vulnerable. It had started to rain. He headed back towards the pub on Portland Street.

Carl pulled his hoodie over his head, hoping for some protection from the rain. He quickened his pace, intent on finding some shelter in the pub. He hadn't felt any reassurance from his handlers and needed to get his head together on this. If he went on his toes it would look like he was the grass. He could ditch the cops and keep his head down with Jason and Wayne, but it was obvious now the cops were all over them. *Just wait and see. If in doubt, do nothing hasty*, he thought.

Carl had let his guard down, emotions were taking over. As he got out of the van and headed up the road, he failed to spot the fella tucked away in one of the doorways behind a bin. Ryan had been keeping tabs on him since he got back to Manchester. Carl was going to pay the price for helping Jason try to kill him. Revenge would be sweet.

Since he'd shot his mouth off in the pub that night, Ryan had known he had a beating coming his way. But being shot? There was no way he'd deserved that. As for Carl, he at least could have given Ryan the nod. He could have allowed him to disappear. But he had chosen to go along with it. And now Ryan couldn't believe his luck. He had caught Carl with his pants down and even had photos to back it up. The two men that had pulled up in the van had 'cop' written all over them.

After all the shit he had put him through, Carl was a grass after all.

This information would pay a chunk of his debt off to Jason.

As Carl made his way into the centre, Ryan telephoned Wayne.

"Ryan, when I said I would give you another chance, I didn't mean at being my best friend. Ringing me every five minutes wasn't part of the deal. What do you want now?"

"Pipe down, Wayne. I've just found Jason's grass for him." Ryan was on a confident high.

"Really, I thought it was you."

"I've been keeping tabs on Carl since I got back to Manchester. I've just followed him through town. A white van was waiting, with two cops sitting in the front. They stuck out like sore thumbs. The side door opened and Carl got in. He was in there for about twenty minutes. Who'd have thought it?"

As much as he tried, Ryan found it difficult to hide the joy of coming up with the goods and redeeming himself. He felt smug and was enjoying the moment.

"You sure they were cops? Did you get the reg number of the van?"

"Yes, to both. Photos on my phone too."

"Jeez, Ryan, you might redeem yourself yet. Then again, Jason's looking at a long stretch for trying to dispose of you, so maybe not. Leave it with me. And keep your mouth shut. Text me the registration number. I'll get straight onto Frank Burton and task him with making some enquires on the van."

Ryan had an idea where he would find Carl. He made his way to the boozer on Portland Street. But when he walked in and had a quick look around, there was no sign of his former friend. Ryan left and walked the short distance to the next pub. This time, as soon as he walked in he spotted Carl sitting at the bar.

"It must be your round, Carl. Last time we were out together you set me up to get shot."

"For the record, Ryan, I didn't have a clue about what was happening. Jason told me to get the stuff back from you, search the van and get you back to Manchester," Carl said. He ordered two beers and passed one over to Ryan.

"Sure. You're a true friend. So, what you been up to?" Ryan asked.

"I've only just got here. I got a taxi into town." Ryan sensed that Carl wasn't his laid back self. He looked rattled like a condemned man.

"No business on today?"

"Day off, I need to take it easy. The cops are giving us a good looking at."

Nice one, pal, so you don't want to tell me about your friends in the white van, thought Ryan, *keep digging, Carl, keep digging, son.* Ryan knew he just had to bide his time and Carl would get what was coming to him. He was seeing Carl in a different light already. What he had perceived as getting on well with him, was actually Carl working him as a decoy to keep suspicion away from himself.

"All this unwanted attention from the cops means someone is stoking their fires," Ryan said. "It makes you wonder who the grass is. It's not me, so who is it? You got any ideas Carl?"

"It's got to be someone down the chain. We'll flush them out. We've just got to be careful."

Very true, you need to be extremely careful Carl, Ryan gloated to himself.

Chapter Twenty

Wayne arranged a meeting with his associates in Liverpool. He would only work with people within his network. People he knew, and more importantly, people who feared him and would be unlikely to betray him. Not some unknown assassin. Jason's blunder had proven how that could shake out.

The meeting went well. The scousers knew just the man for the job. He had a good reputation and was trusted, having been the gun for hire for a few of the recent shootings around Merseyside. His track record proved that he was definitely not an undercover cop.

Jason's request would be carried out soon, properly this time.

A few days later, Wayne met up with Carl to sort out some routine business.

"Jason's been in touch," Wayne said. "He wants Ryan punished, then we can move on from this mess."

"I'm surprised it's not happened already. Ryan must know it's coming. You happy he's not the grass? I still have my doubts. We know he's reckless."

"I can't rule it out, which is worrying."

You snake in the grass, Carl. You know damn well who the grass is. Wayne mused.

"There's a plan in place. Tomorrow morning you are going to take Ryan to one of our dealers, on the pretext of collecting some cash takings. Make sure he goes to the usual place, then leave. It won't be pretty."

The following day, Ryan was chilling at home when his phone started to ring. It was Wayne.

"Morning, Wayne."

"Looks like you're right, Ryan. Our enquiries confirm you made the right call. Burton's bent cop has confirmed a few points for us. I've set things in place to smoke him out. You're going to get a call from Carl in a bit, so go along with what he wants. All will be revealed. Don't fuck it up, Ryan," Wayne said, and ended the call.

No sooner had he finished talking to Wayne than his mobile rang again. Sure enough, it was Carl.

"We've got a job on. Where are you? Carl said.

"I'm still at the flat."

"Okay, I'll pick you up in half an hour."

"What are we doing?"

"Just a pick up for Wayne, it's all hands on deck, mate. See you shortly."

Ryan was waiting outside his flat when Carl arrived. He got in, feeling tense. His best hand had been played, but Ryan knew how things panned out in this game. Was he being taken for a punishment beating, or was that on hold for now? Had Carl jumped the punishment queue ahead of him? He doubted it. Wayne was meticulous and would be making further checks on Carl before jumping to conclusions. Carl seemed like his normal self. There was no weirdness between them.

"It's the usual score," Carl told him. "I'll park at the end of the street. You walk down towards the shops and the courier will hand you the package. Walk through the park and I'll pick you up on the other side."

It sounded simple, yet Ryan felt vulnerable. He wondered if Carl had set him up with the cops, to be caught in possession of drugs in the park. Although the punishment beating still seemed more likely. Jason could be harsh but that didn't make him a fool. Surely, he must know that Ryan would be of better use to them as part of the firm with a debt to pay than locked up for possession with intent to supply.

"Mate, if I'm going for a kicking, at least tell me. Then I can take some gear to numb the pain."

"Not my call, Ryan. I know nothing about all that. It's down to Jason and Wayne. You know the score. This is just business as usual. Wayne can't do it all on his own."

"Just saying, you do owe me one. Last time you took me on a job I was being set up to be shot."

"Fuck off, Ryan. I'm sick of your victim sketch. You played with fire and got your fingers burned. I didn't have a clue what was going down. I thought I was taking you back to Manchester."

The tension between them went up a notch. Things were different now. Their trust in each other was at an all-time low.

A short while later Carl pulled the car up to the kerb. Ryan got out and started walking down the street. It was a picture of poverty. The majority of houses were boarded up with rusted metal sheeting, and those that weren't still looked to be in a shit state.

After a few minutes he reached the end of an alley near to the shops. Only the off-licence had survived. It looked like Fort Knox with all the iron bars over the doors and windows. It didn't have cctv cameras, if it did have them they would be nicked.

This wasn't right. The courier on the BMX bike was usually slick and on time. As he thought this, Ryan heard a motorcycle being revved at top notch. It appeared at the opposite end of the street from under the railway bridge. It was two up and speeding up the road towards him. Ryan looked back towards the car. It was still there. Carl was still sitting there. It was a set up. He sensed something wasn't right.

Ryan knew he had no time to run. He stepped further back into the alleyway and bent down, making himself as small a target as possible behind a bin. To his amazement and relief, the motorbike sped past him, just as he was about to roll onto the floor in a token attempt to avoid being shot. He started walking back towards the car, wondering what the hell was happening.

He didn't have long to think it through.

The motorbike stopped alongside Carl's car. Four gun shots rang out, along with the sound of breaking glass. As soon as the gunfire stopped, the passenger jumped off the bike and leant into the car. No doubt he was searching through Carl's pockets. Within moments he jumped back on the bike and off they went.

Every man for himself, thought Ryan. He pulled his hoodie over his head and got on his toes. As it happened, he knew this housing estate well. The back entries provided a labyrinth of rabbit runs, perfect for evading the cops. He was long gone before the police and ambulance turned up.

So, it was Carl, and he's paid the price. I need to get away from all this, and I mean well away. It's all going mental.

DI Statham was in her office when the call came through. She grabbed her coat and walked into the main office.

"Pete, we've got a job on. A shooting at Hulme. One dead, two offenders on a motorbike. Looks like a gangland feud." They made their way to the scene.

DS Higgs parked the car close to the police incident tape that cordoned off the crime scene. They saw the Crime Scene Manager at the back of her van. She too had just arrived.

"Helen, how you doing?" DI Statham asked.

"Too busy, could have done without this. It's like Gunchester is rearing its ugly head again. Looks like another gang shooting."

She handed the DI her forensic suit, gloves and mask, and they both got ready to enter the scene. The PC on the cordon logged them in.

"Did the paramedics pronounce life extinct?" DI Statham asked.

"Yes, looking at the poor sod, I don't think they were in any doubt."

DI Statham and Helen the CSM approached the car. The driver-side door was open, giving a clear view of the male sitting behind the wheel. He was indeed clearly dead. He had bled from the side of his head and chest. Leaning into the passenger seat, supported only by the seat belt. Smashed windscreen glass was everywhere.

"No problem with an identification," Andrea sighed. "That's Carl Smith, one of Hamilton's boys."

"Never heard of him," Helen replied.

"This lot are keeping us busy at the minute. Hamilton is inside, so it's probably a rival gang fancying their chances whilst he's out of the way."

They agreed a forensic strategy for the examination of the scene and DI Statham made her way back to DS Higgs, who she could see was talking to the uniform Inspector.

He approached DI Statham and said, "The uniform guys reckon the victim was Carl Smith. They've completed the initial house to house. There are no witnesses and no cctv in the vicinity, nothing. The informant number was withheld."

"Yes, they're right about the ID. It looks like our team will pick up the case because of the potential links. A rival gang is a possibility. Let's get back to the nick and brief the team."

"I could do with getting a kebab on the way back, I've not eaten yet," DS Higgs said.

"You're a bad influence on me, Pete. I only eat salad when I'm not with you."

Andrea's protest wasn't much of a show. They stopped off and bought two kebabs just as Pete suggested. They tucked into them in the car outside the takeaway.

"I had an interesting chat with the uniform Inspector back there," Pete said. "Turns out he's known Carl Smith for years. Smith had previous convictions for burglary and thieving, but he was surprised when I mentioned his drug dealing. The Inspector said Carl Smith despises druggies and dealers. Apparently, his girlfriend from years ago got hooked and died from a heroin overdose."

"What's all that about then? Something doesn't add up."

"I've got the fast-track actions being looked at by the teams. I'll run you through them when we get back."

"We might get the bullets back and there were cartridges on the floor, so hopefully we may get something from the firearms comparison data base. It looks like a classic drive-by shooting. The residents around there are either scared of the ramifications of speaking to us, or drug users in fear of their dealers. We might pick up something with a wider cctv trawl though, maybe the vehicle involved."

"It might even be linked to the canal shooting," suggested Pete. He looked down and saw chilli sauce had dripped down his tie. *Another tie ruined, expensive kebab that one.*

"I'd be surprised if it's not linked, it will all come together for us this."

As DI Statham and DS Higgs arrived back at the police station, Ryan arrived back at his flat. He made a coffee then selected Wayne from the contacts on his burner phone.

"You had a busy morning, Ryan?"

"Mate, it's a nightmare. When I saw the motorbike, I thought they were coming for me. Or did they get the wrong target?"

"I'll pick you up at the end of your road in half an hour," Wayne said, ignoring his last comment.

Ryan finished his coffee. He'd managed to stay off the coke for over two weeks now and felt better for it. For one thing, he was able to think straight. He knew he wanted to get his act together. He knew he'd gone into self-destruct mode again through his hedonistic behaviour. But he also knew that he'd been lucky and had come out at the other end. Pissing Jason off had nearly cost him his life. But now Jason was doing time inside and Ryan was partly to blame, at least in Jason's eyes. On top of all that, Carl was dead. Ryan had definitely played a part in that.

His efforts to look after the care home boys were producing results too. As a result of his anonymous tip offs, security at the home had been heightened. A predatory paedophile who preyed upon the younger lads at the home had been arrested and three of the county lines dealers had been relocated to a quieter backwater care home, in attempt to remove them from the danger.

Time to get out of this mess and make a new start. Ryan was developing a new positive and smarter mindset.

He left the flat and walked to the end of the street. He didn't have long to wait before Wayne pulled over.

"I didn't want to talk on the phone," Wayne said, as Ryan jumped into the car. "We don't know how much damage Carl has done to us with his grassing. I think we'll be getting some heavy attention from the cops after this."

"Was Carl done on Jason's say so?" Ryan asked.

"Yes, there was no doubt he was grassing. Frank Burton's man on the inside confirmed it. I didn't see Carl as a grass, but that's this game for you. Trust is a risky business."

"Where do we go from here?"

"You've got a massive debt to pay off, Ryan. You're lucky not to be keeping Carl's company pushing up the daises, but I think you know that. In your favour, Jason doesn't think you'd have taken his legs. Whilst he's inside I'll steady the ship, but you'll need to up your game. Are you still on the coke?"

"No, I've been off it for more than two weeks now, I'm off it for good."

"Yeah, of course you are Ryan," Wayne laughed. "Enough of that, we've got things to do and people to see. I'm going to need you with me for the next few days, and we need eyes in the backs of our heads watching out for the cops. Here, I've got you a new burner phone. Give me your old one."

Ryan did as he was told.

"Is this the one you had with you when Carl got shot?" Wayne asked.

"Yes, just that one."

"Just in case things escalate, give your flat a good search. Get rid of any old phones and stuff that might be incriminating."

They had circled the estate a couple of times. Wayne dropped Ryan off near to his flat before making his way into the city to meet a few of his boys. Ryan knew that he would get rid of the SIM cards and burner phones. It seemed he really was back in the fold, whether he wanted to be or not.

Chapter Twenty One

DI Statham and DC Higgs were back at the office. They had briefed the team of detectives, who were now out pursuing their allocated lines of enquires. There was a knock at the door.

"You got a minute boss?" asked the intelligence officer.

"Yes, come in, grab a seat. Good timing, I wanted to sit down with you to review our intelligence strategy," DI Statham said.

"We've just received some interesting intel. It appears there was a dispute between Wayne Davies and the deceased Carl Smith. Basically, the deceased was accused of grassing in relation to the contract kill which was set up by Hamilton." She handed the intelligence report log to the DI.

"Right, we'll move on that one pretty quick I think. It's very credible. Let's get Wayne Davies brought in and arrange for a prison visit to interview Hamilton. Can you also produce a package into rival drug gangs and disputes?"

"Yes, I'm on with that, it's nearly done."

DI Statham's mobile rang. She knew this was just the start. Everyone would want a piece of her over the next two days or so. There would be hard work and long days ahead.

"Hi, pal," the caller said. "It's Harry from the Informants Unit. I need to speak fairly urgently, are you free to come across?"

"Yes, I'll be with you in the next half hour. I've not had a chance for a coffee yet, so stick the kettle on."

Before heading out, DI Statham checked through the main lines of enquiry with DS Higgs. Both felt confident that all priorities were being investigated.

They made their way to the next meeting at the Informants Unit.

DI Harry Roberts answered the door and directed them to his office.

"Sorry but I'll need you to sign the usual confidentiality agreements," DI Roberts said.

Both DS Higgs and DI Statham scan-read the forms and signed them.

"I need to put you in the picture about Carl Smith. He was a registered covert human intelligence source with us."

"That last intelligence log makes a lot more sense now," DI Statham said.

"Obviously his death will have massive implications for our unit because of our duty of care to him. Internal affairs have been onto me already and we are being referred to the Independent Police Complaints Authority. I'm confident our risk assessments are watertight, but it doesn't help the poor bastard now I suppose. Still, it will keep the wolves from our door. I've got a package of relevant intelligence logs for you. It was decided by Force Command at a Gold Meeting today that full access would be given to you and DI Dave Ferguson for your respective investigations."

DI Statham took the package.

"We're arresting Wayne Davies and Jason Hamilton in relation to the intelligence, so we're on to it already. I'll keep you up to speed."

"Thank you. Give me a call if we can be of any further assistance. I want to help you to nail the bastard who did this."

DI Statham and DS Higgs left his office.

"He gave us a pile of paper and didn't even offer us a coffee!" DI Statham said.

"I'll let him off this time. His plate is full and all the vultures are circling over him. He looks like a man under a lot of pressure. He'll probably be moved back to uniform pretty soon. The top brass do like a scapegoat."

Wayne left his meeting and began the walk back to his car. He was more than happy. Business was still running smoothly, despite Jason's arrest. The fear factor amongst the dealers had been reset to a high level. The word was out about Carl's demise. It provided a good wakeup call about the risks of grassing. It was time for anyone who thought Jason was out of sight and out of mind, to reconsider their naivety. He showed his ruthlessness and power, even from within a prison cell.

Wayne got into his car and set off for home.

A short time later he turned into the parking area of his flat. Immediately he sensed something was wrong. Too many unknown cars were parked up, most of them occupied. Wayne wasn't fazed. It was not what he had wanted, but it was what he had expected to happen sooner or later.

As soon as he got out of his car, he was approached by four plain-clothes cops. Wayne was unconcerned. He knew that the next few days would be more of a hindrance rather than an actual problem. He was confident the police had nothing on him.

He recognised two of cops as local CID. The first one stepped towards him.

"You're under arrest on suspicion of the murder of Carl Smith." The caution followed, which Wayne could recite word for word anyway. A pair of handcuffs was placed onto his wrists and he was patted down by one of the cops, who took his mobile phone and wallet. *Unlucky boys, the phone you wanted is at the bottom of the River Irwell*, thought Wayne.

He was taken to the police station and booked in by the custody sergeant. Once in his cell, he made himself comfortable on the thin mattress and closed his eyes. It was time for a kip. He hated the smell of cells. Yet he fell asleep despite the banging doors, the shouting and the obvious lack of heat.

Wayne was awoken by the noise of the cell door being opened. A uniform cop informed him that his solicitor had arrived. Wayne followed him to the consultation room.

Frank Burton looked at home in his surroundings.

"Sorry for the delay, Wayne," he said. "I got here as soon as I could."

"I need to get out soonest. Things to do, people to see. Can we get on with the interviews? I've nothing to do with Carl's death. It was probably down to rival gangs."

"Of course, I'll do my best. We'll be given their disclosure shortly. If there is nothing of interest we'll press on with the interviews. 'No comment' will suffice at this stage. They've searched your flat and found nothing."

Burton pressed the button by the door and a Detective appeared at the cell door.

"We're ready for disclosure when you are."

"We are good to go, so let's go straight through," the detective said.

The scant disclosure explaining the suspicions of the police didn't worry Burton or Wayne. *No evidence whatsoever was mentioned, no witnesses mentioned, no CCTV. It was probably all based on intelligence*, thought Wayne. The disclosure referred to associations between Carl, Ryan, Jason and Wayne, as well as Intelligence on drug dealing, and suggestion of a dispute between Carl and Wayne.

After the introductions and the caution, the questions began.

"Do you know Carl Smith?"

"No comment."

"Do you know Jason Hamilton?"

"No comment."

"Have you been in dispute with either of these people?"

"No comment."

Further questions followed, but Wayne made no comment throughout the interviews, which continued through the day and into early evening. They were concluded around eight hours, later after which Wayne was given police bail and released from the station. At this point Wayne considered the process to be an occupational hazard. He had things to be getting on with. Jason could still assist by using his influence from the inside, but the graft was now down to Wayne and his prodigal sidekick, Ryan.

"Jump in the car. I'll give you a lift home," Burton said.

They both got into Burton's sports car.

"Is this car what they call a mid-life crisis?" Wayne laughed.

"You can always walk, Wayne," Burton said dryly. "Anyway, how's business doing? Anything that Jason needs to know?"

"Same old, really. Dirk has been in touch about the next shipment. Same route as the last one through Felixstowe. We had no issues whatsoever. That's now on the streets. He wants me to go over. I got the impression it was a bit of 'The king is dead, long live the king'. And he mentioned meeting the Columbian again, but I won't get excited. He didn't show up last time."

"I've got my boy on the inside working hard. Poor bastard wishes he'd never met us."

"How did you turn him?" Wayne asked, out of curiosity. *Probably tell me it's none of my business.*

"Usual things. His gambling debts were building; living beyond his means, he was in danger of his house being repossessed and he befriended the wrong people, namely my clients. Now he's up to his neck in it with us we have him over a barrel."

Wayne winced. *Crazy bastard, that's never going to end well.* "The cops sounded me out for grassing on Jason. They said his empire was about to come crashing down and I needed to think about my own self-preservation. They must be struggling to get any evidence. I told them they couldn't afford my witness protection bill."

Burton dropped Wayne off in town. He went for a beer and takeaway on his way home, as if nothing significant had happened today.

Chapter Twenty Two

DI Statham and DS Higgs had just completed a debriefing with their staff. It had been a long day, with not much in the way of results to show for it. The main office had an eerie silence about it, contrasting with the busy hub it had been for the last few hours. The team had been stood down, ready to return refreshed in the morning. DI Statham glanced over towards DS Higgs, who looked knackered. She wasn't surprised. He was a grafter. He needed to lose a bit of weight as well. She couldn't help but worry about him.

It made her feel a little better to think that Pete would be loving the overtime. He had a big mortgage, a wife, and two kids to look after, in addition to his growing collection of motorbikes.

"Not much from the interviews today," Pete said. "Both made 'no comment'. Jason Hamilton is on technical bail and Wayne Davies is on police bail. The Section 18, PACE search at Wayne Davies's house was negative too. His flat was spotless. We took a mobile off him, but it looks like a new burner phone, nice and clean. The informant unit team had a word with him about turning on Hamilton. They'd have been better saving their petrol."

"The rival gangs line of enquiry isn't coming up trumps either," DI Statham said. "But there's time yet. It's in their interests to keep Jason Hamilton and Wayne Davies inside for good. It's looking like their rivals might be our best chance at the moment."

"We need a stroke of luck from somewhere. No witnesses or cctv. The search was negative. I'm not holding much hope for the forensics at the scene. It's going to be a long haul I think."

“Maybe for now, but I think an approach to Hamilton might be worth a shot. At least once he’s resigned to a long stretch. Stranger things have happened, you know. If it takes years off his sentence he might be tempted.”

“Big call though. His suppliers would hunt him down no matter how good he was at hide and seek. Still, I see your point. Nothing ventured, nothing gained.”

“Let’s look at this again, from the beginning. Hamilton has a confrontation with Smethurst and comes off best. He then has a dispute with Ryan Young and puts out a contract on him, which results in him ending up in prison. Somehow, he is made aware that Carl Smith is grassing and Smith gets shot, leaving Wayne Davies and Ryan Young to run their drugs dealing operations.”

“And his partner Kirsty. I wonder where her loyalties are now. Must be worth another visit to her at some stage. Bad time at the office for Hamilton and a mountain to climb for us in getting the evidence. At least he’s inside for the contract kill.”

“Let’s knock off. Fancy a quick drink before we go home?”

“Very kind of you,” Pete said. He switched the lights off as they left.

Ryan had been at the gym for most of the afternoon. Part of his new health regime. He got home about 6pm and put the kettle on to make a coffee. He’d been doing a lot of thinking and had decided that it was time to make a call. A call he had been wanting to make for a couple of weeks now. It felt like the right time to do it.

He grabbed his mobile and scrolled through the contacts.

The phone was ringing out. He was just about to hang up when it was answered.

"Hello," Kirsty said.

"Hi, Kirsty, it's Ryan. I've got a new phone. Listen, I really need to meet up for a chat. Do you fancy a coffee or a beer or something to eat?"

"Hmm, that's an offer I can refuse. Don't think so, Ryan."

"I don't blame you for saying that. But hear me out. I've been off the booze and charlie for a good few weeks now. I'm loving being clean. My life is back on track for the first time in years. It feels good. There's been lots going on. I really need to talk to you."

"Not that I believe you, Ryan, but I'll meet up. Purely out of curiosity, so it had better be good. And don't bother booking a hotel room, because it's not happening."

Ryan laughed, "That's a shame. Shall we meet for a coffee on Portland Street? Then we can have a Chinese buffet for lunch."

He knew that would seal the deal.

"Okay, see you there tomorrow, about one o'clock."

Ryan felt excited. His mind had not been as clear as this in years. He had a vision of what he wanted. Hopefully this was the start of a new life. He had told Lisa that he couldn't get down to Bristol for a while. He was hedging his bets in case plan A failed.

He went to get a shower.

The next day Ryan arrived early at the coffee shop. He was apprehensive and excited at the same time.

The shop was about half-full of customers. They were mostly office worker types, sitting at laptops or tablets. He felt at home here, like it was part of his new way of life.

He went to the counter and was served by a woman who looked to be in her early twenties. She seemed friendly and welcoming, actually interested in what she was doing. Ryan indulged in a quick fantasy about being on the other side of the counter, maybe in a chic cafe in Spain, starting a new life. He avoided the array of cake and biscuits.

Once his Americano arrived, he found a comfy-looking sofa in the corner. He sat down and took his first sip of coffee. He was getting to the bottom of the cup when he saw Kirsty walk in, dressed all in black, with her blonde hair up in a pony tail.

Kirsty approached the table. Ryan noticed she didn't seem as confident as usual. She came over as a bit awkward, as a matter of fact.

"Hiya, Ryan, you ready for another?"

"Thanks for coming, Kirsty. It's great to see you. I'll have another Americano please."

He watched her walk to the counter. *Which way is this going to go?* he wondered. Kirsty returned with two drinks. She took off her coat and slung it over the back of the chair.

"I'm ready for this. I've just got back from the gym. What have you been up to?"

"Having an epiphany," Ryan said. They both burst out laughing. If there was any tension, it was slowly dissipating. "Seriously, I'm off the charlie, off the beer, and training hard. I've never felt better. It's taken me a while to get here and I'm not going back. I feel liberated. It took a near-death experience to knock me into shape."

"That's great to hear. I'm really happy for you. I can see it, too. You've got your Mojo back. Good for you."

"The next thing is to get out of the firm and move on to a normal life. I tried before but just failed miserably and created a shit-storm, so I'm not messing it up this time. It's all changed for the worst. I've always been bottom of the food chain, the cops are all over us and Carl's dead. Jason's inside and I've pissed him off good style. He probably still wants a piece of me, but at least he knows Carl was the real grass."

Ryan couldn't be sure, but he thought Kirsty's eyes gave away some warmth towards him and his new plan.

"I'm right behind you. It all sounds like the right thing to do. I wish I could move on. I've been living with my mum and dad since he went inside. The house is for sale and it should go quick. I've put it on the market at a realistic price.

"I've been on at Jason for years now to go legit. He's got the money to move on, but I'm beginning to wonder if he enjoys it too much."

All Ryan really heard were the words 'I wish I could move on'. *I might be in with a chance yet.* He drained the last of his coffee and sat back into the sofa.

"I asked to meet up with you for a reason. It's either a chance to have a nice lunch and say goodbye before I move on, or my last chance to ask you to get back together with me. We can both move away and start a new life together."

He almost spat the words out, as if he couldn't say them fast enough. He felt relieved that he had asked her. His proposal was now in the open. It was out of his hands now. It was down to Kirsty to decide.

"You don't do anything by halves do you, Ryan? Have you considered Jason's position in this plan?" Kirsty laughed.

"Well your laughter hasn't filled me with hope, but what do you think? You know we are good together, think back to our night at your house. How right did that feel?"

"My initial thought is that you must be mad, you've just dug yourself out of a right mess and you're going to risk creating yourself a bigger problem."

"I know, what you're saying is spot on, but that night at your house left me in no doubt at all. We are great together and we should be together. I've never stopped loving you Kirsty. If you feel the same, which I think you do, you've got to consider it."

"If only it was so simple Ryan, unless you've forgotten, I happen to be in a relationship with Jason. We would be putting our lives at risk. Are you not better just moving on for a fresh start, you'd meet someone else who wasn't in a relationship with a psycho wanting to kill you." Kirsty's words had a sobering impact on Ryan. *Maybe she's right, but she certainly doesn't sound interested either way.*

Ryan felt he'd given his pitch and he didn't want to labour it. All he could do now was hope that Kirsty felt the same, however unlikely that felt at the moment. They left the café and walked into China Town. Ryan had already accepted today was probably now about a goodbye lunch.

As they entered the restaurant Ryan felt relaxed. He'd been here many times. It had a modern décor of white walls and mirrors, quite minimalistic, unlike the traditional type of Chinese restaurant. They were seated at a table and ordered drinks.

"I'm glad you asked to meet up. You've spoken a lot of sense. It's good that you want to leave it behind you. I'm pleased for you."

The drinks arrived at the table. Ryan noticed that Kirsty took a big glug of her prosecco before she continued.

"Since the break-in at the house it's all got out of hand. You and Jason fell out, and then he tried to get you killed, now he's in prison. And now Carl has been shot dead. It's worse than a nightmare. I didn't sign up for this," Kirsty said.

"I suppose I've just gone with the flow since the Warrington days. It was better then, but watching you hook up with Jason was very hard."

"Yes, well, we've both done a lot of growing up since then. Maybe we're all a bit wiser too."

"Everything just happened. But it's all too violent these days. Even the care home kids are being dragged into it, to deal for him. It's like life means nothing. It's cheap and easy to get somebody killed over nothing."

"Unless you're Jason and you ask a cop to do it," Kirsty said, with mock disdain.

"Ouch, a bit harsh," laughed Ryan.

"He's really pissed me off, you know. I was worried sick when I overhead him talking about hitmen with Lee. This should all have been left behind us a few years ago. I can't believe he was happy to have you shot. Surely it could have been sorted. And to top it all I'm racked with guilt when I should feel justified being angry with him."

Kirsty went quiet, as if she had said too much.

"There's no need for you to feel guilty. You've done nothing wrong," Ryan said.

"I wish that was the case. I was the first to meet Lee at the gym. I liked him and thought he'd be a good mate for Jason and a good influence on him. It was me who told him that Jason was at the arches on the night they met. I helped him to befriend Jason."

"Don't beat yourself up over that. He deceived you. He's trained to do just that, no one saw it coming. He looked like the real deal, not an undercover cop. Anyway, Carl was grassing, so it was going to happen sooner or later. I reckon the stuff we lost to customs at Liverpool was down to Carl."

"It gets worse though. I overheard Lee and Samantha talking at the gym. Something wasn't right about it. It wasn't like a couple talking. They were talking about Jason like he was a target or something. I could have alerted Jason then, but I didn't. I knew something wasn't right about them. I should have worked it out. I should have warned Jason. Then Jason, Carl and Wayne were talking about you. I sensed trouble. I'd had a few drinks and confided in Lee. I should have known better, but I thought he'd calm things down a bit and talk some sense into Jason. Jason was asking if Lee knew any hit-men. I told Lee he couldn't let it happen. The crucial moment was when he said something like, 'Don't worry, I won't let it happen, you've got to trust me.' In hindsight that was a policeman talking to me. It wasn't Carl who introduced Lee to Jason, it was me. And I should have warned him about what I'd heard."

Ryan was concerned for her. She looked really cut up about it all, but probably better for talking about it to him.

"I've got a part to play in creating the shit-storm, as you call it," Kirsty went on. "I feel guilty, angry, and fucked up by it all. My head's all over the place. He won't even let me visit him in prison to talk."

Ryan held his hands out across the table to her. She took hold of them and said, "What a mess."

"You really shouldn't be beating yourself up. None of that is your fault. You had good intentions and got caught up in a situation that you shouldn't have been exposed to."

The food arrived with perfect timing. It was a good place to have a pause in the conversation.

Ryan's thoughts were racing whilst he ate his meal. If Kirsty was right, should Carl have been shot? Even so, he was still grassing. He may have put the undercovers onto Kirsty at the gym in the first place. None of this made sense to him, which was all the more reason to get away from it all.

His mind took off in a different direction. His future chances were looking good. He hadn't expected Kirsty to be in this state of mind. He just needed to be patient. Feeling sorry for Kirsty only made him want her more, to be able to look after her and to give them a great life together, away from all this shit.

They finished the meal, passed on the coffee and left the restaurant. Neither said much on their walk to the car park. Enough had been said already. Now it was time to think it over.

After Kirsty had gone her own way, Ryan returned to his flat.

Kirsty awoke earlier than usual. Her mind was running through the conversation with Ryan. She felt all over the place. This was what it felt like to be in love with two men. She had history with and loyalty to both. With one she was trapped in a world of crime and danger, the police hovering like hawks. He was also in prison and not allowing her to visit him. He made her feel angry, frustrated and guilty at the same time.

The other man was her first love from the same world, who wanted to start afresh and leave the crime behind him. Most importantly, he wanted her to join him in leaving this mess behind. She was finding it difficult to make the choice. If she went with Ryan, she expected trouble with a capital T from Jason. His relationship with Ryan was already broken and this would be the final kick in the bollocks.

Kirsty picked up her mobile phone and selected Ryan from the contacts. She waited a moment and put the phone down beside her. She walked to the kitchen to make a coffee. She needed to let her subconscious work on this one. With time the answer would become clear. She knew where her heart wanted to be, but life wasn't that easy.

She took her coffee back to the sofa and sat down. The caffeine was good for her. She picked up her phone and made the call.

"Morning, Kirsty. How are you? I know it can't be easy for you. Is there anything you need?" Burton asked.

"I need to see Jason. I've not spoken one word to him for weeks now, unless it's a message via yourself. Can you arrange a visit for me?"

"Kirsty, my sympathy is with you, but you've got to understand Jason's position. He doesn't want you to see him caged up. To survive in there, he needs to be fully focused and in the right mindset. It really is dog eat dog, survival of the fittest and all the rest. He can’t afford the distraction and emotional impact of seeing you. He fears it will weaken him. That’s why he has asked me to look after your interests.”

“I understand all that. But just one visit, is that too much to ask?”

“I will ask the question again, but I honestly can’t see him changing his mind. Leave it with me.”

Kirsty ended the call and finished off her coffee.

Chapter Twenty Three

Whilst Kirsty was trying to make sense of her thoughts and emotions, DI Statham and DS Higgs were back in the office. They had only been away from it for six hours, but felt refreshed for it. The detective teams were out progressing their enquiries. It was very early days but nothing of significance had come to light.

"The intelligence work on rival gangs isn't producing much. Nobody wants to risk grassing and there are no flash points which may have resulted in this," Pete said.

"That points us back to the internal dispute. We know he was an informant and that they suspected it too. They might even have known for definite if there was a leak on the police side. From reading the intelligence logs of his disclosures, he only seemed to be grassing on rival gangs. He provided information which helped customs to seize some drugs at the Port of Liverpool. The information he gave on Hamilton was just lifestyle and associations, nothing of any evidential value."

"It helped Covert Operations to infiltrate Hamilton. Probably he was just giving the handlers information for his own ends. Maybe even with the bigger objective of getting more info from them and putting a cop in his pocket."

"Apparently his motivation for grassing was revenge for his girlfriend dying of an overdose. She had a good job and was in a good place until she succumbed to Hamilton's dealers." Andrea said. "A sort of payback I guess, which makes sense of what the uniform Inspector said at the scene. We can leave the bent cops enquiries to internal affairs and the anti-corruption unit. If it's right I hope they nail the bastard. We have got to approach Wayne Davies and Ryan Young about coming across to us."

"Agreed, but I'm not holding any hopes. Jason Hamilton and Wayne Davies must have an idea we haven't got much evidence on them. We are way off the charging threshold."

"Start the ball rolling, Pete. Remember, nothing ventured, nothing gained."

"Okay, I'll speak with the informant handling unit. Those two are answering their bail next week, so I'll aim to do it then."

Kirsty was on the running machine at the gym. She had struggled to motivate herself to get off the sofa, but knew she would feel better for it afterwards. She saw her phone activate on the control consul of the treadmill. It was Frank Burton.

She pressed the red stop button on the runner and the running belt came to a halt.

"Hiya, Frank. Cheers, you've just got me out of some exercise. I was struggling there!"

"Glad to hear it. I'm here to assist. I've spoken to Jason. It's a no go I'm afraid, but I did expect that answer. Just give him some time. I'm sure we can sort something later on. He's got a lot on his plate at the moment."

"And does he just expect me to carry on as if everything's normal?"

"He wants you to do your own thing and put him to the back of your mind for now. Why don't you book a holiday, get some sun and take some time out?"

If only you knew who I was thinking about taking a long holiday with, thought Kirsty.

"Okay, well thanks for asking him, Frank. I might just book a holiday, good thinking."

She couldn't put the other call off any longer, it wasn't fair. She selected Ryan's number.

"Hi, Kirsty, how're you doing?"

She could tell by his voice that he was anxiously awaiting her decision.

"Ryan, I need to take a break. I'm going to book some last minute sun and think things through. I need to get this one right."

"I'll come with you. I can give you some space whilst we're away. It will do us both a world of good," he sounded desperate.

"I'm really tempted and it would be good, but I just need some space. I'll see you when I get back. You can buy me another Chinese."

"No worries, I understand. Enjoy your break. Give me a bell if you fancy a chat."

She hung up the phone, suspecting that Ryan would take this as a knock-back. It was how he worked. He wasn't patient. But he should also know how her mind worked by now. She wasn't one for making rash decisions. Apart from getting this holiday booked.

Two weeks had passed since Ryan had last spoken to Kirsty. It was now time for him to answer his bail. It didn't cause him much concern. He suspected the cops didn't have any evidence on him. He was more concerned about Kirsty's decision. She would be back any day now, with an answer he hoped. He got a taxi to the police station, confident that he wouldn't be there long. He hadn't even bothered to get a solicitor. If needs be he could use the duty solicitor.

Ryan arrived at the police station reception and approached the enquiry counter. A middle-aged woman, who looked tired and stressed, raised enough enthusiasm to say hello. Ryan informed her he was here to answer his bail. As requested, he took a seat and looked around him. It was a soulless place in need of some TLC.

A door opened and a young Detective held it open.

"Ryan Young, follow me please," the detective said. Ryan stood up and followed him along a corridor and into the custody suite.

DS Higgs was standing at a desk. The custody sergeant went through the booking-in procedure and informed Ryan that he would be going straight through for interview. DS Higgs beckoned him to follow and they walked the short distance to the interview room, followed by the young detective constable. They each took a seat, all familiar with the routine and expectations.

Following the introductions, offers of free independent legal advice and the caution, DS Higgs began, "Ryan, as you are aware, Jason Hamilton is in custody at Strangeways. He has entered a guilty plea at the case preparation hearing. He knows he's banged to rights. He is likely to receive a substantial custodial sentence for conspiring to have you murdered." DS Higgs paused to let his words sink in. "We know you are part of his organised crime group and play an active part in the unlawful supply of controlled drugs."

"Well, charge me then," Ryan challenged. He started to laugh. "But that would be difficult for you I suppose, because you don't have any evidence against me."

"Yet," DS Higgs retorted. "We are still building a case and we are not going away any time soon."

After a pause, DS Higgs questioned Ryan further about his activities and associations with Jason, Carl and Wayne. Ryan answered 'no comment' to all of the questions. He knew when to answer and when to keep his mouth shut. He also suspected that the cops hadn't gathered any further evidence since the last time he was interviewed.

The interview was terminated. The three of them started to stand and walk to the door. DS Higgs stopped, blocking the way of the others. "Ryan, I know you will not give evidence at Hamilton's trial, but to be honest it won't weaken our case. He's banged to rights," DS Higgs said again.

"All good then," Ryan replied. "Everyone's happy."

"But you need to give some thought to coming across with evidence about his drug dealing business. We know he's involved in the shooting of Paul Smethurst on the canal and the Carl Smith murder. It's over for Hamilton, his days are numbered, and you know that. Someone else will move in and take over. Whose saying he still doesn't want to have you killed? It's time for every man to look after his own interests. It's a shame that Carl Smith didn't talk to us. He may still be alive if he had, eh?"

"From what I've heard he was always talking to you... and that's why he's now dead. Can I go now?"

"Think it over, pal, it makes sense. Look after number one. Witness protection is pretty good these days."

DS Higgs handed him a business card with contact details.

"Give me a call when you realise it's your best option."

They returned to the custody office where the custody sergeant told Ryan he was free to leave.

"You're not putting me on bail? Jeez, you are struggling, fellas. Good luck with your enquires, it sounds like you need it," Ryan said, as he was shown back into the reception area exit.

DS Higgs made his way straight to DI Statham's office.

"How did the interview go?" she asked.

"As expected. He knows we haven't got much on him. I touched on the suggestion of him grassing but I can't see it happening. I mentioned both murders and obviously the dealing."

"You never know, it's always worth planting the seed. We don't know what we don't know. I met with the Superintendent earlier and told him we were struggling with a serious lack of evidence on the Smethurst murder. He wants the Review Team to cast an eye over it in the next few weeks. I don't think they will find anything missed by us, but it can't do any harm. We can keep the main lines of enquiry ticking over. In the meantime, more of our staff can work on the Carl Smith murder full time."

"That's not a bad thing. Forensics retrieved the bullets from the car and cartridge cases. Once they get checked on the database we might get a new line of enquiry. The intelligence points to Hamilton and my money is on Hamilton, but nobody is brave enough to grass him right now. Maybe once he's sentenced for the contract kill, and people realise he is inside for a long time, they may come out of the woodwork. Hamilton's sentencing date isn't that long off now."

Jason had settled into the prison routine. It helped that his reputation was well known amongst the lads on the wing. They had nothing to gain by taking him on, but they would benefit from becoming his associate and part of his network once they were back on the outside.

It was time for another legal visit. The prison officer escorted him to the consultation room. During the walk, Jason was having some banter with the officer, who was a United fan. Jason loved how the tables had turned in recent years. City were no longer the noisy neighbours but holding the bragging rights. He always attempted to get on with the screws. On a day to day basis it made his life easier and there was always the opportunity for preferential treatment. All the better if he could groom one into corruption. It was a challenge he was enjoying.

He was shown into the room where Burton was waiting, reading the paper. Jason could tell Burton wasn't as confident as usual. It must have been dawning on him that it would be a struggle to get Hamilton off the charges.

"Morning, Jason, there's no good news today I'm afraid."

"I do wonder what I'm paying you for at times," Jason said, whilst holding a long stare at Burton. He watched Burton wince.

"The prosecution case is pretty watertight. It always is with undercover officer's evidence. There's nothing in the unused disclosures to hook onto either. I think you should stick with the guilty plea we entered at the plea and case management hearing. I've not uncovered anything to make us change that to not guilty. Let's keep our powder dry."

"Fuck me. It's great to see you're so committed to fighting my corner."

"Wow, cut me some slack here. I've served you well over the years. We are all in this together. The problem here is that you allowed the police to infiltrate you. Sorting that out isn't easy," Burton countered in a raised voice. He was looking somewhat ruffled.

Jason knew Burton was right but he still had to keep him on his toes. He was still in Jason's pocket and it was probably in Jason's interest to keep him there. In truth, they were all in this together because of the knowledge and black they had on each other, including Burton's bent cop.

"What about the other option, an armed attack, getting me out of the sweat-box on the way to court? It worked for the Salford lads."

"Wayne's not up for it. He thinks it's too high risk and would have to involve outsiders. The chances of success aren't good. There are too many variables to cover and if it went wrong the sentences would be high to make an example. He's struggling to keep the day to day stuff going at the minute without you and Carl. It's too early."

"When the going gets tough, eh?" Jason said. He started to tap the table impatiently.

"It's a plan for the future that we can keep on the back-burner, when the time and circumstances are right. You've just got to keep your head down in the meantime. We'll get you out at some stage. An emergency hospital admission might be more feasible."

Although it wasn't what he wanted to hear, Jason knew Burton was talking sense. Besides, he needed Wayne on the outside to keep the business running smoothly.

"Kirsty has been on at me again. She wants to visit. To say she's getting pissed off with you is an understatement. Are you going to sort her with a visiting order?"

"She needs to wind her neck in. It's not happening yet. I've got enough on my plate to be getting on with."

"Okay, I'll let her know. I think she should be back from Spain."

"Good idea. It may be best for us all if she moved on. She's not looked happy with the relationship for a while now."

The visit was concluded and Burton left the prison. He walked towards the metro link, quietly glad to be away from the cacophony of shouting and banging. The open space and fresh air made him feel alive. He selected Kirsty from his contacts.

"Good afternoon, Kirsty. How did the holiday go?"

"Really well thanks. Sun and sangria can help a girl sort anything out. I've got my head cleared and to make things even better, the sale on the house has gone through."

"Excellent, that's good. You've got to put yourself first and look after yourself. I asked Jason about a visit. His head isn't in the right place yet I'm afraid. I did my best, sorry."

"You know what, fuck him. He creates this mess and bullshits me that he's going legit, and then can't even be bothered to speak to me. If he thinks I'm putting my life on hold whilst he's inside, then he'd better think again because you know what, he's never going to change."

Kirsty ended the call without allowing Burton to reply. Burton sensed there may be trouble ahead. *That was one pissed off woman, and who can blame her? I need to make sure she behaves herself.*

Kirsty was angry, but her mind was already made up from the holiday. She rang Ryan on her mobile phone.

"Hiya, Ryan, can you come and meet me at the house? It's sold and I need a lift with the last few bits and pieces."

"No worries, how was the holiday by the way?" Ryan said.

"I had a great time. I'll tell you about it later."

Kirsty ended the call. She felt great and empowered for the first time, for as long as she could remember. Her relationship with Jason had been in a rut and stagnating for too long. This latest episode was the straw that broke the camel's back. He'd blown it. It was over. There was no going back.

Ryan felt optimistic after speaking to Kirsty. He'd known that she had been home for a few days but he didn't want to be pushy or look desperate, so he refrained from calling her. As the days went by and she hadn't called, he was resigned to the fact, they wouldn't be getting together. But this call presented him with hope and that's what he was holding onto. He hired a van online and made a coffee whilst he waited for it to be delivered.

Just after lunch the buzzer on his intercom broke the silence. It was the guy with the van. Ryan made his way down to the parking area. He saw the van and approached the young lad standing next to it holding a clipboard. They carried out the usual visual checks of the van and the lad went over the conditions of rental before Ryan signed the papers. The lad was skinny, probably in his twenties. He was cheerful and looked happy with his lot. He was in a place where Ryan wanted to be, enjoying a straightforward life, off the drugs and booze and as far away as possible from his life in the firm. He took the keys and set off for Kirsty's house.

As he approached, Ryan saw the estate agent's sign which confirmed that the house was 'sold'. The gates were open. He turned into the drive and parked up, apprehensive about what Kirsty's decision would be. Either way, he accepted that it was out of his hands. One way or the other his fresh start began today.

He pressed the doorbell and waited.

The door was opened by Kirsty. He immediately noticed her holiday tan and how good she looked in her gym gear.

"Hiya, Ryan, come in, how you doing?" she said, and led the way to the kitchen.

Ryan followed on behind her.

"Living the dream, Kirsty, life's just a one big blast. How were your hols? You look good for it."

"It was just what I needed, Ryan. Jason still won't let me visit him so I can't sort anything out with him. Coffee?"

Ryan wasn't sure whether the visiting thing was good or bad for him. *What was it she needed to sort*?

"Cheers, I'd love one," he replied, struggling to restrain himself from saying, *well what's it to be,*

Kirsty? She handed him a coffee then took a sip of her own.

"I feel like there's an elephant in the room here, Ryan, so here goes. I'd like us to get together and see how it pans out."

As soon as the words left her mouth, Ryan gave her a big hug, lifting her off of the ground and spilling her coffee onto the floor.

"Kirsty, I can't tell you how happy I am. We're going to be great together." "How do you fancy making a new start in the sun? We can get some bar work for starters with a view to getting our own business set up."

"Perfect, it's exactly what I would have suggested. That's what we used to dream about years ago."

"I'll have plenty in the bank from the house sale and I can let my managers run the salons for now. You've got the money from the sale of your flat. We should be fine. At least for a few months whilst we figure things out. I'm going to tell Burton my plans. If Jason doesn't want to see me, he can tell Jason for me. I would have done it myself but he won't let me."

"He's going to go ballistic."

Kirsty didn't reply. Nothing needed to be said. They both knew the risks involved. They finished their drinks and loaded the cardboard boxes into the van. Kirsty locked the house up and they set off to Warrington, where Kirsty planned to store some things at her mum and dad's house. It was only a quick detour to drop the keys at the estate agents on the way.

Later that evening they checked into a hotel at Manchester Airport and booked their flights. They also booked themselves a villa in Spain. Their new adventure together was becoming a reality.

Chapter Twenty Four

Jason's sentencing at Crown Court was only weeks away. Although it was getting late into the evening, Burton was still at the office scrutinising the prosecution case and disclosure schedules. He thrived on the challenge and if he found a crack or a loophole he would exploit it. He was going over the evidence of undercover officer Lee for the umpteenth time when his phone rang. He could see it was Kirsty and rolled his eyes. *I could do without this. Involvement in a domestic is the last thing I need.*

"Hi, Kirsty, how are you?"

"I need you to speak to Jason for me."

"It's not happening, Kirsty. He won't arrange a visit, I've done..."

Kirsty interrupted, "I know that. This is different. I wanted to tell him myself but if I can't see him you'll have to do it for me. You may want to sit down."

"Okay, what do you want me to tell him?"

"I've written him a letter. I need you to let him read it on your next visit. It should be delivered to your office first thing in the morning, recorded delivery. I am leaving him and moving abroad with Ryan for a while. I need a break from all this. I've taken as much as I can. I need to get away. There's nothing definite with Ryan, but we're both needing to get away so it makes sense."

"Jesus, are you serious, Kirsty... with Ryan?" Burton was shocked.

"You need to make him understand it's for the best. It's been a sham from the start but I was young then and didn't know any better. It's always been about him and his power. He wanted me because Ryan had me.

Because Ryan had to know he was second best. Since then I've just been an accessory for him."

Kirsty paused to allow Burton to speak. He was conscious that this was quickly turning into a rant, but he couldn't think of anything to say. Taking cue from his silence, Kirsty continued to speak.

"Frank, I know what you're thinking but you've got to help me here. It's in Jason's best interests too. He won't be surprised. Like I said, it's been a sham and he knows it. He's never shown me love or affection. Christ, we've not had sex for as long as I can remember."

This last disclosure was too much information. Cringing, Burton finally said, "I can't say I'm surprised at what you're telling me, Kirsty. I will do my best to protect you from the backlash. But you know Jason better than anybody. His sentencing is in two weeks so the timing isn't good. I would prefer to keep this under wraps until afterwards."

"Let's be honest, Frank, there's never going to be a good time to tell him. But I'm one hundred per cent on this. He's promised me he's going to go legit for years but it's now worse. Then trying to get Ryan shot which has landed him inside. And what about poor Carl?"

"I can't argue, Kirsty, but I also can't guarantee there won't be repercussions for you and Ryan. You two will always have to be looking over your shoulder."

"Like I said, do your best to make him see sense. It's in everyone's interest... including yours Frank. I'm not stupid, I know you are all in it together. Me and Ryan know enough to take you all down... it's best if you leave us be. I bear no grudges and hope things work out for him. This isn't a threat but if he does come after us we will go down fighting. Or we can all move on from this. Nobody needs to lose face. We will keep our heads down and cause him no issues."

"Leave it with me, Kirsty." Burton clearly understood that it was in all of their interests for Jason to allow them to move on without incident.

The call was ended.

The following day wasn't going too well for DI Andrea Statham. As usual, she had pressed the snooze button once too many times. She had been at a leaving do the night before in Manchester. Although she had made sure it wasn't a boozy night she still hadn't had too many hours sleep. She locked the front door and walked to the car. *That's all I need, a flat tyre. It's going to be one of those days.*

She took out her mobile phone.

"Morning, Ma'am," DS Higgs said.

"Pete, I'm having a 'mare. I'm on the last minute and now I've just found a flat tyre on my car. After you've debriefed the troops can you come and pick me up please?"

"No worries, are you not putting the spare on?"

"No, I'll do it later. I'm suited and booted, so I don't want to get covered in crap. I'll stick a cafeteria on for when you get here."

Andrea went back inside and booted up her laptop. She was only half way through her emails when the doorbell rang. It was Pete.

"Morning, pal, thanks for coming, I appreciate it."

"Too many bottles of wine last night?"

"I wish. I only had two glasses, you cheeky sod."

"I know you are capable of changing a wheel yourself, but do you want me to sort it? I've had a look. There's a screw in it, near to the wall, so they probably won't repair it."

"Thanks for the offer, chivalry appreciated and no offence taken. I'll sort it later. I got engrossed in the emails so I didn't put the kettle on. Come on, the Costa's on me."

Andrea locked the house up for the second time that morning and joined Pete, who was already in the driver's seat.

"I've just read an email from DI Dave Ferguson. It's Hamilton's sentencing in a week. Apparently, he's banged to rights. He's thrown a guilty plea in, looking to reduce his sentence."

"It takes the pressure off us I suppose," Pete said. "He's limited to what he can do inside and people may be more willing to talk to us about the murders?"

He drove onto the retail park and got a parking spot near to the coffee shop.

"If it's you're shout, I will have a piece of tiffin as well," he said.

"You're pushing your luck now, sergeant. Do you want ice with your glass of water?" Andrea laughed.

They found a seat in the corner, facing the door. Pete tucked into his piece of cake.

"Very nice, do you want to share?"

"No thanks, I've got a toastie on its way. It's a bit early for cake."

"Anyway, to business, we've had the results back on the weapon used to kill Carl Smith. It's been used in two shootings on Merseyside," Pete said.

"Good news. That will open more lines of enquiry. Have you allocated liaison with Merseyside?"

"Yes, I gave the actions to Rita and Gary this morning. They were setting off to Liverpool as I left. Initial enquiries suggest it's a pistol for hire used by the local crime groups, so with a bit of luck it will open some doors in time."

"It's more than we've got on the Smethurst murder. The intelligence is spot on, Hamilton's boys stepped on his toes and he wasn't having it. Trouble is for him, he underestimated Hamilton. I spoke with the review team yesterday. They couldn't come up with any lines of enquiry that we hadn't covered and agree the solvability factors are pretty low at the moment."

They finished their coffees and headed off back to the police station.

Frank Burton had arrived in his office and checked his mail. He found what he was looking for straight away, an envelope marked private for his personal attention. He opened it and started to read Kirsty's Dear John letter. He was impressed. It was an articulate letter which made a lot of sense. To Burton's relief it was respectful to Jason, albeit honest in Kirsty's perception of their relationship, or lack of it. Even so, the potential of Jason seeking revenge, particularly on Ryan, seemed inevitable. *I'm not looking forward to delivering this bombshell.*

Burton telephoned Wayne. He wanted a second opinion on this. He needed to handle it right. The repercussions could be massive. For all of them. Wayne answered after a few rings.

"Morning, Wayne, I've got some urgent matters to discuss with you. Are you free to pop by?"

"Sounds ominous, you free about one o'clock?" Wayne suggested.

"See you then."

Burton placed the letter in his drawer and locked it. He wouldn't be telling Wayne about that, just the facts of the situation. Burton was feeling uneasy now. He had a fear that this whole situation could implode. If Jason lost the plot they could all go down like a house of cards. Whether he liked it or not, he was in Jason's pocket and Jason had serious dirt on him, including the bent coppers. But he also had serious dirt on Jason too. It bonded them all together like glue, which also meant that it had the potential to get very messy. *I'll sort it, I always have,* Burton tried to convince himself.

An hour later Burton was still analysing the evidence of undercover officer Vinny. There was a timid knock on his door prior to it opening. One of the new legal executives, an awkward, lanky and shy young man, showed Wayne into the office. Wayne took a seat and the door was closed behind him.

"Nice office, Frank, thought you would have gone for the modern minimalist look to match your sports car. This looks more like Rumpole of the Old Baily."

"I like to think of it as traditional. Wayne, we've got some pressing matters to discuss when you've finished with your schoolboy humour. How are business operations progressing?"

"Are we okay to talk here?" Wayne whispered.

"Yes, we're fine. If the police wanted to monitor this office they'd need a damn good reason for an application to be authorised. Legal privilege and all that. Besides, I have it swept for listening devices frequently enough."

"Business is fine on the ground. I've just got back from Amsterdam. The next shipments are sorted and on track. The lads there seem to have taken to me. I've planted the seed that Jason won't be inside for long. I met the Columbian too. It was a bit of an anti-climax to be honest. No way was he the main man, more like the bin man! Talking of the main man, how did he react to our reluctance to spring him from the sweat-box?"

"He wasn't happy but accepts it's probably for the best. Now, before we move on, any other business issues that Jason needs to be aware of?"

"No, in fact it's all running nice and smooth. The recent shit-storms have put everyone on their toes. The fear factor is high. I've pulled the lads out of Chester and North Wales for obvious reasons and moved them to Crewe and Stoke. We're doing some good business down there. I've also reviewed our network just to make sure the cops can't link us to the street dealing. A couple of extra layers of couriers have done the trick. Surveillance will get the cops nowhere near us."

"Okay, I'll update Jason on my next visit before his court appearance for sentencing. The reason I asked for the meeting was to make you aware of Kirsty's new position. I can't say I'm too surprised, but I'm not sure how Jason will react. My main concern is ensuring he remains rational and does not go ballistic. We have the bigger picture to think about and our own skins to save, more importantly."

"Go on. What's she done?"

"She's moved abroad with Ryan, her childhood sweetheart, to start a new life."

"Jeez, thank god for that, for a minute I thought you were going to say she'd gone over to the cops."

"Yes, I suppose it could be a lot worse. I've spoken to her, obviously. She has no intention of causing us any mischief. They want to disappear into the sunset and be left alone. So, if I can manage Jason's reaction there will be no harm done."

"She was never going to wait whilst he was inside. If we're honest, it was always going to happen. It just complicates matters that she chose Ryan. He's got a death wish, that lad."

"So, do I tell him before sentencing, or get that done and dusted first?"

"You've no choice, Frank, if you don't tell him and he finds out he will be well pissed off."

"Decision made then. Happy days," Frank said. "If we can keep a lid on this, we are almost returning to normal-business-resumed. My man on the inside tells me the canal investigation is about to be pended. They have an idea obviously, but no evidence. Our only weak link there is Ryan."

"That doesn't worry me. I think he's over his 'heads gone' moment and it's not in his interests to blab. He's out of the picture now. If we let sleeping dogs lie, he'll be fine."

"Let's hope so. I'm not as optimistic. He seems to be on a mission to self-destruct. If his new relationship goes tits-up I can see him back on the booze and charlie. Anyway, Jason will have the final say."

"How good is your bent cop?" Wayne asked.

"Very. He's in the thick of things and has been very reliable."

"What about trust? Could he do us harm?"

"He's too far down the line with us. If we exposed him he wouldn't see the light of day for a long time and he knows it. Whether he likes it or not, he's one of us now. His gambling and money problems made sure of that. A few years ago, he was getting ideas above his station, so Jason sent a couple of lads to a retirement do he was at in a Manchester pub. They started chatting to his boss. The message was received loud and clear."

"They couldn't use him as a double agent, could they? Sort of mitigation on his wayward ways?"

"You've been watching too many cop dramas on television, Wayne. In a word, no."

"How about the other investigation?"

"Similar story, the best they've got is identification on the pistol, nothing else other than intelligence. If the pistol turns up they can arrest and question whoever's in possession of it and work backwards through those that have handled it."

"Other than that, then it's the same, only you, Jason, Ryan and me in the loop. The kid who did it hasn't a clue who set it up. Just a gun for hire. I made sure there were no bread crumbs left to be followed back to us."

"It could be a lot worse," Frank said. "We can manage this, onwards and upwards."

"If you could get Jason to see fit, I think it's best if I keep Ryan in my pocket. Friends close and enemies closer and all that. We've still got the fear factor on him and he knows which side his bread is buttered."

"Makes sense to me," Frank said.

After the meeting, Wayne put a call in to Ryan whilst he was walking back to his car. The line was dead. No surprises there then. He was a man who didn't want to be contacted. Wayne tried Kirsty's number, which went straight to voicemail.

"Hi, Kirsty, it's Wayne. I need to get hold of Ryan but I've not got his new number. Can you get him to ring me on this one please? It's in his best interests to speak. I've no issues with either of you and want to smooth the waters best I can with Jason, which is the best way forward for all of us. Hope you are well, catch up soon."

Two days later Jason was being escorted to the consultation area for his legal visit. It was the same prison officer as usual, Dean the Man United fan. They chatted away almost like mates. Jason had sorted Dean out with contacts for free gym admissions and cheap steroids. Present circumstances aside, Jason thought Dean was okay and suspected the feeling was mutual. Jason entered the legal consultation room. It always felt like Groundhog Day. The same cheap plastic chairs, windowless walls and stench of Burton's aftershave.

"Morning, Jason," Frank said. "You're looking good, considering the circumstances."

"Well, you know. I'm making a few improvements. I've got one of the screws coming along nicely. Free gym memberships and steroids. He's now working out with some of our boys. They're getting to know him quite well. Could be useful, you'll need to do a bit of background research on him."

"Poor bastard, it's the start of the slippery slide downwards towards membership of the firm."

"I've thought about what you said last time. I'm with you. Guilty plea, and put forward mitigation of me being taken in with all the Special Forces talk. It's not agent provocateur but I was led into a situation of proving myself as an equal and got out of my depth. Events spiralled out of control to which I felt threatened and feared for my safety if I tried to backtrack."

"It's for the best. The guilty plea will be gratefully received, saving court time, tax payer's costs and witness attendance. It also allows you to hype the remorse and then be the model prisoner. Less of a media spectacle too. We won't lay it on too thick at court. I don't want to give them the opportunity for a Newton Hearing. Once it's all settled down you can decide whether to do the time or whether we arrange an early release. It sounds like a plan. All is good on the business front, operations will continue as you direct. Wayne has stepped up to the plate he is working hard."

"Jeez, Frank, you make it sound like I've won millions on the lottery, not time inside."

"There is one other thing I need to update you on. Kirsty has left you. She was gutted and wanted to tell you herself but obviously you wouldn't let her visit. She still thinks a lot of you and still respects you, but it has all got too much for her. She's gone living in Spain with Ryan for a while to sort her head out. Here, read this letter before you say anything."

Frank passed Jason the letter. There was a silence whilst Jason read Kirsty's explanation. Jason handed the letter back to Frank.

"Fucking priceless. We just need to keep an eye on them. Tell Wayne to keep in touch with Ryan. I'll decide what action needs to be taken." Jason showed no emotion and was very matter of fact about it.

"Anything else, Frank?"

"No, that's everything covered. We can have a final meeting before sentencing but I think we're good to go now."

Jason was escorted back to the wing by a different prison officer, a woman who looked like she could do with one of his free gym passes. Shifts and fast food were doing her no favours, she was carrying far too much weight. She wheezed as they walked up the stairs, and always looked stressed and anxious. Maybe he could help her out... she looked vulnerable and could be an asset.

His mind started to wander. He wasn't surprised by Kirsty's decision. In fact, it seemed to be the natural conclusion under the circumstances. He knew he wouldn't miss her because his focus in life had now changed. He had to batten down the hatches and focus on what he was good at, running the firm. He had to make his time in prison work for him. Ryan was a different matter. He could be dealt with at a later date, but he wasn't a priority right now.

Ryan's surroundings were in total contrast to Jason's prison cell. He was sitting at a white metal table by the pool, at the villa they were renting just outside Marbella. Kirsty was lying on the sun-lounger reading a paperback.

"Do you want another glass, Kirsty?"

"I'll have a beer instead please." Ryan fixed the drinks and placed a beer on the table next to her.

"I think you should return the call to Wayne," she said.

"I know. I'll do it now. It makes sense to keep in touch with him. It also gives me the heads-up for stuff going on over there."

Ryan sat back down at the table. He took a swig of his lime and soda and selected Wayne from the contacts.

"Wayne, it's Ryan. I got your message mate, how you doing?"

"Hey, Ryan, thanks for getting back to me. I believe you've headed for the sun, and you and Kirsty are back together?" Wayne said.

"Mate, I had to get away. I needed a new start. I'm off the booze and charlie for good. I've never felt better. And by the way, Kirsty had already decided to leave Jason before I offered to give her some support. We go back a long way mate. She really needed a break. So, we've no definite plans, we will spend some time out here and take it one step at a time. How's Jason took it?"

"Frank Burton has spoken to him. Frank was surprised that Jason's been pretty cool about it. Let's be honest, mate, you and Kirsty were together before Jason swept her off her feet with money, houses and cars. She was young and impressionable."

"Look, Wayne, I'm not stupid. I know I need to watch my back. But remember, I'm never going to cause any issues. You and Jason have my total loyalty. I didn't cooperate with the cops when he tried to kill me and never would. Getting back with Kirsty isn't meant to be a kick in the bollocks, either. She left him and I took my chance, besides it not even definite that we're in a relationship. The situation just works out for both of us."

"I know, mate. I can't make any promises, but I'll do what I can to keep him off your back. We all need to move on. It's been a shit-storm of a few months. Normal service has resumed with the business. By the way, I've listened to what you said and cut the care home kids out of the from dealing the gear for us. I know you were one of them once... looking out for your own and all that."

"We just want a quiet life out here. We'll keep our heads down and Jason won't hear a peep from us. I've got bar and door work sorted. Kirsty's hairdressing again for the time being. It's just what we need."

"You might even be able to manage shipments from Spain for us," Wayne said.

"I'm out, mate."

"I was joking, Ryan. I know."

"Keep in touch, mate," Ryan said. He pressed the red button and placed the phone on the table.

"Did you catch that, Kirsty?"

"Yes, it went well. Don't forget it benefits them too if we all move on. They've got a lot to lose if it all goes tits-up again. I reminded Frank Burton of that. Did he sound genuine?"

"Yes, and he didn't ask where we were. Time will tell." Ryan knew he had one more call to make. He couldn't put it off any longer. "I'll go and get some more ice." He said. Ryan walked straight through the villa and took a seat in the front garden. He put the phone to his ear, cowardly hoping it wouldn't be answered.

"Ryan how you doing?" Lisa said.

"Lisa it's not good. I've got into a lot of trouble with some bad people. I've had to move Spain to keep my head down. I'm going to have to split with you, I can't risk you getting mixed up in this. Let's remember the great times we had together and go our own ways."

"That's a bit knee jerk and sudden. Are you over reacting here? I can come out to Spain too?"

"It's the best way Lisa, you'll always have a place in my heart and I will miss you."

"Fucking hell Ryan, you're like the rest of them. I thought you were better than that" There was a short silence, then Lisa started on a rant at him. Ryan listened to the rant, said sorry, then ended the call. He felt like shit, he had dreaded making the call and still had feelings for Lisa. But once Kirsty was on the scene, there was only one winner. He returned to his seat and placed the replenished ice bucket on the table. He looked across at Kirsty and felt the need to pinch himself. But he also felt very pensive. Lot's had happened over the last few weeks, and he suspected that more was to come. This wasn't over by a long stretch.

Chapter Twenty Five

DS Higgs tapped on the door and walked into DI Statham's office.

"How did the management meeting go, Ma'am?"

"Jason Hamilton was the main subject. He's up for sentencing tomorrow. He's thrown in a guilty plea to reduce his sentence, as you know."

"He had no choice really."

"Well, he's not off the hook. The boss thinks we have a good chance to bring the whole Organised Crime Group down now. All of this disruption may present an opportunity. The regional crime group are carrying on working with our drugs squad and economic crime Unit."

"Where does that leave us?" Pete asked.

"It was decided that our team have the capacity to take on the next murder. We'll keep the other two on the back burner. We've exhausted our lines of enquiry for now but let's see where their investigations take us. We can pursue any lines of enquiry that come to light. An informant would be perfect at this stage. I need to discuss the possibility of offering a reward for information leading to charges, I don't think the command team will go for it though."

Jason was escorted up the steps to the dock. The journey to the court was a blur, albeit still a break from the monotonous prison routine. He took his seat next to the guard. The room felt bright and the air nicer to breath than the stifled, rank prison air. He detected the aromas of aftershave and perfume straight away. He could see Frank Burton huddled in conversation with his barrister.

The Judge entered the court room giving everyone the cue to rise to their feet. The Judge, hidden behind his red robe and grey wig, introduced proceedings and invited the prosecution to outline their case. The barrister for the prosecution stood up. She began her summary of the prosecution case. Jason watched and listened. She was about forty years old, well spoken with a slow and clear delivery. She obviously took pride in her appearance and was a good looking woman. In different circumstances Jason would have been attracted to her.

She continued, "In conclusion Your Honour, the defendant before you has shown total contempt for the rule of law. He has callously taken the law into his own hands and directed the calculated cold blooded execution of an innocent member of the public after a dispute which should have been settled more proportionately over a pint of beer in their local pub. He is a danger to the public with no respect for the right to life of others. A lengthy custodial sentence is the obvious and only disposal for the court."

The Judge made notes, creating a silent pause in proceedings. He then directed the barrister for the defence to present the mitigation on behalf of the defence. The barrister rose to his feet. He wasn't a tall man, probably 5'8". He had a thin build, and was bespectacled with short black hair. *Good choice, Frank.* Thought Jason. The barrister was unthreatening, with a studious demeanour, a man to be trusted.

"Act in haste, repent at leisure. We all know only too well the consequences of such behaviour. Following a dispute with a known associate, this is where the defendant found himself. He makes no excuses for that behaviour. He pleaded guilty to the court at the earliest opportunity. He has shown sincere regret and remorse about the actions he took. He has expressed massive relief that his intended victim is still alive.

"He is a working man who has got to where he is through working hard, in spite of a poor and interrupted education. He allowed himself to be taken in and overawed by the company of supposedly ex-Special Forces soldiers and, out of character, made ill-judged decisions in an attempt to be accepted into their fold. Events ran away with themselves to an extent that he felt threatened and feared for his safety, were he to call off his business agreement. He was in far too deep for his own good. A custodial sentence is the only appropriate sentence for the court to pass, however I question the need for a lengthy sentence. The defendant fully accepts and takes responsibility for his actions. He has cooperated with the police investigation. He has pleaded guilty and without doubt is clearly remorseful. A short, sharp, shock sentence will clearly suffice. Of his own volition he is helping and supporting fellow inmates already, voluntarily giving his own time to the prisoner peer support project. He is a respected businessman in Manchester and uses his influence to support the needy and other community projects. He knows he has crossed the line and he is regretful. He stands at the mercy of the court, showing genuine remorse."

The court adjourned prior to sentencing.

Not a bad effort. I almost felt sorry for myself. Jason sat back into his chair and waited.

"All rise."

The call brought his attention back into the room. The Judge entered the court and took his seat, looking down on everyone else. Everyone sat down, with an eagerness to move on and hear the result.

"Would you stand please, Mr Hamilton?"

Jason stood up and adjusted his tie. He was doing his best to portray the image of the respectful and remorseful fool, who had stepped way out of his depth.

"I have considered the presentations heard before us today. I accept your cooperation with the police and the court. However, the objective of your behaviour was to have another man killed. In view of the seriousness of this offence, you will serve a custodial sentence of ten years. Take him down."

The guard stood up and led Jason through the gates and down the stairs to the holding cell.

Jason sat on the bench and pulled the tie from around his neck. He felt indifferent, if not relieved that he now had no uncertainty. Ten years. He had already come to terms with doing prison time. *Life goes on, time to get this show on the road again, Wayne and Frank are going to be busy, and my cosy retirement is on hold.* He heard the approach of footsteps in the corridor and the rattling of keys before the door opened. Frank entered the cell and the door closed behind him.

"It could have been a lot worse, Jason. I think we did okay."

"Well done, Frank, it's not a bad result. Time to crack on with business."

"Business is good. Wayne is doing a fine job. It's time to steady the ship. With good behaviour you could be out in four years, unless, of course, we make alternative arrangements for an early release."

"One day at a time, Frank. I'll take stock and consider our next moves. I'm building my support network inside. Dean will help to facilitate us in time and I'll recruit a couple of enforcers on the wing to keep things running smoothly. I need you to get your man on the inside working hard. I want to know all about our friend Lee, or whatever his real name is. He's my next project. That's a need to know between me and you, Frank. That's all."

"Right, I need to go and speak with counsel. I'll set up a legal visit for next week. Leave it with me."

"One more thing... make sure Wayne keeps close to Kirsty and Ryan, I've got unfinished business there."

Frank rang the bell; a guard opened the door allowing him to leave. Jason watched, whilst deep in thought, he had lots to do.

About the Author.

CJ Wood is a retired career detective. He served in the Royal Military Police and police service in a career spanning over 30 years. For his last 15 years he undertook the role of Detective Inspector investigating Serious Crime and Major Incidents.

CJ is an avid reader and passionate about writing, when not engaged with a book he can be often be found hiking the mountains of the Lake District.

Website; www.cjwoodauthor.co.uk

Facebook CJ Wood-Crime Fiction Author

Twitter. @CjAuthor

Acknowledgements.

I would like to thank the following people for their help and support. Many thanks to Andrea Wood for her encouragement and motivational support.
To Charlotte Gormley and Mark Crossfield for their editing.
Many thanks also to Audrey Harrison for her expertise and guidance.
Also, to my family and friends for their support.

Disclaimer.

Printed in Great Britain
by Amazon

23205824R00158